D1160815

FIGHTING FOR AMETHYST (POLICE AND FIRE: OPERATION ALPHA)

BADGE OF HONOR: A TARPLEY VFD NOVEL

DEANNDRA HALL

This book is a work of fiction. Names, characters, places, and incidents are products of the author's imagination or used fictitiously. Any resemblance to actual events or locales or persons living or dead is entirely coincidental.

Dear Readers,

Welcome to the Police and Fire: Operation Alpha Fan-Fiction world!

If you are new to this amazing world, in a nutshell the author wrote a story using one or more of my characters in it. Sometimes that character has a major role in the story, and other times they are only mentioned briefly. This is perfectly legal and allowable because they are going through Aces Press to publish the story.

This book is entirely the work of the author who wrote it. While I might have assisted with brainstorming and other ideas about which of my characters to use, I didn't have any part in the process or writing or editing the story.

I'm proud and excited that so many authors have loved my characters enough that they wanted to write them into their own story. Thank you for supporting them, and me!

READ ON!

Xoxo

Susan Stoker

CHAPTER 1

"Craven, please! Just listen to—"

"No. Forget it. This is your problem, not mine. I told you … I *told you.* Not my problem. Not. My. Fucking. Problem." The door slammed and she was left standing there, alone.

With a positive pregnancy test in her hand.

What the hell am I going to do? She'd have to figure that out later. At that particular moment, she had an environmental sciences exam to take.

"Miss Meadows?"

Amethyst rose and stepped through the open door. Two of her professors sat there, and the third had ushered her into the room. "Have a seat. We need to go over your records," Professor Perry said as he pulled out a folder.

Professor Fogerty looked at some papers in her hand. "You've failed the last three exams. I offered an opportunity to retake the last one, and you failed that one too."

"I know. And I'm trying to … I mean, it's …"

"Miss Meadows, what can we do to help? Your grades were exemplary until this semester and, quite frankly, I don't think there's anything you can do now to pull it out of the dumpster fire that it's become. I checked with Professor Singleton and Professor Camden, and they both said you're failing in their classes too," Professor Anderson reported. "The dean said he got word this morning that your scholarships will not be renewed." There was silence in the room until Professor Anderson added, "Miss Meadows? What's going on?"

"Nothing. Nothing anybody can help me with anyway. I'm sorry. I need to go." She stood and looked around. All three professors looked at her with mercy in their eyes, and she had nothing to say. What could she say? Without another word, she turned and left the room, headed down the hallway, and stepped out into the early spring air.

When she got back to the apartment, there was a note on the door.

Note from management:

We're sorry, but your eviction is proceeding. We've tried to work with you on the rent, but we've gotten nothing for two months. This is your notice before legal action is taken.

That was that. She didn't know what to do. Calling Sapphire had occurred to her, but she was the big sister. She was supposed to help the little sister, not the other way around. And calling her mom would be a waste of time. The woman was only interested in two things—younger men and herself. Nothing else.

And then there was Daddy. She knew he'd do whatever she asked, but that wasn't fair. He had a new wife and a new life, and she had no right to just dump everything in his lap. Amethyst gazed around the apartment. So many memories, happy memories, with Craven. He'd warned her when they met that he had a "map" of his "road to success," and that anybody who got in the way would be left in the dust. She'd assumed he meant friends and relatives. It had never occurred to her that he'd treat her that way.

With a few boxes nabbed at the corner liquor store, she started packing her things. Where would she go? As much as she hated it, there was only one answer.

THAT WAS ONE VERY LONG DRIVE. SHE'D ONLY BEEN TO Tarpley a few times, and every time she went, it seemed like it was farther than the time before. Amethyst drove for a while, and she'd find a convenience store, go to the bathroom, grab a snack, and nap for a couple of hours, then get up and start out again. At the rate she was going, it was going to take her almost all day to get there, but she'd just keep driving. Eventually it would happen.

She was being very careful with her money, but it was getting low. By the time she got to Galveston, she was exhausted, but there was no money for a hotel, so she kept pressing on. Relief washed over her when she realized she was close to San Antonio. That meant she was almost there. She drove on, listening to the mapping program on her phone—her old Toyota didn't have any of that fancy onboard stuff—and pretty soon, she was crossing the Medina County line. That made her feel pretty good. She was getting closer and everything was starting to look a bit familiar. There was a little sign that read "TARPLEY 15 MILES" and she breathed a sigh of relief. And then the unthinkable happened.

The car sputtered, shook, choked, and rolled to a stop as she steered it to the side of the road, no small feat since the power steering quit working as soon as the engine died. She stared at the gauges and realized what had happened—she'd simply run out of gas. It was almost dark, and she couldn't remember how far she'd come since she'd seen the sign, or where the next gas station was. The battery on her phone had run down hours before and she'd looked everywhere for her charging cable but never found it, so she couldn't call her dad. All she could do was sit in the car and hope an ax murderer didn't come along to chop her into pieces before a sheriff's deputy spotted her, so she settled down to wait.

About twenty minutes passed before she heard an engine behind her and looked in her rearview. Sure enough, there was a large vehicle reflected in the mirror, its grill as big as the back window of her car. *Maybe a wrecker operator saw me and has taken pity on me*, she mused, hoping against hope that would be the case. But the driver's door opened and a lone figure in what looked to be jeans and a tee sauntered up toward the car. The hair on the back of her neck rose and she held her breath.

In seconds, there was a tap on the window and she turned to see a face. It was a man about her dad's age, and he motioned for her to roll her window down, so she did—about an inch. "Ma'am, do you need some help?"

"I've run out of gas."

"There's a gas station about five miles down the road. Want me to go get some for you? I'd be glad to."

Something about the man looked familiar. "Do I know you?"

He chuckled. "I dunno. Do you?"

"Do you live in Tarpley?"

"I do now. I used to live in Bandera. Had a little farm over there. Got a bigger farm over here in Bandera County now. Name's—"

"Frame. You're Jackson Frame." It all came rushing back, the horrible accident her dad had been involved in and how an EMT with the Medina County Volunteer Fire Department had cut him down out of a tree. The man had saved his life.

"I am. Do I know you?"

Amethyst opened the car door and stood. "I don't know if you'll remember me or not."

He looked her up and down for a few seconds and smiled. "Yeah! You're one of G-man's girls!"

"I am." Amethyst smiled and relaxed. Jackson would take care of her. She was sure of it. "The oldest one."

"I bet your dad's going to be happy when you get there. He's probably worried sick."

She sighed. "He doesn't know I'm coming."

"Oh! A surprise! Well, I bet he'll be thrilled. So do you want me to go get that gas for you?"

"I don't have any money …"

"Doesn't matter. You need gas and I can get some. No problem."

"Uh …" She shifted her hips just a little. "Could I go with you? I kinda need to, um—"

"Of course. Lock 'er up and come on. You're welcome to come with me. Wouldn't mind the company."

As they drove along, Amethyst watched out the windows. She loved the rolling meadows of hill country. It was a pretty place, especially in the spring. "So have you seen my dad lately?"

"Oh, yeah. I see him every other Tuesday night when the VFD has their meeting. I moved over here so I could join Tarpley's VFD and I like all the guys. He's doing real good. If you didn't know he'd been in an accident, you'd never guess. He's barely got a limp. It's a miracle, really."

"You're the miracle. You saved his life."

"Oh, naw, I just figured out how to get him down. The doctors did the real work."

"He never would've gotten to the hospital if it hadn't been for you, so thanks again. He's really the only family I have that I can count on."

"Yeah, I've heard him talk about your mother. I mean, he's not disrespectful or anything, but he said she's not much on standing still."

Amethyst laughed. "That's a good way to put it! She's a rolling stone for sure. Woman cares nothing about roots, and that's all Dad really wanted. And I'm glad he has them—I'm glad he has Lorna. They seem very happy together."

"They *are* very happy together. He dotes on her and she worships him. They're so cute, and to think she almost threw it all away because she was so worried about the difference in their ages."

"Yeah. He was a lot younger than my mom too."

"So what do *you* think about that?"

"I think it doesn't matter as long as two people love each other and want to have a solid relationship. As long as they're willing to work at it, it doesn't matter what their ages are."

"I agree. Okay, here we are. I've got a can back here, so I'll pump the gas and you can go, um, whatever—"

"Yeah. I will. Thanks. I'll be right back." She made

her way into the store, looked until she saw the sign, and headed to the ladies' room. When she was finished, she washed her hands and started back out to the truck. Jackson was standing at the register, so she stopped and waited, and he smiled when he turned and saw her. "Thanks again."

"You're welcome. I don't have a daughter but if I did, I'd want somebody to do this for her. Come on. Let's go get you started up so you can get going."

They chatted on the way back too, and they rolled up behind her Toyota in no time. She watched as Jackson poured the contents of the big gas can into her filler pipe. When it was empty, he set it down and pointed at the car. "Start 'er up."

Amethyst slid behind the wheel, turned the key, and listened to the engine purr. "Yep. That's all it was. Thank you again, Jackson. I'll repay you, I promise."

"Not necessary. You have a good evening and tell your folks I said hello."

"I will. Goodnight."

"Night. Drive safely, honey." She watched in the mirror as he closed the door on his truck, but he didn't drive away, and she realized he was waiting for her to pull out so he knew she was good to go. As she pulled off the shoulder of the road, his truck did too, and he followed her all the way to the Bandera County line. They were less than a mile across when she heard a horn blare and saw him turn off onto another county road.

She drove through the tiny town and on out to the other side until she got to her dad's road, then turned in and rolled slowly toward the house. It had gotten dark, and lights were on in the living room. As she pulled up to park, she saw a figure open the door and peer out. "Can I help you?" a male voice called.

Tears rolled down her cheeks. "It's me, Daddy."

"Amethyst? Lord, honey, what are you doing here?" Gant was right in front of her in a heartbeat, his arms wrapped around her tightly. Nothing felt better than her dad's strong arms enveloping her in that moment—nothing. They were like a salve to her battered, broken heart. "Why didn't you tell me you were coming? Have you been driving all day? Are you hungry? Coming in?"

"Dad, slow down! I wanted to surprise you, yes, yes, and yes. How's that?"

"Okay! But what are you doing here? You're supposed to be at school. If your mother's pulled some stunt—"

"No, Dad. And I really don't want to talk about it right now, okay? Please?"

Gant eyed her suspiciously, but she held her ground. She just didn't think she could bring herself to say the words. Then he gave her that smile, the one that said everything was going to be okay. "Lorna's gonna be so happy to see you."

I sure hope so, she told herself. If her stepmother wasn't happy to see her, she didn't know what she'd do. There was nowhere else to go.

Nowhere.

KEYS DEPOSITED IN THE BOWL BY THE DOOR, HE TOED HIS boots off, dropped the mail on the coffee table, and strode into the kitchen. The beer he'd brewed a few weeks earlier was waiting for him, and he couldn't wait to try it.

His last brewing attempt had been great. The one before it? Eh, not so much.

As he sat down with the bottle, he flipped through the mail. Junk, junk, junk. Bill. Junk. More junk. Postcard from Autrey, one of his army buddies. That lucky bastard couldn't help showing off, and Jackson looked at the picture. Fiji. It was beautiful, apparently. *I'll never know*, he chided himself as he thumbed through the rest.

The remote was right beside him, so he pulled up a news channel and watched. Nothing new there. The Asian continent was in an uproar, as usual, and so was the Middle East. Brexit had become old news, but the newest scandal in London had everyone on the edges of their seats—everyone but him. He didn't give two figs what the Brits were doing. As he flipped through the channels, he found an old western and settled down to watch it. Oddly, it was one he didn't remember ever seeing before.

But he couldn't concentrate on it. He kept thinking about Amethyst, alone there on the side of the road. Something in her eyes had made his chest tighten. She was in some kind of trouble, he was sure, but he didn't know her well enough to ask. G-man would take care of her. He and Lorna loved those girls. He thought for a second or two about Sapphire—he'd seen them at the hospital and at the engagement party—but he hadn't really thought much about either of them since then. They were pretty girls, and he wondered what their mother looked like. She had to be stunning to have daughters that beautiful.

Then he thought about Cassidy. She would've been eighteen. He wondered if she would've been as pretty as the two Meadows girls. Of course she would've. Her mother was a beautiful woman. Georgie was gorgeous.

He hadn't seen her in years, but Georgie's mother had been attractive when she was his age, so she probably was too. Thinking about them was almost too painful, even after all those years, and he tried to tamp it down and go back to watching TV.

Two more beers and he wasn't thinking about them anymore. Two beers after that and he wasn't thinking about anyone or anything anymore. When he woke, he was looking straight up at the ceiling, his head resting on the back of the sofa, and he struggled to get to his feet and drag himself down the hallway. Leaving a trail of clothes behind him, he was down to his boxer briefs when he made it to the bed, and he fell across it, too gone to care. As he drifted off, he could see Amethyst's eyes, and he recognized the look there. Tormented. That's what it was.

Of course he recognized it. It was exactly what he saw in his own eyes when he looked in the mirror.

TWO WEEKS. FOR SIXTEEN DAYS, SHE'D BEEN AVOIDING anything that looked like a conversation, but she knew that was going to come to an end. Her dad was patient, but eventually he'd sit her down and tell her to come clean. She owed him that, she reckoned, him and Lorna both.

She also knew he'd been trying to find out what was going on and he'd called Sapphire. She hadn't been able to bring herself to call her sister either. She was the big sis, and she was supposed to set an example. Fine example she was! A single, pregnant, homeless college dropout. Great role model material there. He'd called the college too, but she'd filed paperwork before she left that required her signature to release any of her information. She wasn't a child anymore, and she didn't want just anybody accessing her data. Of course, Gant wasn't just anybody, but still …

He and Lorna had gone to the farm store right outside San Antonio to get bedding plants and she'd begged off with a lie about an online class when she heard his truck out in the driveway. At least she thought it was his truck. But when she peered out the glass in the front door, she was surprised.

Jackson Frame was making his way up onto the porch, and she opened the door before he had a chance to knock. "Hey! He's not here. They went to get flowers or something."

Jackson gave her a lopsided grin. "I swear, he'd do anything for that woman."

"Yeah. He would. Anything I can do for you?"

"Nah. I was going to talk to him about shoeing a couple of my horses, but it can wait."

Amethyst chuckled. "Why didn't you just call him?"

"I was already in town and figured what the hell. How are you doing?"

"I'm good." *No I'm not. I'm a wreck*, she wanted to say, but she couldn't. And yet there was something about Jackson that made her want to spill her guts to him. He had a quiet, purposeful demeanor about him that left her feeling comfortable around him. Every time she'd talked to her dad while he was recovering, he told her how thankful he was for Jackson, how the EMT checked on him at least every third day, brought food over so Lorna didn't have to cook, helped her while he was laid up at the fire station, and sometimes just came and sat around to talk with him. It had meant the world to Gant, and Amethyst wondered how Jackson had that much free time. Didn't he have a job? Didn't his family need him?

"That's good. Well, I suppose I should go and—"

"You're welcome to come inside and wait. They've been gone an hour, so I can't imagine they'll be gone much … Yep. There they are." The sound of tires crunching gravel grew louder as Gant's truck rolled up the drive.

"Hey, Boss, whatcha doin' here?" Gant yelled in greeting to Jackson.

"Just came to check up on you and see if Lorna's tired of you yet."

A feminine laugh sounded from the other side of the truck before Lorna's face popped into view. "Not yet, but getting closer every day!"

Gant laughed too before he asked, "We've got pizza. Can you eat?"

"Can I eat? Do chickens have beaks? Hell yeah, I can eat! But you don't have to feed me."

"Nonsense. We're back, we've got food, and it's mealtime. You've fed us so many times that the least we can do is share some cheap pizza with ya." Gant climbed the stairs to the porch and the two men shook hands, Gant balancing the pizza boxes on his left palm. "Just glad to see you."

"Glad to see you too. And thanks for the offer. Guess I'll take you up on it. Don't want to ruin my chances with your girl there," he said as Lorna stepped up beside him and wrapped an arm around his waist. "You doin' okay, darlin'?"

"Yeah, I'm fine. You're lookin' good! I think Bandera County living is treating you well."

"It is. I didn't think it would make such a difference moving here from Medina County, but you guys know how to welcome somebody into your fold. Tank came over last week and helped me with a fence, and Dirty-D and Buff were over there a couple of days ago looking at my tractor."

"Did they get it fixed?" Gant asked as he dropped the pizza boxes on the counter and started helping Lorna pull drinks from the refrigerator.

"Nah. They said it needed one very large, very expensive part."

Gant grinned. "Yeah? What's that?"

"A new tractor."

Gant laughed loudly. "That bad, huh?"

Jackson was laughing too. "Apparently!"

They sat around the dining room table, eating pizza and talking. Well, the three of them did. Amethyst intentionally kept her mouth shut. She responded when she was asked a question, but that was about it. The less she talked, the better things were.

And it was interesting to watch them interacting. Gant kept asking questions that bordered on military issues, and every time he did, Jackson said something to shut it down. There was a story there, but she had no idea what it was. She remembered someone had said something about Jackson being a field medic, so apparently he'd been military, and she got the distinct impression he did not want to talk about that. Her dad had asked him about his U.S. Army Reserve duty, and he'd answered a few of the questions, so she knew he was still involved in the military in some way.

She was totally unprepared when Jackson turned to her and asked, "Now, where is it that you go to school?"

"Um, University of Alabama."

"Tuscaloosa?"

She nodded and swallowed hard. "Yeah."

"What's your field of study?"

How do I make this stop? she wondered as she panicked. "Communicative disorders."

"Oh, so you've got some neuro classes, some speech pathology, things like that."

I'll give it to him, he knows the world around him. "Yes. Exactly. And some social work classes."

"Right. That would be an interesting field. Got any job prospects for when you graduate? Anywhere you'd like to work?"

Amethyst could feel her hands start to shake, and she knew her face was burning. "I, um …" Things started to look like they were wiggling and waving a bit, and breathing was getting harder and harder …

The next thing she knew, she was looking up into Jackson's face. "Honey? You okay? Amethyst?" Over his shoulder she could see Gant's worried face, and Lorna's was above his. "Can you sit up? Are you in pain?"

"Uhhh, no. Um, I dunno. Yeah. I think …" She let him take her hand, and he grasped her upper arm with his other hand as he helped her sit up. "I'm fine. I'm …" There was nothing to say. Pure panic had set in, and that hadn't entirely gone away yet.

"Here, sweetie. Take a few sips." Lorna's hand held a large glass of ice water, and Amethyst took it, sipped some, and handed it back. It made her feel a little less shaky, but that feeling of dread was still there. "Better?"

"I think so. I, um, I need to get up off the floor."

"Sure. Here. Let's get up. Ready?" Gant asked as he grasped her other arm.

"Yeah. Sure." Between her struggling and the two men, she managed to get onto her feet. "I don't feel so good."

"Come on. Let's get you into bed. You can take a nap. Lorna, got a thermometer? We need to take her temperature," Jackson called back up the hallway as he walked on one side of her, Gant on the other, until they reached the bedroom.

"Yeah. Here ya go." She passed the thermometer off to Jackson just as Amethyst plopped down on the side of the bed.

"In the bed you go, young lady," Jackson said, his voice gentle and low as he lifted her legs and spun her to lie down. "Put this under your tongue. Thatta girl."

She wasn't running a fever. She knew what was wrong, but she couldn't say anything. A firm grip took her wrist, and she realized Jackson was taking her pulse, so she held still.

When she glanced up at him, he smiled. "Your pulse is normal. Let's see …" Pulling the thermometer from her mouth, he held it up and looked at it. "Nope. No fever. Did you eat something that's making you sick?" She shook her head. "Any symptoms of anything else? Headaches? Sore throat? Cough?" Amethyst just kept shaking her head. "Maybe you're just tired. Why don't you stay here and rest? I don't think that'll hurt a thing, right, Dad?" he asked and grinned at Gant.

"Nope. Won't hurt a thing. Take a nap and we'll see how you feel when you wake up. Okay?"

"Okay."

"I'm going, but I'll be checking on you, girl. You do what your dad and Lorna tell you and let them take care of you. You'll be fine." When he patted her hand, she almost felt like things would be okay.

Almost.

She could hear the three of them talking in low tones as Jackson made his way to the door, and the tears started. There was no one she could talk to, no one who'd understand, and she knew she was going to have to tell her dad. There was no way around it. Maybe it was time. She'd start to show pretty soon, and everyone would know. What would he say? What would Lorna say? Her stepmother would influence her dad in his decision.

And if he kicked her out? Emerald's wandering camper wouldn't be a good place to raise a child. Therein resided the problem.

She wanted the baby. Raising that child would be the only thing she might succeed at, and she wanted that chance. It would be hard to ever go back to school with a child, but maybe she could do it. But no way did she want to put it up for adoption, and an abortion was out of the question. It was *her* baby, and she wanted it desperately. That hadn't been her first reaction, but the more she thought about a child, the more she thought about the way she was raised, especially before Gant had come into their lives. It had been chaotic and unanchored and constantly in flux, but she wanted better than that for this baby. She wanted it to have a home and a family and a stable base. Problem was, she wasn't sure how she'd do it alone, but she would. That was something she wouldn't fail at. She just couldn't.

There was a sound at the bedroom door and she turned her head to see Gant standing in the doorway. When she didn't speak, he shuffled over to the bed, pulled up the little chair from the corner, and sat down.

For a full minute, he said nothing, just stroked his chin like he was thinking about his next words, and she was sure that was the case. When he spoke, every fear she had gelled into a hot mass of terror. "Amethyst, something's going on. I don't know what it is, but I've been patient. I can't help you if you don't talk to me, so talk. Tell me what's happening, baby. You're not in school. You're not talking to your sister. Your conversations are stilted and limited, and that's not you. So tell me, please. You're breaking my heart because I can see you're in pain and you won't take my hand and let me help you."

Amethyst couldn't stop the sobs that tore from her chest. She knew how her dad was going to react. But when his hand took hers and he gripped it tightly … It was like she finally had a lifeline. Every time she'd trusted Gant, he'd come through for her, and she wanted to believe this wouldn't be an exception. "I … I … I … I failed out of this semester."

"You're a smart girl. You've done so well. Why would you fail out?"

"Be … Be … Because Craven and I broke up."

"Well, that explains why he didn't answer the phone when I called him. What happened? You guys have been together for almost four years now! That's quite a while. I can't imagine—"

She couldn't stop herself when she blurted out, "I'm pregnant!"

"How far along are you?"

Shit! He's going to suggest I have an abortion! I knew it! "Um, about seven weeks."

"And you've considered all your options?" She nodded. "And what do you want to do?"

"I … I … I want to keep it!" She couldn't control

herself anymore, and she sobbed so hard that her throat ached and her head hurt.

Two strong arms wrapped around her and she dissolved against his shoulder when her dad whispered, "Then that's what you'll do. I don't know how we'll work it out, but we will. I'm gonna be a grandpa, and I can't wait to meet that little boy or girl. Whatever you need, you'll get it."

Why had she ever doubted him? Her daddy had never let her down—never—and he wasn't going to start at that point, not when she needed him most. In her heart, she blessed the powers that had brought that brave, strong, loving man into her life to give her someone to cling to in her worst moments. "Th-th-th-thank you, Daddy. I love you."

"I love you too, baby girl, you and your sister. You're the only kids I'll ever have. Okay, well, I've got Tank and Bree and Carly and … Well, yeah, they're not that much younger than me. Anyway, you girls, you're my legacy. And if you're bringing another level of that legacy to the table, you think I'm going to just turn my back on that? No. I want whoever that little person is to be a better person than me, to be my contribution to society, one that's better than I could manage to be myself. And I'll help that along any way I can."

"And Lorna …"

Gant pulled back and ran a calloused hand down her face. "Honey, she loves you like you're her own. Whatever you need, we both stand ready to do whatever we can. Now, our first order of business should be getting you feeling better, and then we need to find you a doctor. Probably have to be somewhere else—if we've got a lady's doctor here, I don't know about them—but we can find somebody. Bree can probably help you with that. Justice too. But this? This is going to be fine. You're going to be fine. *We're* going to be fine. And you don't worry about Craven. You never have to see him again. I'll make sure of that."

"Daddy, please …"

"Don't you worry yourself about it. Now, take a nap and when you're rested, we'll all sit down and figure out what we need to do. But you're not alone, Amethyst. *You're not alone*." He leaned in and kissed her cheek. "I love you, baby girl."

"I love you too, Daddy." She wrapped her arms around his neck and squeezed tightly, and those arms encircled her again. She felt safe. She felt loved.

And, for the first time in weeks, she felt hopeful.

"GOING OUT TO THE SHOP FOR A FEW MINUTES. I'LL BE right back." Gant knew Amethyst was listening from down the hallway, so he pointed to Lorna and then to the shop, and she nodded. He'd barely made it to the forge when he saw her slip out the back door and make her way across the yard, so he grabbed her hand and ran with her down the drive until he got to the trail to the creek. Once they were out of sight, he slowed, but he kept leading her that direction and, to her credit, Lorna said nothing. They reached the rocks they both loved to meditate on and Gant dropped to sitting, then took her hand and pulled her down. That was the moment when she finally asked, "What's going on?"

"She's pregnant." Lorna didn't say a word. "Did you hear me?"

"Yeah. I did. What does she want to do?"

"She wants to keep it and raise it."

"And what about you? What do you think about this?"

"It's not up to me. It's up to her. My job is to support her however she needs me to."

Lorna's hand rose and she stroked his cheek as she smiled. "That's my man. That's the right answer. What about the father?"

"What about the father? I'll show you." Gant pulled out his phone, hit a contact and waited. A voicemail answered.

"You've reached the voicemail of the awesome Craven Bradshaw. Leave a message and if you're worthy, I'll call you back. Otherwise, get lost." *BEEEEEEEPPP!*

"Craven, it's Gant Meadows. You know, the grandfather of your child? Just wanted you to know that we're handling everything and if you so much as step into Bandera County … I'd suggest that you don't, for your own safety. When word gets around what's happened, I'm pretty sure *no one* here will welcome you. Not that you give a shit, as if I was unaware of that, but just don't. Don't call her, don't come here. I won't tell you a second time. In regards to my daughter, you're history—ancient history." And he hung up.

"So I take it he's the father and he's not supportive?"

"Nope. Not at all. I'm not sure what happened, but I know she failed out of her classes and came here, so I have to believe he either kicked her out or moved out and she couldn't afford the apartment." There was only one question he had for Lorna. "Are we okay?"

"We're absolutely, positively okay. I didn't marry you

to limit you. I married you to stand beside you, and I will."

"Thanks, babe. I have a feeling this is going to be a rough road."

"Then I'll buckle up and hang on!"

She had no idea how thankful Gant was for her, and in that moment, he didn't think he'd ever been as thankful for anyone. Lorna had been a huge blessing in his life, and he could never give her as much love as she'd shown him.

But he'd sure try.

AMETHYST WOKE TO THE SMELL OF SOMETHING delicious. She wasn't sure what it was, but her mouth was watering and her stomach growled. As soon as she'd finished a trip to the bathroom, she wandered up the hallway and into the kitchen.

"Hey, sleepyhead! You feeling better?" her smiling stepmother asked from the stove.

"Yeah. What's cooking?"

"Potato soup. And I've got sourdough bread baking. I'll have some chicken tenders out of the air fryer to go with it all, and a salad. Does that sound good?"

"It sounds amazing. Can I help?"

"Sure. Get the stuff out for the salad. We can all put whatever we want on them. There's mixed greens in there, and tomatoes, two kinds of cheeses, diced onions, about five different kinds of dressings … Oh, and some crunchy condiments to put on them, and sunflower seeds up there in the cabinet," Lorna added and pointed, so Amethyst got busy.

"Where's Dad?"

"Out in his shop."

Amethyst waited, but Lorna didn't say anything, so she finally asked, "Did he tell you?"

Lorna turned and put the spoon she'd been stirring with in a spoon rest. "Honey, we don't have any secrets. So yes, he did. And whatever he told you, I'm right there with him. I'll be here for whatever you need from me."

Amethyst started to cry again. Damn, it seemed that was all she did those days! There was warmth next to her and she felt an arm encircle her shoulders. "Oh, honey, it's okay. You're not alone. We're right here. Is there anything I can do for you?"

She nodded and sniffled. "Yeah. Do you know a doctor? Or does Bree know one?"

"We both go to Dr. Everett in Hondo. She's really nice. Carly went to her too. And the hospital over in Medina is pretty nice, if you want to consider it instead of going all the way into San Antonio."

"Okay. I'll call and make an appointment if you can get me the number."

"I'll be glad to. Let's just take this one day at a time, okay?"

"Okay." Amethyst felt better, and she wasn't mad at Gant for telling Lorna. Someday she'd like to have a relationship like the one they had, and that kind of relationship required honesty and trust. If she really thought about it, she was kind of glad he'd told Lorna. The fewer times she had to say it all, the better off she was.

CHAPTER 2

He didn't have her number, so Jackson called Gant to check on Amethyst. Something about the way she'd looked when she collapsed had caused him great alarm, and he hoped she was feeling a little better. "Hey there, Boss!"

Jackson smiled. For reasons he didn't understand, he'd picked up the nickname Boss right after he'd been there on scene for the take-down with Gant, and it had stuck. "Hey, just calling to check on your girl."

"She's okay. I'm out in the shop, but I just saw her through the window, helping Lorna in the kitchen, so I'm pretty sure she's okay."

"Good. She really had me worried there. Something just seemed off about the way she went down, and I—"

"It was anxiety, pure and simple. I think when she started talking about school and job prospects and all that kind of thing, it just caused her to spiral."

"She's anxious about graduating? Most kids are happy to get out."

"No. She's not going to graduate. She dropped out."

He was about to ask when Gant said, "Jackson, she's pregnant."

That was so *not* what he'd thought Gant was about to say. "Holy hell. I'm so sorry. I mean, not sorry that there's a baby, but sorry that her plans … You know what I mean."

"Yeah. I do. And she wants to keep it, so we're going into this for the long haul."

"And the father?"

He heard Gant snort. "Jackass either kicked her out or left so she couldn't afford the apartment. That's how she wound up here."

Jackson remembered their conversation in the truck that first night. "That explains why she didn't tell you she was coming."

"Yep. And if she wanted to surprise me, she did a great job of it. If it had been Sapphire, I mean, she's younger and kinda silly sometimes, so I guess I wouldn't have been so surprised, but Amethyst has always been so mature and grown-up. This was the last thing I ever thought I'd hear her say to me."

"Well, look, if I can do anything or you need anything, don't hesitate to ask. Call me anytime."

There was silence for a few seconds and then Jackson heard Gant's voice break as he said, "Thanks. I appreciate it. I know not a lot of people around here know me and I haven't been real social, but you're somebody who's very important to me, and I value your friendship, Jackson. I really do. I wouldn't still be alive without you, so I appreciate you."

"Just doin' my job, but it couldn't have been done for a better person. I value your friendship too, and I meant what I said. Call me. Anytime. Even if it's just to talk.

This is going to be stressful. Don't be afraid to reach out if you need to."

"I will, I promise."

"Well, tell her I said to take care of herself and I'll be seeing you guys."

"Yep. Will do. Thanks again, Boss. Later."

Jackson sat with the phone in his hand and thought about everything. Amethyst was pregnant. Gant and Lorna were going to have their hands full. They'd never thought when they married that they were going to have a woman and a baby with them. That certainly wasn't something they would've wanted.

But Jackson? It was all he'd ever wanted and never managed to keep.

THE MEETING WAS ALMOST OVER WHEN THE DOOR opened. "Well, well, well! Decided to grace us with your presence, beautiful?"

Lorna laughed as she crossed the room with a large cake-keeper in her hands. "I'm just bringing in treats."

"Of course you are! Who's that behind you?" Pops asked to encourage an introduction to the rest of the fire-fighters.

She smiled. "Guys, this is Gant's oldest daughter, Amethyst. She's going to be staying with us for a while. I know some of you met her at the hospital." The young woman nodded to the gathering of guys as she carried in a big bakery box.

"Oh, so now you have reinforcements in the plot to thicken us!" Pops said as the rest of the guys laughed.

"Whatcha got in that box, darlin'?" he asked in Amethyst's direction.

"They're just no-bake cookies. Nothing special."

"Hey, if you made them for the lot of us, that's pretty special!" Buff called out as the rest of the guys laughed.

Ten minutes later, the cake-keeper and box were both open and the men had plates with slices of beautiful, golden pound cake on them and two or three cookies apiece. Lorna had transferred the rest of the cake to a plate she'd taken from the cabinet when Jackson walked up. "Hey, girls, thanks for this! It's nice to have something homemade every once in a while."

"You're welcome," Lorna said, beaming. "And I was glad to have some help tonight."

"Oh, it's no big deal," Amethyst responded. Even under her dark skin, Jackson could see her blush.

"Yes it is. Just having someone think about us is a big deal. So thank you. You feeling okay?"

"Yeah. I am." She stopped for a second, then dropped her gaze to the countertop. "I know you know. Dad told me you called to check on me. I hope you don't see me as—"

"As what? A beautiful young woman who's made a courageous decision?"

"No. An idiot who did something really stupid and is planning to ruin a kid too."

Lorna had walked away, and Jackson moved a little closer to Amethyst so the rest of the guys couldn't hear their conversation. "I don't see you as an idiot who's going to ruin a kid. I see you as a beautiful, capable woman who's decided that bringing another person into the world to make it a better place sounds like a good idea, even if her plans have to be disrupted for a while."

That was the moment when Amethyst glanced up at Jackson and their eyes locked. He couldn't remember ever seeing a more beautiful pair of eyes in the whole world. They were clear and bright and framed by the most glorious dark lashes he was sure he'd ever witnessed. There was a noticeable *click* somewhere in his chest, and it was almost as though his heart and breathing hit a reset. *Kiss her!* a voice shouted in his head, followed by *Oh, holy hell, do NOT do that!* He couldn't if he wanted to—there were too many people around. And he did want to. *Shut it down, Frame*, he told himself, but it was too late. He didn't know what she'd felt, but there'd been a spark for him, something warm and wonderful, and he wanted to know what that was.

"Well, I suppose I should go. Lorna's going to be looking for me. I'm glad you're enjoying the treats." The young woman turned to walk away, but then spun back and looked him in the eye. "You've been so nice to me. Would you let me cook dinner for you sometime?"

"You don't have to do—"

"I'd like to, but if you don't want me to—"

"Oh, no. I'd really like that. But …" One of her eyebrows quirked upward and Jackson thought it was the cutest thing he'd ever seen. "Okay. When?"

"Tomorrow night?"

"Okay. What do I need to buy?"

"How 'bout I send you a grocery list? I'd buy it but I—"

He knew what she was about to say. "That's okay. I don't mind at all. You just tell me what to buy and I'll get it."

"Okay. Sounds good. Dad's got your phone number, right?"

"Yep. Get it from him and text me so I've got yours and you can send me the list."

"Works for me. So, bye, Jackson. Guess I'll see you tomorrow night." As she brushed past him, she touched his hand briefly with hers, and he understood.

What he'd felt? He hadn't been the only one.

FEED THE COWS. FEED THE HOGS—WELL, HOG. THERE was only one. He'd had the other one butchered. Feed the horses. Make sure everybody had water. That was hell for him, so all the while he had the hose in his hand, he talked to himself. Out loud. That surely meant he was mentally ill, he reasoned.

"She's young enough to be my daughter!"

"No, she's not. Well, technically, she is, but she's not my daughter."

"No! She's my friend's daughter!"

"That's even worse!"

"No, it's better. He knows me. He'll understand."

"He won't. She's his little girl. He'll kill me."

"She's a grown woman. She can make her own decisions."

"She's a down-on-her-luck pregnant college dropout. Do I really want to get involved in that?"

"She's also beautiful, smart, and kind, all things I value highly."

"But she's pregnant!"

"So what? I love kids! After Cassidy ..."

His ruminations ended abruptly. After all those years, it was still dreadfully painful to think about, even though remembering kept her alive in his mind. He pulled out his phone and looked through his contacts until he found her number. When she answered, all she said was, "Hi."

"Hey. How ya doin'?"

"I'm pretty good. What about you?"

"I'm pretty good too. Just hadn't talked to you in a long time and figured I should. You guys doing okay these days?"

"Yeah. Jonathan got a promotion a few weeks ago so we're doing quite well."

"What about the boys?"

"God, they're growing like weeds. I mean, Seth is eight now, and Cody's six. Seth's playing elementary soccer and Cody's all wrapped up in baseball. That's all he thinks about. What about you? What are you doing these days?"

"Moved to Bandera County from Medina County. Farm's a little bigger, town's a little smaller. Otherwise, there's not much difference. Got a hog, a few cows, five horses, and I take care of those. Think I'm going to buy a border collie to help work the cows."

"How many cows are we talking about here?"

"Fourteen."

"Oh! I thought you were going to say three! That's quite a few."

"Yeah, and they're a little hard to manage if they're not behaving, but a dog could really help."

"A dog would keep you company." It got quiet, and he knew what she wanted to ask him.

"Before you ask, no. Nobody. Although I've met somebody I'm a little interested in, but I doubt she'd give me the time of day."

"You should take the plunge, Jackson. It's high time."

"I don't move as fast as you do, Georgie. It takes me a

good while to make up my mind to something. You know that."

"Didn't take you any time to decide to reenlist." He was about to say something when she blurted out, "I'm sorry. Ancient history. And I don't want to alienate you. I know we'll never be that close again, but we have a shared history, and I don't want to lose that. You and I, we have a history no one else can share because of the things that happened. You're the only one who understands it for me, and I'm the only one who understands it for you. So I apologize. I didn't mean to take another swing at you."

"That's okay. We all have things we wish we'd done differently. That's my biggest one."

"Make peace with it. You won't outlive regret, Jackson. It'll still be around when you go to your grave."

"That's true. I suppose it will. Well, I guess I'll let you go. I just wanted to check on you, see how you are. I'll talk to you again sometime."

"Yeah, I'll still be here. And Jackson?"

"Yeah?"

"I love you. Not the way I used to, but I do love you as a friend."

He pinched the bridge of his nose with his thumb and forefinger. "Same here. Love you too. Bye." Jackson ended the call and stood there, suddenly weak and tired. He wanted to talk to her, wanted to keep in touch, but it drained him. He was thinking about that picture, the one of the three of them together, and how he still had it in his office, propped up on the shelf behind the desk so he couldn't see it when he was sitting there. He didn't want to stare at it all the time, but it was all he had left of them.

That old pity was washing over him when his phone

pinged and he checked it. Strange number. Then he opened the text message and laughed.

Hey. Grocery list headed your way. What time?

Good question. *Five?*

Sounds good. I hope Dad knows where you live because I don't.

That made him laugh again. *I think so. You send a grocery list. I'll send directions. See you at five.*

She sent him a thumbs-up emoji followed by a smiley. That counted for something, right? He laughed and shook his head. No young, beautiful woman with her whole life ahead of her would want a washed-up former Army reservist who'd gone through hell and back and lost his entire family. Oh, and one who was twenty-one years older than her. Why the hell would he even think about that?

But if he was honest with himself, it was all he'd thought about since he'd seen her the night before. The grocery list popped up. When he'd taken a look at it, he shook his head and laughed again before he shot off a reply: *I hope you have suggestions for substitutions, because I can tell you our store won't have half of that stuff.*

There was a long pause before she texted back: *Do your best.*

He laughed aloud at that. "Lawd, girl, you have no idea how pathetic my best is!" He was still chuckling when he headed to the house. It was time to get cleaned up and go to the store. And while he was there, he'd just get a couple of surprises too.

"I'M GOING," AMETHYST CALLED OUT AS SHE STOOD BY the front door.

"Okay. Have fun and cook good. God knows that poor devil could use a homecooked meal," Gant called back. "What time do you think you'll be back?"

"I dunno. Gotta cook it, gotta eat it, gotta clean up after it, and gotta at least spend a little time with him. No eating and running."

"No. That would be rude, even if you *did* cook it," her dad agreed as he stepped into the living room. "Be careful and let us know when you're headed back so we'll be watching for you. And let me know when you get to his house and—"

"I'm supposed to be there at five. If I don't go, I'll be late. And if I'm late, don't you think he'll call you and ask where I am because he'll be afraid something happened to me?"

Gant chuckled. "Yeah, probably."

"Okay. I'll see you guys later. Bye, Lorna!"

"Bye, sweetie! Have a good evening."

She looked at his directions and followed them to the letter. Stay on the highway. At the junction of FR 462, keep going. Another mile. Past the produce stand on the right—yeah, there it was. The bridge, Williams Creek Depot, and WCD West, whatever that was, should be in view on the left up ahead. Just a few hundred feet more but right before the bridge, turn left on … Yep. That was it. He hadn't been joking—some kid had covered up the actual road sign and written *HELL HOLE* over it with white paint. Very funny, that one, and she wondered why they'd done that.

It didn't take her long to find out. There were three or four dilapidated mobile homes and a little shack of sorts, and she kept her fingers crossed that those weren't Jackson's place. Nope. Not far enough out. He'd said two miles down that road, so she kept going. As soon as she crested the next hill, she gasped. There, sitting on a prairie-like expanse, was a cedar-sided home with dark brown shutters. Yards and yards of fencing came from the house out to the road and then down the road in both directions, and a few black cattle grazed under the late afternoon sun. Behind the house was a huge ridge, and when she thought about it, she realized Williams Creek was probably on the other side of it. Sure enough, there was a pickup truck in the drive, and she recognized it as Jackson's. There was a big garage attached to the house, and a huge one out in back. She assumed that was where he kept his tractor. Out in the middle of the field was a wooden structure with a tin roof, probably as shelter for the cattle, and a bigger barn off to one side where she imagined he let them stay when the weather was really bad. Hell, she didn't know anything about cattle.

She was surprised, though, when she pulled up and no dog ran out to greet her. Didn't everybody there have a dog? Well, her dad and Lorna didn't, so maybe nobody had one. Maybe dogs weren't popular there. She was getting her bag and climbing out of the Toyota when the front door opened and he stepped out onto the porch. Amethyst sucked in a breath at the sight of him there. The man was fine, all broad shoulders and chest, and that flat waistline and tight ass. Oh, yeah, and he was plenty tall enough too, at least six feet and two inches. His skin was dark and golden, and his medium brown hair was streaked with gray and sun. But the gray at his temples was extra sexy, and that button front shirt and form-fitting jeans ... Oh, god, she had to stop thinking that way! He was her dad's friend and a lot older than her. "I see you found it!" he called out as she stood from the car.

"Yeah. No trouble at all, although I don't think I've ever known anybody else who lived in a hell hole!" she answered, laughing.

"Yeah, wish I knew the little bastards who did that, but it's funny and everybody gets a laugh out of it."

"Honestly, the first few places I saw on the road made me think maybe it really was a hell hole."

Jackson shrugged. "I know. I own that too, and I need to tear those down. Nobody's lived up there for a few years, and I could use the property."

"You own that too?"

He nodded. "Yeah. Own almost two hundred acres out here."

"That's a lot!"

He laughed and held the door open for her. "Not if you live in Texas. It's just a drop in the bucket. To most Texans, that's a hobby farm!"

One look around and Amethyst wasn't sure what she'd expected, but that wasn't it. The hardwood floors gleamed, and the furniture was beautiful shades of navy and tan with dark wood trim. The coffee table was some kind of wooden slab with a blue river running down the center of it, and it was shiny enough to be a mirror. She'd never seen anything like it. Rustic art hung around, but it wasn't the sort of things she'd seen at roadside vendors or art fairs. This was art, high art, but still with a country, outdoors feel about it, made of all kinds of natural materials. One wall sported a huge woven wall hanging into which was incorporated feathers and twigs, and the beads here and there on it looked to be hand-flinted. Everything whispered *home*.

"Come on in. Want something to drink? I've got tea and sodas and all kinds of juice ..." She followed him and when they stepped into the kitchen, she almost fainted.

Stainless steel gleamed everywhere. The light wood cabinets sat above a stone-like floor, and they and the big white island in the middle of the room were topped with concrete countertops. "My god."

"Like it?"

"I love it. It's beautiful, Jackson. Just beautiful. You do a lot of cooking?"

"Confession time, I suppose."

She laughed and gave his arm a playful slap. "You *do* do a lot of cooking!"

"No. But I enjoy baking. I make all kinds of bread. Love it."

"Why have you never brought any to Dad and Lorna?"

"Because I'm afraid it's not good enough to share."

"That's ridiculous! I bet it's delicious! So, did you have any trouble getting the things on my list?"

"Nothing except the beets. Nobody had any, but I bought carrots. Will those work?"

"Perfectly. Okay. I'm going to get started and you can just go sit down and relax."

The smile he gave her was gentle, and it warmed her all over. "Would it be okay if I just sat in here and visited with you while you're cooking?"

"Sure. That would be nice. So I need a dish I can roast in, and a couple of saucepans, and ..." In just a couple of minutes, Jackson had retrieved every item Amethyst asked for, and she set about prepping everything.

Twenty minutes later, dinner was in the oven, and Jackson pointed to it. "How long does that need to cook?"

"About an hour."

"Good. Want me to show you around?"

"That would be fun! Sure!"

Once they were outside, she spoke the thought she'd had in the car. "I was surprised that a dog didn't meet me at the car."

"That's funny, seeing as how I just told my ex-wife earlier that I think I'm going to get a dog."

That was the first Amethyst had heard about an ex-wife. "You were married?"

"Yeah. Long time ago."

"You're not old enough for it to be a long time ago."

Jackson shrugged. "I'm forty-three."

"So she's around here?"

"No. She's outside Philadelphia with her husband and kids."

That was weird. "You still talk to her?"

"Yeah, a couple of times a year we check on each other. Things were … bad when we divorced, and since we were the only two who went through all that, it makes sense to at least stay in touch. You know, sometimes when you've been through something traumatic, it helps if you've got somebody who knows exactly what you went through."

"You went through something traumatic?"

Jackson nodded. "Yes." And that was all he said.

Amethyst waited, but he never spoke. "Well, did you feel better after you talked to her?"

He snorted. "No. Not really."

"Oh."

He kept walking, so she walked alongside him, and he eventually pointed out the different buildings and the cattle. "Oh, and that's the hog."

"Just one?"

"Yeah. I only keep them for meat, and I had the other one butchered a month ago, so I figure I won't need to do that one for another month or two. As soon as he's gone, I'll get two more barrows and keep going."

"Barrows?"

"Yeah. Male weanlings that have been castrated. They're only intended to be raised for meat."

"Oh. Got it." She pointed at the bigger garage and snickered. "Is that the place where you keep the tractor that needs a new tractor?"

"Yep. That would be the place. You'll see." He opened the door to the building and Amethyst started to laugh.

The tractor had to be over a hundred years old. No wonder the guys told him he needed a new one! "I think you need to take their advice."

"I think so too, but I'm thinking I'd like to get this one running. You know, thumb my nose at the gods of machinery and let them know Jackson Frame won't take their bullshit lying down!"

"Good idea!" They were both laughing, and Amethyst was thoroughly enjoying herself. He was easy to talk to, had a great sense of humor, and seemed to be pretty stable. "So you work?"

"No. I left the military and joined the reserves. But my enlistment there is up and I decided not to re-enlist."

"That didn't pay much."

"I've got a military pension."

"You were old enough to retire?"

"Yeah. Put in twenty years."

"But you're forty-three?"

"Yep. Retired five years ago."

"You joined when you were eighteen?" She could hardly believe it. Guys really did that?

"I did. I was ROTC in high school. I originally thought I wanted to be a doctor, but I really liked the life of a soldier, so I went the medic route."

"So were you like a major or a colonel or something?"

Jackson laughed. "No! I was E-8. Master Sergeant. Assigned to a battalion in Afghanistan."

"You went to war?"

"Yeah. I did. And I trained combat lifesavers too."

"What's that?"

"They're regular soldiers trained by a medic to do lifesaving steps. Sometimes if there's not a medic around when a soldier is hit, a combat lifesaver can do exactly what the name implies—save his life—by doing stop-gap measures that can keep him alive until medics or medical surgeons can get to him or her."

"Were you ever shot at?"

He sighed deeply. "All the time."

"Were you ever hit?"

"No." An odd look passed over his face. "But sometimes I felt like I had been. It was like I could feel every wound I attended to. It was horrible. The gunshot wounds, explosive injuries, vehicle accidents, dozens of things. I had guys who'd been knifed by people they thought were civilians or friendly forces."

"So you were a medic the whole time?"

"No. I was a medic the last fourteen years I was in. Before that, I was just a soldier, but I'd been trained as a combat lifesaver and one of my sergeants thought I had the aptitude to go on to E-8, so he talked to the sergeant major, who put in a request for them to consider me, and they took me almost immediately."

"Cool. But you enjoyed the army?"

"Honey, nobody enjoys the army, but I felt like I was performing a service for my country, and that meant something to me. Still does. Afterward, one weekend a month and two weeks out of the year, I got to be with other people who were in the reserves, and I got to train some of them as combat lifesavers."

"But they're reserves."

"Yeah, but they still need training. I've also gotten requests to train members of the Texas National Guard. Honestly, every time I replicate my skills in a new person, I feel like I've done the greatest service. If one of those guys goes out and saves five lives, those are five lives that might've been lost if there'd been no one to train them, so I'm happy to do it."

"So I guess you lost a lot of men over the years."

"Yeah. Quite a few."

"I guess that was the worst."

He shook his head. "No. The worst is losing somebody you love and being able to do nothing about it."

She didn't know what that was about, but it made her curious. Then she looked down at her watch. "Oh! It's almost ready! We should head back."

"Sure. Let's go." She waited as he closed the door on the big building and followed her back to the house.

An hour later, Jackson leaned back in his chair and sighed. "Whooo! I'm stuffed! Lawd, girl, that was delicious!"

"Thanks. I learned to do the vegetables from a friend

on the faire circuit. The chickens were something a friend's mom made and I loved them, so I learned that from her."

"Well, *I've* got a surprise for *you*!" Jackson opened a large pantry cabinet and pulled out a pan. "Hope you like it."

Amethyst lifted the top of the foil to find something chocolatey, cherry, and gooey. It smelled heavenly. "Oh, god, I love cherries."

"Good, because it's sure full of them. Of course, be careful. Sometimes the people at the packing plants miss a pit, so I wouldn't want you to break a tooth."

"Okay. I'll remember." She waited as he scooped out a big serving and slid the bowl to her. One bite in and she stared up at him. Still chewing, she said, "Oh my god, this is delicious."

Jackson laughed. "Good! Now that you've tested it out, think I'll have some!"

Twenty minutes later, everything was cleaned up and the dishwasher was running. "Have a seat," he said and swept his arm toward the sofa. When she sat, he took up residence in an adjacent chair. For reasons she couldn't quite put a finger on, Amethyst was a little disappointed. Something about him sitting beside her … *No. Stop that right now*, she told herself, but she knew she wouldn't. She'd watched him all evening and those hands were made to touch her, she was certain. "So, do you think you'll go back to college eventually?"

She nodded. "Probably have to if I'm going to make a living for me and a child."

"True. But who knows? You may change your mind on your major by then."

"I don't think so." She waited a few seconds before she asked, "You have an ex-wife. Do you date?"

He seemed a little surprised, and that surprised her. Could he not tell how much she liked him? "Uh, no. I haven't."

"Why not? You're a good-looking guy, and a nice one too."

He snorted. "Have you seen the dating pool in Tarpley? I think the only decent women in town have been snapped up by the other guys with the VFD. The rest aren't exactly my type."

"And what's your type?"

He shrugged. "I dunno. Somebody who's smart and funny. Somebody who's quick-witted and will give me shit when she needs to. Somebody who'll let me take care of her but won't let me boss her around. Somebody who wouldn't mind a simple life because, god knows, mine's not too complicated."

"Do you have family here?"

"Nah. Just a brother in Wyoming close to where we grew up. He thinks I'm crazy for living down here with the heat and the dust and the scrub, but I love it. It's like everything I love about Mexico and none of the things I don't!"

"And you still have tequila here."

"I do! Which makes everything okay, I suppose."

"Are you interested in dating?" She was going to get to the bottom of this thing if it killed her.

"I am."

"Maybe I should've asked, are you interested in a relationship?"

"Yes. Maybe I should've answered that I'm interested

in a relationship, not just dating. I'm not into casual dating. If I'm going to be with somebody, I'm going to be with them. It's not going to be a drop by, sleep with me, go home and we don't talk for a week until there's another booty call. That's not me. That's one of the reasons I moved here. I figured if I met somebody here, they'd be an 'all in' kind of person, not just a fly-by-night girl. I've gotten used and mistreated a few times in the past, and I'm not interested in going down that road again."

"Apparently so have I. Only it was with somebody I'd been with for almost four year. And that sucks."

"It does." She watched his face carefully. Something was going on there, something she couldn't understand. When he finally spoke, he said, "There's something I think I need to tell you."

"Okay."

It seemed to be hard for him to get started. Several times it looked like he'd start to speak, only to stop. When he finally did, he sighed before he began, and something about that sound told Amethyst just how difficult it was going to be for him to utter the words necessary. "I had a daughter."

"Had?"

"Yes. Cassidy. Beautiful little girl. Her mom's eyes, my smile. Dark hair, hazel eyes, skin the same color as mine."

"Which is beautiful, by the way."

"Thanks. Munsee." What did he mean? "Algonquin. Part of the Lanape tribe in New Jersey. My grandmother's people. Anyway, she was adorable. I was deployed and Georgie called me one day, said Cassidy was acting kind of weird and she was taking her to the doctor."

"Georgie is your ex?"

He nodded. "So she took her, and then she called me and told me I had to come home right that minute. I told her it would take time, and she told me there wasn't any." He shifted in his seat, and Amethyst found herself as uncomfortable as he was. "She had a brain tumor. Glioblastoma." Amethyst had heard of those, and she knew what that meant. "They told Georgie she might have six months. I talked to my CO, told him what was going on. He told me if I left, I would only have a window in which to travel, so if I wanted to be there for her at the end, I should probably wait. When I called Georgie and told her, she went off the deep end. Called me every name in the book, said I didn't care, that I didn't deserve to be a dad, that I was a horrible person and she hoped she never saw me again."

"What did you do?"

"I waited like I was told. The doctors were wrong. She didn't have six months. She only had three. The hospital called me and told me I should get on my way but by the time I got home, she was gone. There was a war because Georgie didn't want to wait for me to get home, even for the funeral, and my brother hired an attorney and blocked that. By the time I got there, the funeral was arranged and only two hours away, and my marriage was over."

"God, Jackson, I'm so sorry. I can't even imagine."

"Me either. Even now it seems like a nightmare. I wasn't here to hold her, to kiss her, to tell her goodbye. Georgie was furious with me because I hadn't been there to hold her, kiss her, or tell her it would be okay. I let them both down. All that was left for me to do was to get on a plane and go back. I worked my ass off trying to save as many soldiers as I could, but I couldn't even be there for my own child, much less save her."

"But I thought you said you just talked to Georgie."

"I did. About five years after Cassidy died, she called me out of the blue and wanted to talk to me. We sat in a coffee shop in New York and talked for about three hours. I told her over and over how sorry I was and how I wished I could change how everything had gone. She told me she forgave me, and that since we were the ones who'd remember Cassidy best, it would be nice if we could at least be friends. I agreed, and we've worked hard to stay civil over the years. A year later, she called me and told me she was remarrying. Now she's got a good husband and two boys, cute little guys, and she's happy. She deserves to be. I've been alone ever since. And I deserve to be."

"Nobody deserves to be alone. Not even you." When he wouldn't lift his head to look at her, Amethyst dropped to her hands and knees and crawled across to him, rose upright, and pressed his face upward until he was looking at her. "What happened was horrible. There's no script for that, no protocol, no timeline. Everything about it has to be made up as you go along, and you did what you thought you should do. No one can fault you for that."

"I fault myself."

"You shouldn't."

"But I do. I guess I always will."

Those eyes … Amethyst had never seen eyes so sad. He was hurting, and he'd been hurting for quite some time. "How long ago was that?"

"She was three and a half, so that was over fifteen years ago."

More than fifteen years of torturing himself every

damn day. Fifteen years of lying awake at night, wondering why he could save people he didn't even know and couldn't do anything for his own child. Fifteen years of being alone and feeling like that was all he deserved. He went off to war to serve his country and came back to nothing, his whole world dissolved and wasted away. Amethyst didn't even think about it. She just leaned in and pressed her lips to his.

In mere seconds, his arms were around her shoulders and he was kissing her back with a tenderness that Amethyst had never known. When he ended that kiss, he looked down into her face and smiled. "Don't do this. You deserve so much better."

Her eyes filled with tears. "There is nothing better. There's no one better than you."

"I wish I believed that."

"Believe it. I can promise you this. I believe it, and I'll treat you like it's true until you finally believe it too. I can believe enough for the both of us."

"What's your dad gonna say?"

Amethyst laughed through her tears. "Based on what he and Lorna went through, I don't think he can say one damn word."

Jackson rose and reached down for her hand. When she was standing, he pulled her toward the sofa, sat down, and pulled her down to sit beside him, then took both her hands in his. "I just want you to know that I'm not going to push you. I'm not going to rush you. I'm not going to demand anything. I wouldn't do that to you. Whatever you want, that's what I want too."

She nodded. "Okay. And I'm not going to ask things of you that aren't fair. And one of the things that wouldn't be fair would be for me to ask you to help raise this baby. That wouldn't be fair to you at all."

"Why not?"

"Because it's not your responsibility."

He lifted one hand and stroked it down her cheek. "But if it's yours, it is."

"But it's not yours."

"No one has to know that. Who else knows you're pregnant?"

She realized in that moment that no one did. No one but her dad, Lorna, and Jackson. Oh, and Craven, but that sonofabitch didn't count. "Nobody. Just the three of you. No one else. I haven't even told Sapphire, and I sure haven't told Mom."

"Then we don't tell anybody else. And when it comes, everybody will think it's mine. What ethnicity is the biological father?"

"His dad's white. His mom is Italian or Jewish or something, so he's actually … His coloring is a lot like yours."

"Well, there ya go. How far along are you?"

"About seven or eight weeks?"

"And how much time have you spent around people here?"

"Uh, more than I should've, I guess. All the guys at the station have seen me coming in and out."

"Yeah, but for all they know, we've been seeing each other on the sly for months, ever since your dad was in the hospital. So they know nothing. Will Gant and Lorna go along with it?"

"I don't know why not if I ask them to. Tank's my stepbrother, so if he asks, I'll tell him the truth, but he and Callie won't say a word. Bree and Slade won't either.

But I don't know how I'm going to tell my dad about this."

"You don't worry about it and let me handle it. I'll cook tomorrow night if you'll get them to come over here, and we can talk to them here."

"And if he kicks me out?"

Jackson laughed. "Well, looks like you'd have a place to go!"

"Do you want me to come over and spend the night?"

"Do you *want* to come over and spend the night?"

"Uh, yeah. I mean, Jesus, after that kiss, hell yeah."

"Ever been with an old man?"

"No, and I won't be with an old man if I'm with you. Unless you're going to do like that actor did in that commercial and start taking off your muscles when you walk through the door, I don't think that's going to be a problem."

"Nope. They ain't much, but they're all mine."

"They're pretty fucking fine from where I sit."

"Oh, you've got a dirty mouth on you?" That made Amethyst laugh. "I like it!"

"Good thing, because I've tried to calm it down over the years and it just doesn't work."

"By the way, how old *are* you?"

Amethyst grinned. "I'm twenty-two."

"Hot damn, this old guy's got it goin' on!" Jackson cranked up a little gyrating dance as he sat there on the sofa and Amethyst screamed with laughter. "What? You think this is gonna keep? Naw, girl, you gonna have to get on it! My 'best if used by' date is coming up soon!"

She was laughing so hard that she couldn't breathe. "Oh, is that right?"

Then Jackson grabbed her hand and gave it a squeeze.

"I do have one thing to say. There will be no sex until you've seen the obstetrician. I want to know that you're okay and everything looks fine. No risks here. And ..." He stopped and took a deep breath. "It's obvious to me that you and what's-his-name didn't use condoms. I mean, you'd been together for four years. I probably wouldn't have either. But you don't know where he's been, so I think you should be tested."

"How long has it been since you were with anybody."

He blew out a breath and gazed ceilingward. "Oh, let's see, um ... three years?"

"*Three years*? Are you serious?"

"Yeah. I'm serious."

"Do you even remember how?"

He winked at her. "Oh, little girl, you just wait. I'll show you how much I remember."

"Promises, promises."

"Obstetrician, obstetrician."

"Gah, you're a hard ass!" she said, laughing again.

"Yeah, well, when I care about somebody, I care about them. What can I say? I'm just an old guy who cares about people."

She grasped his chin with her thumb and forefinger and moved in closer. "And I find that very sexy." When she kissed him that time, there was a hunger between them that she could feel. He wanted her. She wanted him. He was a kind, decent man who'd treat her right and never, never betray her trust. Of that, she was certain.

That time she was the one who broke the kiss. "I should probably head in. Dad's already said I should call him when I leave to let him know I'm on the way."

"He cares about you. And I want you to call me when you get home so I know you got there okay."

"If they're asleep, I'll text you. That okay?"

He kissed the tip of her nose. "That's fine."

"Okay. So you really want to do this tomorrow night?"

"Yeah. Rip the damn bandage off."

"Okay then. I'll see you tomorrow night. Same time?"

"That's fine."

"Okay. Seems like I'm saying okay a lot."

"I'll walk you out."

"Good. Be a gentleman."

He chuckled. "I have every intention of it!"

When they reached her car, she turned, and he kissed her again, her hands resting gently on his shoulders and his arms around her waist. "You be careful," he whispered to her as he kissed her on the forehead.

"I will. Night."

"Night, angel."

As she drove away, she could see him standing there, watching her go, and Amethyst sobbed as she drove. She'd endured weeks and weeks of crying almost constantly, but this time was different.

They were tears of joy.

CHAPTER 3

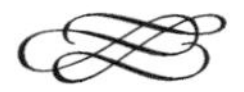

He grinned when the text message came in.

I'm home and safe. They're not asleep, but he's hovering. IDK WTH's wrong with him. Thanks for everything. Can't wait to see you tomorrow.

Everything inside him lit up at her words. *Can't wait to see you too. Night, angel.* The text he got back made him smile even wider.

Night. XOXOXO

"Oh my Jesus," he said aloud to himself. "I'm in love with a girl half my age. What the hell is wrong with me?" He didn't have to ask himself that question. He knew.

He'd known that evening when he found her stranded on the road that something was going on, and he'd felt that attraction, the one that told him he needed to keep an eye on her, that she was vulnerable and ripe for exploitation. For a split second, he let himself have the luxury of thinking about a little boy or girl with dark, curly hair playing on a jungle gym he'd built with his own hands, riding a bike up and down the long drive, and riding on the tractor with him. He could just envision them chasing chickens around in the yard, and him laughing and telling them to cut it out at just the moment Amethyst stepped out the back door and called them to dinner. His family, the family he thought he'd never have. It could be a reality.

It was going to be a long, sleepless night. He just knew it. His mind was racing with happy thoughts, things he hadn't let himself feel for years. With a cup of fresh coffee in front of him and the carafe full, he looked over his finances. She probably didn't have insurance, but that didn't matter. He had plenty of money he'd banked away during the years he was still in the military after Cassidy was gone. The hospital bills would be no problem. College … That would be a little harder, but they could swing it. Hell, the kid would probably be so damn smart that they could get a scholarship! But the cost of living would go up, and there would be shoes, and dance classes or baseball, and Amethyst might want to go back to school … He might have to get a job, but that would be okay. Surely he could find something. That could be managed. He thought about re-enlisting in the reserves, then decided against it unless it was absolutely necessary. But finding a job doing training sounded like it might be possible.

He picked up a notebook lying on the coffee table and opened it. Then he started making a list.

Pros:

Stable home life

Two parents

She's not alone

I'm not alone

Everybody thinks the baby is mine

She has family nearby

Her parents and I get along well

Cons:

Age difference

My age when child graduates high school

School distances from here

Low cultural involvement

Few social opportunities

He looked the list over. It wasn't too bad. Several of the things in the "Cons" section were things that every parent in the area struggled with. There was the age difference, but that didn't seem to bother her, and it didn't bother him. Unlike most of the young women her age, she was extremely mature. Not once had he heard her say, "Oooo, that's sick!" or any of those other weird phrases college kids used. She wasn't a college kid. She was a young adult, and she behaved like one. That was something he credited Gant with. He'd also heard Gant talk about her upbringing, and he knew she'd had to be a grown-up with a mom like hers. He had a feeling she'd been the parent to her sister before their adoptive dad had come on the scene.

Jackson took another swig of coffee and dropped his head back onto the back of the sofa, then closed his eyes. In his mind he could see her there, kneeling on his floor, her hands on his cheeks. Her eyes were bright and beautiful, and she looked like an angel there, smiling at him. He'd only been home for the last little bit of Georgie's pregnancy with Cassidy, but he remembered his little daughter kicking inside her mommy's tummy, remembered Georgie's swollen, tight breasts, remembered watching her nurse Cassidy and the joy on her face as she held their child. What would Amethyst look like, her belly round and huge, her breasts heavy and their blue veins prominent? Oddly enough, part of his training in combat medicine had been devoted to childbirth, in case he was nearby and a woman was going into labor, or if a female soldier on the battle lines found herself in the middle of a miscarriage or worse. He'd only had to use that training a few times since he'd been part of a VFD, but would she want him to deliver the baby? God, he'd love that!

"Shit, my mind's running away with me," he muttered aloud to no one as he sat there, thinking. But the prospect of a family had never crossed his mind until she'd rolled down that window on the side of the road and he'd seen those beautiful dark eyes. His family. His child. His wife.

His *wife*. That one word took every thought Jackson had and compressed it down to one simple truth. He wanted to make her his, hold her, care for her, provide for her, and raise her child—*their* child. It was everything he'd ever wanted, and with that one simple word, his life would be complete.

THE STILLNESS OF THE EARTH IN THE MORNINGS WAS HER favorite time, and Amethyst loved it. Most of her friends were night owls, but she loved sunrise, the birds chirping and the clouds moving through the sky. She made a pot of coffee and poured a big cupful, careful to make sure she didn't accidentally turn it off before her dad and Lorna had a chance to have some. She'd give them about forty-five minutes and they'd start stirring because Lorna had to go to work. When they did, she'd hustle back inside and cook them some little breakfast of some kind. It was the least she could do.

As she sat there in the chaise lounge on the back porch her dad had built for Lorna, she smiled. The coffee was strong and warm and her fuzzy socks were keeping her toes toasty in the cool spring air. A few beams of sunlight fell across her legs and warmed them. She hadn't even noticed which side of Jackson's house was turned east, and she made a note to check for eastern exposure when she went that evening.

Her mind raced ahead. Would he let her have a garden? Would he insist she have one? How much would he expect her to help him out around the place? Would she ever have to go near that hog? Damn thing scared the shit out of her. So ugly. The first time she spent the night there, would he get up and fix her bacon from his own hogs? That made her smile, thinking about the time and effort he put into having things there that were special. The house was beautiful, and he'd gone to a lot of trouble to make it look nice. She hadn't asked, but she was pretty sure it had three bedrooms. That meant Sapphire could come and spend time with them in the summer. She'd love that, and Saph would be a lot of help with the baby too. Playing auntie was something she'd fall right into.

She wanted to call her sister and her mom and tell them, but she and Jackson had agreed not to tell anyone else until they could start their little ruse. God, she hoped Saph didn't call Dad for some reason until they'd all had a chance to talk! That would throw a monkey wrench in everything for sure.

"Hey, you're up early!" a male voice said, and she turned to see her dad step out onto the porch, barefoot and in his pajama pants and a tee.

"Yeah, I love sunrise."

"Mind if I sit down with you?"

"Of course not! Want a cup of coffee?" she asked, setting hers on the table beside the chaise.

"No, no. Don't get up. I'll go get it. Be right back." She watched him disappear into the house, but he was back in under a minute, and he took up residence in one of the glider chairs, his feet up on the little coffee table in front of the furniture. "Ahhh, you sure know how to make a cup of coffee, girl!"

"Thanks. It's gotten me through a lot of mid-terms and finals."

"I bet." They sat there in the chirping, rustling sounds of the outdoors until Gant said, "You know I don't miss much."

Uh-oh, Amethyst heard a voice in her head say. "What do you mean?"

"I know you wanted to cook for Jackson to repay him for rescuing you as a damsel in distress on the side of the highway, but I got the distinct feeling there was something else going on there."

"There wasn't." *God, I hate lying to him!* she scolded herself, so she added, "Not when I left here yesterday."

"And when you came back?"

Holy shit balls, what do I say to that? Many things her dad was, but clueless wasn't one of them, and sometimes she wished he was. "Jackson wants to talk to you."

"About …"

Amethyst shrugged. "Things."

"And would these 'things' have anything to do with you?" he asked with air quotes.

"Like I said, Jackson wants to talk to you."

"Do you want me to talk to Jackson?"

She nodded. "Yes."

"I swear to god, you and Pops … The two of you are

the most frustrating people I've ever talked to. You talk and talk without saying a damn thing, and when you do, you act like I should've already known what you were thinking." He took another swallow of coffee. "So that's what this dinner is about."

"That and all of us spending time together, which I thought you'd welcome."

He set his coffee cup down, dropped his feet to the porch floor, and stared at her. "You know full well I like spending time with Jackson. He's a great guy. I can see where anybody would like spending time with him. I think it's the *kind of time* I'm asking about here."

"I can't say. That's his discussion to have with you."

"So you're not going to tell me anything?"

She shook her head. "Nope."

"So I should just let my imagination run wild?"

"*DAD!* For the love of god, stop! You'll find out tonight. I mean, that's not that long from now. What, eleven hours and some change?"

"Fine, fine!" Gant picked up his coffee cup and put his feet back up on the table. "But I wish you'd just *talk* to me!" Then he fell silent.

Amethyst waited, but he didn't say anything else, and she felt terrible. She'd shown up on his doorstep with a problem she couldn't handle alone, and he felt like she'd conspired behind his back. Her phone was in her pocket, so she stood. "Gotta get more coffee." Gant just grunted at her. When she stepped inside, she texted quickly: *I have to tell Dad. He knows something's up and he's mad.*

Do what you think is best. I trust your judgment.

She smiled. *Thank you.*

She instantly got back a reply.

I'd do anything for you, angel.

There was no doubt in her mind that he meant what he said. When she opened the door and wandered back outside, she stood by the chaise for a few seconds before she asked, "Do you really want me to tell you? Because I will if you want."

He snickered. "And how would Jackson feel about that?"

"He told me he trusts my judgment."

Gant's head snapped around and his eyes widened. "Okay. So yeah. I want you to tell me."

Amethyst tried to figure out how to start. "Well, um, yeah. He rescued me. And while he was taking me to get gas and bringing me back, we talked and laughed, and I really liked him then. And I really respect him because he saved your life."

"That's not a reason to sleep with him."

Okay, that just pisses me off! She couldn't believe her dad would say that to her. "I haven't slept with him! My god! What, now I'm a huge ho because I'm knocked up?"

"I didn't mean it like that!"

"Yeah, well, how the hell *did* you mean it?"

Gant sat there for a few seconds, staring into his mug. "I meant, I thought, I dunno. I don't think that. I'm so confused right now …"

"Okay, so let me see if I can straighten this out. I went over there last night to cook dinner for Jackson to thank him for rescuing me. And we sat down to talk. There were a lot of things I didn't know about him, and I doubt you know either. Did you know his little girl, a toddler, died?"

Gant's eyebrows shot up. "No. Had no idea. When?"

"Over fifteen years ago. And he was in the military. Didn't even get to say goodbye. She had a glioblastoma and went a lot faster than the doctors thought she would. That was what ended his marriage."

"My god. That's horrible. Poor guy."

"Yeah, well, he thinks he doesn't deserve to be happy. He and his ex-wife are civil and keep up with each other because of their shared history, but other than that, nope. Nobody."

"You shouldn't be with somebody because you feel sorry for them."

Amethyst blew out a deep breath and rolled her eyes upward before she leveled her gaze with his and spoke. "Look, I haven't slept with him. I just know that we're very, very attracted to each other, and for all the right reasons. Not just sex. Matter of fact, he won't touch me until I've gone to the obstetrician, and he wants me to be tested too because we don't know where Craven might've been."

"Asshole," Gant muttered.

"Exactly. And he's right. He said it wasn't just for him. It's for me and the baby, to keep us healthy."

"How does he feel about the baby?"

Amethyst's lower lids filled with tears. "He wants it, Daddy. He said nothing would make him happier than to take care of me and a child."

"A child that's not his."

"Nobody knows I'm pregnant. If we're together and claim we've been together since you were in the hospital, nobody will be any the wiser and his name can go on the birth certificate."

"He'd agree to that?"

She chuckled. "He's the one who suggested it." Gant started to say something, but Amethyst cut him short. "Look, let's all just go over there tonight. You can see us together and decide for yourself. But I can't think of a finer man to spend the rest of my days with. Except maybe you. And you're my dad. So … Anyway, please? Just go with an open mind?"

Gant set his coffee mug down again and smiled at his daughter. "You know, I can't think of a finer man to take care of my daughter and my grandchild. How does he feel about you going back to school?"

"He's all for it. Said I might even want to change my major, although I know I won't. But yeah, that's fine with him. There are colleges around here. I can find a place to go to school, and I can take some online too. He's not in the reserves anymore, but I guess he could reenlist if he wanted to."

"What other sources of income does he have?"

"I don't know. I didn't ask. But I will, if that matters to you."

"It does." Gant reached out his hand and Amethyst put hers in it. "I love you, sweetie. I don't want to see you make a bigger mess than you already have."

"I'm sorry you see this baby as a mess."

"No, but it has forced all your plans to change."

Amethyst smiled. "Isn't change what life is all about?"

"Now that you mention it," Gant said, picking up his coffee mug, "it is."

Two hours later, with Gant in his shop and Lorna at work, Amethyst's phone pinged and she opened the messaging app to see a simple message.

Well?

She sent back two words.

He knows.

A ONCE-OVER AROUND THE HOUSE. CLEAN TOWELS IN THE bathrooms. Everything straightened up. Dirty dishes washed and put away. Drinks in the refrigerator. Shoes in the closet. And fresh sheets on the bed. He laughed at himself as he thought, *Hey, a guy can hope, right?*

He'd started the pork chops on the grill and the broccoli and sweet potatoes were ready to go on too when Lorna's car pulled up. He was a little sad to see the three of them get out. His earlier hope had been that Amethyst would drive herself and stay. Yeah, there wasn't much they could do, but he would've been happy just to hold her, to sleep beside her, to have her in his arms. He waved from the porch as they all made their way to him. "Come on in. I've got everything going on the grill. Anybody want a drink?"

"Yeah. I'll take a beer," Gant announced.

"Got some wine for you, Lorna," Jackson told her and held up a nice merlot.

"Oooo, that looks good!"

"I'll take a glass too," Amethyst said, and when he wheeled to say something, she burst out laughing.

"Oh, you think you're so funny!" he said, shaking his head and laughing. "I got you something special to drink too." He handed her a bag and when she reached in, she screamed with laughter. "That'll be safe enough."

Gant stared at her as she laughed. "What is it?"

She pulled out a packet. "It's frickin' Kool-Aid! I haven't had that stuff since forever! Are you kidding me?"

Jackson was quick to snatch the lime-flavored drink mix out of her hand. "And now I'm going to show you the magic of Kool-Aid. Watch and learn." He mixed the packet into water and when it was completely dissolved, he poured a glass of ice half full of it, then poured ginger ale in on top of it. When that was almost finished, he dropped in about a tablespoon of grenadine, stirred it all up, and handed it to her. Then he leaned back against the countertop and waited.

Amethyst took a sip and looked up at him. "What manner of magic is this that you've wrought, wizard?" she asked with a fake British accent, a wicked grin on her face.

"Like it?"

"No. Love it. It has a certain … *je ne sais quoi*," she answered.

"I'm going to make it for you all the time if it'll make you speak French to me," Jackson said, laughing. "I should probably go check the grill. Y'all excuse me, please." He grabbed the aluminum pans on his way out.

"I'll come with you," Gant offered, and Jackson really wished he wouldn't. He knew what was about to happen. Couldn't they at least eat in peace?

"Looks like they're ready to turn. Let me put these on there." When he'd found spots for the two aluminum containers, he closed the grill.

"You grill vegetables?"

He decided to keep his answers brief. If Gant wanted the conversation, he'd have to carry it. "All the time. They're delicious that way."

"Hmmm. I'll have to try that." Jackson waited. He was about to say something when Gant said, "So I hear you and my daughter have conspired."

"Not so much conspired. Just confessed our mutual

attraction for each other and decided that we each can be good for the other."

"Ah. I see. So what do you think you bring to the table?"

Well, poke me with a sharp stick, Jackson wanted to yell. "Let's see … I bring experience, stability, patience, a healthy work ethic, a ready-made home, and all the love and devotion any woman could want."

"Your ex-wife didn't want it." Jackson could feel his brows creeping up until Gant said, "That was pretty fucking low of me. I'm sorry. Amethyst told me about … about what happened. And I'm sorry."

"Yeah, well, you weren't there. For however bad you think it was, it was fifty times worse."

"I'm sure it probably was. And no, I can't say I can relate. But I hate to think about that happening to anybody."

"Thank you."

"So I guess we—"

"Look. You're my friend." Jackson dragged a hand through his hair and sighed. "This is *not* the way I wanted to do this, but you're pushing. So be it. What do you want me to do? Tell her I can't be with her because her dad doesn't like the idea?"

"Who said I don't like the idea?"

"Well, god damn it, G-man, what the hell *do* you want?"

"I want to know that you care something about her and you're not just helping her out in her hour of need."

Jackson sighed again. "I don't believe that people just 'fall' in love. I think they fall into attraction, and then the love grows. Thing is, your daughter is a fine woman. No finer."

Gant tried to interrupt him, but Jackson belted out, "And yes. She's a woman, not a kid. She has the ability to make her own decisions. I think she's going to be a great mom. She had an excellent example in the way of a great dad. But I don't mind telling you, that evening when I stepped up to that car and realized who she was, those eyes grabbed me and wouldn't let me go. I couldn't stop thinking about them. And the rest of the package is pretty damn fine too."

"But what about the age gap?"

"You of all people have a lot of nerve asking me that."

"Yeah, but that was a man in his mid-forties and a woman in her late fifties. This is a woman who's barely more than a girl."

Jackson glared at him. "You and I both know she's been an adult for a long damn time. I'm guessing she raised Sapphire, for the most part, until you came on the scene."

"That's true."

"And from what I can tell, she wants a home, not just a place to live. I can offer her that. A home, something to drive, food to eat, clothes to wear, the ability to raise a child, and my total devotion. Because I can promise you, I may not be head over heels in love right now, but your daughter has the ability to make me love her just with her gentle way and that beautiful, soft voice."

Gant's smile was soft. "I think you're already in love with her."

"Maybe. Maybe she's already in love with me. I just know I'm not going to say that to her right off the bat. I'd much rather show her."

The minute those words were out of his mouth, Gant extended a hand and Jackson took it and gripped it tightly. "Then show her. She deserves somebody who'll worship her."

"She does, and I'm the man for the job." Gant slapped him on the shoulder and he felt like he'd won the lottery. There'd be no resistance from her dad, and her mom … Hell, she didn't even know where her mom was. "This will put her down here with you and Lorna, plus Lorna's kids and their spouses, and it'll be good for her to have family around."

"It will, and I'm grateful for that. It'll be nice to have my grandkid nearby too."

"I know we'll be grateful for your help." Jackson smiled broadly. "I just said 'we.'"

"You did. Come on. Let's go inside and see what those two are up to."

Lorna and Amethyst were laughing and talking when the men reached the living room. "What are you two up to?" Gant asked.

"Talking about that show where they do the over-the-top nurseries. Some of that stuff is just crazy!" Lorna said, laughing.

"Yeah. They built a thing like one of those outdoor playlands, you know, with a fort and stuff, and put a bed in it and a desk. It was weird. And I think they spent about twenty-five thousand dollars on it!" Amethyst was still laughing.

"Another one had clowns everywhere! Can you imagine how freaked out that baby's going to be all day and all night?" Lorna was laughing so hard she was snorting.

Amethyst was gasping for breath. "What about the one with the big doggie door so the dwarf goats could get in and out of the nursery? That was insane!"

"Goat shit in the nursery?" Gant asked and turned to stare at Jackson. He just gave Amethyst's dad a shrug of his shoulders.

"You're not going to do something stupid like that, are you?" Lorna asked, still laughing loudly.

"Jesus, I hope not," Jackson mumbled.

"Don't let her!" Lorna barked as she laughed.

Jackson's brow furrowed and he turned to stare at Amethyst, but she just shrugged with upturned palms and kept laughing. "Well, I guess everybody knows now," he said with a scowl. "Who told you?"

"I guessed. I mean, this is like three days in a row that you two have seen each other. I had to believe something's going on. So do we all need to sit down and talk about how this is going to work?"

"Can we at least eat first before we have some kind of over-the-top discussion?" Jackson had started to feel a little frustrated. This was his and Amethyst's relationship. How were so many people getting involved? Then he realized, they weren't "so many people;" they were her parents. They wanted to know what was going on so they could be supportive, and no one could have too many supportive people in their lives.

Amethyst chirped out, "Yes! Let's! I'm starving! Come on. I'll help you get it in from the grill." As she almost skipped through the kitchen, she picked up a tray, so Jackson followed her. He lifted the top of the grill and Amethyst held out the tray, complete with meat platter. "So did you and Dad have a good talk?"

"Yeah. I think he's on board. You and Lorna?"

"Yeah, her too. I think it's fine."

"Good. Because we need to talk."

"Sounds serious."

He leaned over and gave her a peck on the cheek. "It is, but good serious, not bad serious."

"Okay. Oh my god, those chops look delicious. You're a good cook!"

Jackson grinned. "I'm not much in the kitchen, but I love to grill."

"At least we'll never go hungry."

Jackson took the loaded tray from her hands and let her open the back door for him. In minutes, they were all around the table, eating and drinking and talking. Jackson loved it. He'd bought that house and turned it into a home, but it hadn't been much of one out there by himself. In that new moment, there was laughter and light, and he couldn't have been happier. When he glanced across the table at Amethyst, he caught her eye and watched her smile widen.

Every time she smiled at him, something inside him, something cold and frozen over, melted just a little more. He could feel it. She'd be good for him, and he knew he'd be good for her. By the time they'd finished the meal, the dessert was ready, and he pulled hot peach cobbler out of the oven and retrieved a carton of vanilla bean ice cream to go on top of it. All the while, he watched Amethyst eat with gusto, and he realized when he'd seen her that first night, she was a lot thinner than she'd been when her dad had been injured. She'd been worried, upset, tired, and stressed, and probably hadn't been eating right. College students rarely did. As long as she was with him, she'd have three meals a day and snacks if she needed them. She'd stay hydrated. She'd get exercise, but nothing too strenuous. She'd had a rough time of it. He'd make sure things were easier for her from that time forward.

Dessert was excellent, and everyone was stuffed. Gant and Lorna headed into the living room and instinctively took the sofa. Jackson looked around at the seating configuration. There was nowhere for him and Amethyst to sit together, and he'd wanted so much to have them see the two of them as a couple. Two seconds later, he realized he needn't have worried.

Amethyst sat down in the floor and leaned up against his legs, then threw her arm across his knees and looked up at him, grinning. When he pressed his palm against her cheek, she closed her eyes gently and smiled before she opened them again, then took his hand and kissed the back of his knuckles. He didn't look up to see what Gant and Lorna thought. He didn't care. As far as he was concerned, it was just the two of them there in the room in the little space they occupied, their own little cocoon, and it made him happy beyond belief.

His reverie was broken by Gant. "What do y'all think the next step should be?"

"That's something I wanted to talk to her about. I think that's something the two of us need to decide. Don't you, angel?" he asked as he looked down at her.

She glanced up at him. "Yeah. That's kinda personal, and I think that's a private discussion."

"Oh, well, don't mind us. We're just the people you're living with right now," Gant said, sounding a little miffed.

"Dad, I'm an adult. Yes, I know, I came running to you like a scared child, but honestly, I didn't know what else to do. My other options had dried up, and I'm not saying you were my last choice. It's just that it was a long way from where I was and I was hoping to stay in school.

But I'm glad I'm here now. I feel so much better being with people who care about me."

"And we do, honey. You know that, no matter what kind of ass your dad is making of himself," Lorna said and elbowed Gant in the ribs.

"Damn, woman, talk about sharp elbows!"

"You need to quit being so cantankerous. Whatever you decide to do will be fine, honey. We'll support you and Jackson however we can."

Amethyst nodded in respect. "Thanks. I really appreciate that."

"I do too," Jackson added. "I've enjoyed being part of the VFD family. It's nice to think I might have more."

"You already do." Gant looked his friend in the eye. "You're my brother as surely as you were born one."

"I feel the same about you. If I hadn't managed to get you out of that tree, I would've missed out on a great friendship, and I would've really regretted that."

The conversation lightened up after that, and they talked and laughed for the rest of the evening. When the big grandfather clock in Jackson's hallway chimed nine, Lorna sat up. "Oh! It's nine already? I've got to get home. Work in the morning. Thank god we're almost to Saturday. I don't think I could take another week like this one."

"Yeah, you've been worn out," Gant said in agreement. "Guess we'd better get home, but thanks, Boss. It was delicious. And thanks for the hospitality."

Jackson stood. "You're quite welcome." He reached down to help Amethyst up. "We'll do it again real soon."

"That would be great. Thanks, Jackson." Lorna hugged him and he squeezed her back. She was a good woman and Gant was a lucky man.

"You're very welcome. It's nice to have talk and laughter here. It's been really, really quiet for a long time."

"Y'all go on. I'll be along in just a minute," Amethyst announced. With waves and goodbyes, she and Jackson watched Lorna and Gant head out the door. When they were out of earshot, she turned to him. "You said we need to talk."

"It can wait. Wish you'd brought a bag so you could stay."

"I wish I had too."

"That's one of the things we need to talk about, whether or not you want to move in here."

"Do you want that?"

He shrugged. "Well, I don't punch a time clock. You don't either. I don't know of a better way for us to settle in, get to know each other really, really well, make sure we're compatible. And if you want your own room, that's perfectly—"

"Oh, no. I'll want to be in that big bed, cuddled up against you," she said and stood on her tiptoes to plant a soft little kiss on his cheek.

"Why, Miss Meadows, I do think you're going to make me blush!" he said, laughing.

"Oh, if that makes you blush, you can't imagine what else I can do that'll probably cause your head to explode!"

"Can't wait for that! So what do you want to do?"

"Tomorrow's Friday. How 'bout I come out tomorrow afternoon with some clothes and stay the weekend? And if everything goes well, maybe next week I can move more things. Does that sound okay?"

He wrapped his arms around her waist and pulled her

up against him. "That sounds perfect. Know what you want for dinner?"

"Hmmm. Can we cook Italian?"

"We absolutely can. Let me think on it and we can go to the store together tomorrow afternoon. I mean, if we're going to pull this thing off, people need to start seeing us together, right?"

"Yep. I think so."

"You're not embarrassed to be seen with me, right?" he asked, grinning.

"Hell no! I want every woman in three counties to be jealous as hell that I caught the good-looking rancher from Tarpley!"

"Oh, lawd, girl, you're something else." His lips found hers and he couldn't remember a sweeter kiss. Those arms wrapped around his neck and he was in heaven. When he pulled back, he wiped across her lower lip with the pad of his thumb and smiled. "I'm so damn happy."

"I am too. I can't wait to see how things go, but I think they're going to be amazing."

"As long as you don't tell me something is 'totes adorb,' we'll get along fine!" he said, laughing and taking her hand as he led her to the door.

Amethyst chuckled. "Oh, gah, old man Frame, that's so thirty-two minutes ago!"

"What can I say? I'm hopelessly behind times."

"Guess what? Out here, nobody gives a shit." That made Jackson laugh. "I'll see you tomorrow afternoon, babe."

"Yep. See you then, angel. Be careful."

"Will do. And you gonna make me another one-a them special potions, right?"

"You can count on it!"

She'd already made it to the driveway and she started a little shuffling dance. "Uh-huh, that's what I'm talkin' 'bout. Got me a man who makes me magical potions, uh-huh, uh-huh, uh-huh." When she reached the car, she grabbed the door handle, then turned and waved before she slipped inside. Gant tooted the horn as they pulled away, and Jackson stood in the doorway, ankles crossed as he leaned against the door jamb.

He'd offered her a bedroom of her own, but she wanted to be in his bed. In. *His*. Bed. How the hell was he going to control himself with a woman that beautiful lying beside him? He was going to remind her that she needed to get her ass to that obstetrician ASAP. Controlling himself for a while would work, but not forever.

He didn't care what anyone said. There wasn't that much willpower in any man.

AS GANT DROVE ALONG, AMETHYST WATCHED THE lighted windows of the houses they passed by in the darkness and thought about everything. She'd come there barely three weeks earlier, alone and terrified of what would happen if the only person she knew who gave a shit about her and could help her turned her away instead. Three weeks later, there was a very good possibility that she'd met and connected with the man she was supposed to spend the rest of her life with. Jackson was everything she wanted.

Just the thought of lying in that king size bed with him made her almost giddy. God, he was hot! She needed to get the name of that doctor in Hondo and make an appointment. She could control herself, but she wasn't sure for how long.

She excused herself to get ready for bed as soon as they got back home. With a quick goodnight kiss to Lorna and Gant, Amethyst took herself to bed and snuggled down under the sheets. It might be the last night she slept in their house. Wouldn't that be wonderful?

So excited she couldn't get to sleep, she lay there in the bed and stroked down her belly. It was still flat, but it wouldn't be for long. Wasn't that a wonder? Wasn't it just the most miraculous thing in the world, for two bodies to make another person? It was hard to believe that in just a few months, she'd have a baby in her arms, *her* baby. Then she smiled. Her and Jackson's baby.

Voices were coming through the wall, so she concentrated and realized she could hear most of what they were saying.

"So what do you think of all this?"

"Honestly, if it works out, I think it would be the best thing. Jackson's a great guy, and he'll make a good husband and father." Then her dad's voice stopped, and when he spoke again, he said, "At least I think he plans to marry her. Hell, people don't get married anymore."

She heard Lorna laugh. "We did!"

"Yeah, well, we're pretty old fashioned."

"You don't think Jackson is?"

"Yeah, I guess so, but … I'm a little worried."

"Why?"

Gant was quiet, and she waited, holding her breath. "What if they forge some kind of relationship and then she loses this baby? Will she just walk away from Jackson? Will that end the relationship? I don't want to think that's the only reason she's interested in him, but—"

Lorna's voice was scathing. "Listen to you! You raised her better than that! I can't believe you'd think that way. Amethyst's not like that, not at all." *Thank you, stepmom!* Amethyst wanted to yell through the wall. "I'm more concerned that faced with the idea there won't be a baby and family, Jackson will throw in the towel."

"No. Jackson would never, never do that. He's an honorable man. If he tells her he loves her, it won't be contingent on a baby or her weight or her education or his needs. If he tells her he loves her and wants to be with her, that's what he means. There are no ulterior motives there on his part."

"And there are none on hers, so we should just let them flesh this out. They're adults. They can navigate this minefield and come out the other side. I have faith in them. Don't you?"

Gant's sigh could be heard through the wall. "I want to, but this blindsided me so badly that I'm having trouble getting past the shock. I just want her to be happy; I want both of my girls to be happy." He stopped and Amethyst smiled when she heard him add, "I want all three of my girls to be happy."

"That's better, Mr. Meadows. And I want you to be happy too."

"Know what would make me happy right now?"

Jesus, I do not need to hear this! Amethyst put her hands over her ears and hoped they could be quiet. Listening to her dad and Lorna bump uglies was not something she wanted to experience—ever. But even though it creeped her out a bit, she was glad her dad had Lorna. She was a wonderful person and treated Sapphire and Amethyst just as she did her own kids. For years she'd watched her dad struggle along, feeling alone and tired, and stressed over money and schooling them on the road. When she looked at him there in Tarpley, he looked relaxed, centered, grounded, whole. The stress lines on his forehead were shallower, and he laughed and smiled more.

Then she thought about Jackson. Everything about him called to her. As though he could hear her thoughts, her phone buzzed and she picked it up to find a text.

I'm thinking about you. I hope you're thinking about me.

She smiled as she answered: *I am.*

Good. I know you won't believe me, but I miss you.

She closed her eyes and felt a tear trickle down her temple and into her hair as she lay there. *I believe you because I miss you too.*

Sleep well, my angel. I'll see you tomorrow.

His angel. No man had ever treated her the way Jackson did except her dad. Craven sure hadn't. He'd been an asshole extraordinaire. She wasn't sure why she'd stayed with him so long. Probably habit. She was used to him and getting used to someone else would've required effort and energy, both of which were in short supply in her life. But he hadn't been the man Jackson was. She took a deep breath and blew it out before she answered him. *I will. You too. XOXOXO*

Hugs and kisses. Maybe by the next evening she'd be giving those to him instead of texting them. And she could hardly wait.

"HAVE YOU TOLD YOUR PARENTS?"

"Fuck no! Oh my god, I can't even imagine what kind

of disaster that would be. I was hoping she'd come to her senses and do what I asked, but the bitch is just too hard-headed."

"What now?"

"I can't let her have it. It'll ruin my life forever. I'm in line to inherit everything. That would put that … thing in line for inheriting along with any other kids I have, and I don't want a bastard competing for what belongs to my real kids."

His best friend, Hardin, shook his head. "You don't even know where she is."

"Oh, I'm pretty sure I do. She's down there in bumfuck Texas with that loser dad of hers, the black-smith. That's the only place she could run to."

"You going down there to get her?"

Craven Bradshaw sat down on the side of the bed and ran his index finger back and forth across his chin as he thought. "No. But I'm going to call her. I think I can get her to get rid of it. I'll just dangle a carrot and see if she bites."

CHAPTER 4

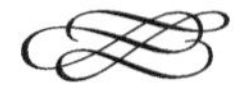

SHE HADN'T BEEN that excited about anything in a long time. Amethyst poked through everything in her drawers, wishing she had some nicer lingerie and a pretty gown or pajamas. As a college student, she slept in sweats, leggings, tee shirts, tanks, whatever she happened to have. It had finally sunk in that Craven hadn't cared how she looked. He just wanted her to spread her legs.

A sound caused her to turn and she found her dad standing in the doorway. "Whatcha doin'?"

"Um, trying to pack a few things. Jackson asked me to come for the weekend. You know, kind of a trial run, to see if we settled in okay together."

"Ah. I see. That's a little bag you've got there," he said and pointed to the backpack lying on the bed.

"Yeah, well, it's pretty empty because I don't have much."

He stepped a little closer and looked down into the drawer. "Oh, honey, you don't. There's nothing in there! How have you been getting by?"

"I've got like three pairs of underwear and I wash

them as I wear them. That's all I've got." She was glad they were already in the backpack so he couldn't see how ratty and shot they were.

"No. Not my girl." He disappeared and Amethyst kept packing stuff. In a minute he was back. "Take this."

She turned to find his arm outstretched and a handful of bills clutched in his hand. "Oh, no. I can't—"

"You can and you will. Go get some things. There's a supercenter in Hondo. You can get enough things there to do you some good. You need clothes, underwear, and that's what my money's for—taking care of my family."

"Lorna's your family."

A sad smile stretched across his face as Gant shook his head. "You're my family too. And don't worry—I'll send the same amount to your sister so she can't claim I was playing favorites. But you're not going to do without, not on my watch."

Try as she might, Amethyst couldn't help breaking down. Everything had been crazy and upside down, and she couldn't tell who was friend or foe anymore. And then she'd shown up there, unannounced and uninvited, and arms and hearts had opened to her. All she wanted was to feel like somebody cared about her, and there, in that tiny little town, she had more support than she'd had in a long time. A pair of strong arms wrapped around her and she cried on her dad's shoulder. "Oh, honey, don't cry. It's all gonna be okay. You should've said something sooner. I don't want you to ever go hungry or naked!"

"I wasn't completely naked, but I was close," she blubbered.

"It'll all be fine. Now, why don't you go on into Hondo and—"

"Actually, Jackson and I are supposed to be going to

the grocery after I get there, so I'll just wait. I'm sure that'll be okay with him, driving into Hondo."

"Yeah, well, there's really not another place to get much of anything around here. So, tell you what." He hugged her and then stepped back and took both her hands in his. "How 'bout we eat a little something and then go down to the creek and do a meditation?"

"Oh my god! I'd love that! I haven't done one in a long time, what with classes and everything."

"Okay. Let's do that. Come on. We'll get some little something and then we'll head that way."

Twenty minutes later, Amethyst settled onto the big, flat rock by the creek, grounded and centered herself, and listened as her dad guided the meditation. Having him there to do the guiding let her mind float free, and that was what she needed more than anything. She felt so peaceful, so relaxed, that she was disappointed when it was over. At least she knew where his "spot" was, and she knew he wouldn't mind if she came there at any time. Maybe she could find a spot like that at Jackson's! That would be great.

As she pulled up in front of the ranch house shortly after two o'clock, she looked around and didn't see his truck. Had he gone shopping without her? Her worry was wasted because, seconds later, he rounded the corner of the house, so she hopped out, grinning. "I thought I heard a car out here! Hey, angel!" By the time she reached him, his arms were open wide, and she snuggled against his chest. "I'm glad to see you too!"

"I'm so happy to be here! Where's your truck?"

"Out back. Come look." Taking her hand, he led her down the side of the house and round the back. "Whaddya think?"

"Oh my god! They're so cute!" Six goat kids romped in a large pen inside the pasture fence, their coats splotched with black and brown on white. "What are they for?"

"I decided I'd get some for milk. It's so much more nutritious than cow's milk. And I guess you've heard of making soap from the milk."

"Yeah, but I don't know anything about that."

"Thought you might want to try it sometime."

"I might. Could be fun. They're adorable."

"That one over there," he said, pointing to one that was almost black, "is the billy. The others are all nannies."

"Will he have horns?"

Jackson laughed. "He'll have horns you'll need to watch out for!"

Amethyst shook her head and laughed with him. "Oh, nice. I can see it now, me on the ground and that goat standing on me!"

"He'd better not or he'll be in a tangine with some garam masala by dinnertime."

Her eyebrows popped up. "I have no idea what you just said."

"Indian food, angel. I'll have to cook some for you."

"Sounds good. But tonight—"

"Italian. Yeah, I remember. Let me get a quick shower and we'll go shopping." He took her hand again and pulled her along toward the house.

Once they were inside, he pointed at the dresser in his bedroom. "That entire half of the dresser is empty. It's yours. And there's plenty of room in the closet."

"I won't need much room. I barely have any clothes."

"Want to go to Hondo and fix that?"

Amethyst nodded. "Dad gave me a handful of money to buy some things."

"No. You give that right back to him. I'll get whatever you need."

"But Jackson—"

"No! No buts. You need it, I'll get it, and I don't want you searching through clearance racks either. Buy the things you need and want. And you'd better start thinking about what kind of car you'd like to have. That Toyota is old and it needs to be replaced."

Amethyst was shocked. "I like my Toyota!"

"Then we'll get you a newer one, but a woman and baby in that? Nope. I won't have it. You'll get something newer and dependable, and something that'll be easy to get the baby in and out of. It won't necessarily be brand new, but it'll sure be newer." She started to say something, but he pressed a finger to her lips. "Don't argue with me. I'm getting in the shower. I'll be done in a few minutes, so if there's anything you need to do to get ready to go, you should do it."

As soon as she heard him start the shower, she retrieved her backpack from the car and started putting what she had away. Her knock on the bathroom door was answered with, "Come on in."

Amethyst almost fainted. Jackson's back was to her, and that was the finest ass she'd ever seen on a man. It was amazing, and his thighs were thick and muscled up. His back was just as muscular. "Um, can I put my stuff in here?"

"You can. Just find places for everything. Doesn't matter where. I'm not territorial," he said, speaking to her over his shoulder. Amethyst pretty much dropped everything on the counter and headed for the door, but she didn't quite make it before he turned around.

Oh my god. JACKPOT! As she closed the door, she saw just enough to know what she could expect, and by god, it looked like being with him would mean she was done with little boys. That was a full out *man*, all man, and what his mama gave him would be more than enough for her. If he had any idea what to do with that thing, and she was pretty sure he did, her nights were destined to be a lot less boring. The water stopped and she called out, "I'll get out of here so you can come out."

The door opened and a laughing Jackson strode through, towel around his waist. "Angel, I spent years in the military. I'm a lot of things, but unnecessarily modest ain't one of 'em!" With that, he dropped the towel and reached for a pair of underwear. Amethyst felt frozen in place until he turned and winked at her, pulling his boxer briefs up at the same time. "If we're going to live together in the same house, might as well get used to seeing each other in the buff. It's going to happen." His hair was still dripping a little when he stepped across the room and laid his hands on her shoulders. "Baby, I'm just me. I don't pretend to be something I'm not. I really am a 'what you see is what you get' guy. If we're going the direction we say we are, what you see here belongs to you anyway."

"I'm sorry. I just—"

"No. Don't apologize. When it comes to relationships, you're still kinda growing up. All you've had were relationships from dating and shared interests. Let's be honest—this is almost like an arranged marriage where we have to decide if we can be together until we finally fall in love with each other. It's not some starry-eyed love-at-first-sight thing. Honestly, that's all fine, but this … This is something that will last a lot longer and be a lot more rewarding if we both give it a shot." When he finished, he chucked her under the chin and gave her a little peck on the lips before he went back to getting dressed.

Amethyst could see what he meant. It definitely made sense to her. As she turned to the bathroom, she said, "Guess I should go in here and actually put my stuff away."

"Wherever you want. If you need to move something of mine, go ahead. As long as I can find it, I don't care where it is."

There was plenty of space in the bathroom. He sure didn't use a lot of product! *At least not like black girls do*, she laughed to herself. "So I thought when we went to the store I'd get some pretty underwear and stuff."

"You get whatever you want, but I don't have to have that stuff. You'd be beautiful in a flour sack to me. But if it helps you feel prettier, you get it. That's fine with me." She couldn't help the little sob that escaped her lips and before she knew what was happening, he was behind her, his arms wrapped around her waist, his lips at her ear. "Don't cry, angel. You deserve all the pretty and wonderful things. I don't think you have any idea what you're worth, but I intend to show you. Now straighten up that gorgeous face and let's go get you some things that'll make you smile, okay?"

"I-I-I-I'm sorry!" she stuttered through her tears.

"Don't. Hormones, babe. You'll cry a lot, and I understand that. But I hope I can make you laugh more than you cry!" He kissed the side of her neck and then disappeared back into the bedroom.

It only took her a few minutes to finish putting everything away and by the time she finished, he was ready to go. The guy sure didn't waste time getting ready!

She hadn't paid much attention in the dark that night when he'd picked her up, but in the daylight, his truck was quite a shock. The only trucks she'd ever ridden in were her dad's, but Jackson's was more like a luxury car. It had every bell and whistle known to the automobile industry, and she was amazed at all the buttons and dials on the dash. And it was huge too, way bigger than her dad's. "What is this thing anyhow?"

"It's a Ford F-250 Super Duty. I wanted it because I knew I'd be hauling stuff and pulling stuff and I needed something that would be rugged and dependable but still comfortable. Like it?"

"Yeah. It's awesome." He pulled into a parking lot and stopped. One look out the window told her they were at a western store. "Uh, what are we doing?"

"We're getting you a pair of boots."

"Cowboy boots? I don't wear cowboy boots!" she yelled.

"No. Boots to wear outside while you're working. Like ropers or something."

"Ropers? I'm roping something?"

"No, no. Come on. You'll see."

Ten minutes later, there were eight pairs of boots spread out in front of her. "You can have whichever ones you want, but they need to be comfortable. And those," he said, pointing to a pair that looked like they were ostrich with some kind of turquoise insets in them, "are not comfortable. You can't convince me that they are."

"Oh, now you tellin' me I gotta have some boots, but

you ain't lettin' me have the fancy boots? Nuh-uh. That ain't right."

"Okay. You get the fanciest ones you like, but pick out a comfortable pair too."

"So two pairs?" Jackson nodded. "Okay then. I'll take those right there and these," she said, pointing first to the ornate ones and then to a pair of plain brown ropers.

"Good choices. We'll take those."

"Can I look at the clothes?"

He grinned. "Sure."

Amethyst started going through the racks. Dear god, everything was pearl snaps and plaid. There was one shirt that was kinda cute, but they didn't have it in her size. Her prowling was interrupted by his voice. "You ready to go?"

"Yeah, I guess so."

Once they were in the truck, he pulled a small bag from the back seat of the crew cab and handed it to her. "What's this?"

"Open it."

Amethyst reached in and pulled out a box. It looked like some kind of presentation box, and when she opened it, she gasped. The bracelet had an intricate pattern of flowers and vines in silver, gold, and rose gold. "Oh, god. It's beautiful."

"Like the girl who'll be wearing it. My first gift to you."

She smiled and pressed a palm to his cheek. "No. Your first gift to me was your friendship."

To her surprise, his eyes reddened ever so slightly. "I'm glad you feel that way. No matter what happens, I hope I'll always be your friend."

"And me yours."

By the time they got to the supercenter, they were laughing and talking about something they'd both seen on TV. "Do you know what we need for dinner?" she asked.

"Yeah. I'm getting pasta, sauce, and sausage, plus some grated parmesan and stuff for salads. And I've got a few other things on my list too."

"Can I just go look at some underwear and stuff while you do that?"

Jackson smiled. "Sure! Have a good time. When you get finished, come find me."

There were so many kinds of underwear! "Lawd, how will I ever choose something?" she mumbled to herself. She found a package of six pairs and almost picked up a second one until she remembered that she soon wouldn't be able to wear them. Maternity panties were in her future, and when she found some and looked at the price for two pairs, sticker shock set in. Baby stuff wasn't all that was expensive. The getting babies there was pretty damn expensive too.

She found four bras that she liked and two more that she was considering when her phone rang. The number looked familiar, so she answered it. "Hello?"

"Amethyst?"

Her heart froze. She'd deleted his number so the ringtone hadn't sounded, and if she'd realized it was him, she never would've answered it. "What do you want?"

"I just want to talk to you for a minute."

"About what? As I recall, we ain't got nuthin' to say to each other, asshole."

"Well, that's some way to talk to your baby daddy," he said and laughed.

She didn't find it one bit funny. "I'm gonna ask you again before I hang up: What do you want?"

"Just wondered if you were still planning on going through with the stupid idea of having that kid."

"It ain't none-a ya business, boy."

"Yes it is. That's my … That kid will have my DNA, and … Look, why don't you do the smart thing and let it go."

"Smart thing? You call abortion a smart thing? You don't get to decide that for me. I'm the only one who can."

"Oh yeah?"

"Yeah. All those anti-abortion laws your white bread brethren keep forcing on women and keeping them from *having* abortions also keep men from *forcing* them to have abortions. So your own damn laws have shackled you. How does it feel?"

"Okay, look, how 'bout this? You have an abortion and I'll give you a hundred and fifty K."

For a split second, she thought she'd misunderstood. "What? What did you say?"

"I said, have an abortion and I'll give you a hundred and fifty thousand dollars. Oh, and I'll pay for the abortion too."

There was a tiny fizzling sound in her brain for a half second, almost like someone had crossed a couple of wires and short-circuited it. The instant it passed, she hung up on him. It took everything she had to keep from throwing the phone across the building. He wanted to pay her to abort her child? What kind of sick bastard did that?

Amethyst's hands were shaking and she felt a little weak. As she gripped the packages and hangers she'd pulled down and stepped away from the display, things were starting to get a bit hazy. A couple of steps in, she staggered just a little and grabbed a column to keep from falling, dropping everything she had in her arms in the process. A lady walked by, turned, and looked into her face. "Miss, are you okay?"

"Yeah. No. I … I need to call …" She handed the phone to the woman as she gripped the column, afraid to turn loose. "Jackson."

The woman rooted around a little and touched the screen a few times. "Hey, is this Jackson? Yeah, my name's Marie. There's a lady over here at the supercenter who told me to call you. Uh-huh. We're in the lingerie department, and she's not looking too good. Oh, you're here! Okay. I'll stay here with her. Thanks." The woman stepped up to her and smiled. "Breathe, honey. He's just across the main aisle over there. He'll be right—"

"Amethyst! Baby, are you okay? What's wrong?" Jackson's arms wrapped around her and she fell into them. She heard him say, "Thank you so much. Marie, right? Thank you. I appreciate it." They spoke for a few seconds before he asked her again, "Babe? What's wrong? What happened? Do you need some juice or something? Is your blood sugar bottoming? Talk to me."

The words didn't want to come out. "Oh god. Oh god, Jackson. Oh god."

"What? Are you hurt? Do I need to call an ambulance? I should call an ambulance." He fished in his pocket for his phone but she pressed a hand to his arm and he stopped. "What?"

"He called me."

"Who called you?"

She stomped one foot. "Craven! He called me!"

"When? What happened? What did he want?"

"He wanted to … to …" It seemed she'd have to

force the words out. "He wanted to *pay* me to have an abortion."

In an instant, her back was pressed to the column and Jackson was gripping her waist. "You listen to me. If he calls back, do *not* answer the phone. If you're not thinking and happen to answer it, you tell him to go to hell. And if I'm around, you hand the phone to me and I'll … I'll … He won't call you again after I talk to him. He'll *never* call you again. Do you understand me?" Her voice just wouldn't come. "Amethyst, answer me. Do. You. Understand?"

"Yes. I understand. Yes."

She could hear him rustling around, picking up the things she'd dropped and depositing them in his cart. "Come on. Let's pay and get out of here. You need to go lie down. Hang onto the cart and let's go." Instead, she wrapped her arms around one of his and let him lead her through the store.

The minute the truck door closed, she started to wail. How could he call her and try to *pay* her to abort her child? What kind of monster was he? She cried until her eyes were swollen, until snot ran down her face and she gagged and heaved. Instead of trying to hush her, Jackson just held her hand and sat with her. He could never, never know how grateful she was for that.

She'd settled down a little, and he reached into the back seat again. That time, he pulled out a bottle. "Here. You're probably dehydrated. Drink this." Amethyst looked down and found a sports drink, a lime one, pressed into her palm.

"Thank you," she whispered as she unscrewed the top and tipped the bottle up to her lips. Three swallows and she could feel her heartbeat leveling off. "I'm sorry."

"It's okay, angel. I can't imagine how that must've felt. Now you don't worry yourself about it again. He can't touch you, and he won't. Put his number back in your phone so you know if it's him and don't answer it again, okay?"

"Okay." She took two more sips as Jackson started the truck and pulled out of the parking lot. If he called back and she handed the phone to Jackson, what would he say to Craven?

She didn't know, but she sure hoped she got to hear that.

SHE COULD HEAR VOICES, BUT NOT THE ONES SHE expected. One of them was Jackson's and the other, Lorna's.

"So is there anything we can do?"

"Oh, yeah. There's plenty you can do. Call Jack."

"Okay. And tell him what?"

It took a couple of seconds before she heard Lorna's answer. "Get a restraining order against him so he can't contact her."

"He's in Alabama. That's not going to help much."

"It'll help more than you think. He'll be forced to deal with the authorities in Alabama when they're told to enforce the order, and it'll all stop."

"What about harassment?"

"Oh, yeah. If he keeps calling her, definitely. And bullying. Both are considered hate crimes in this state, so he could be prosecuted. Arrested and extradited. I assume he's white?"

Jackson shrugged. "I have no idea. I never asked."

"Yeah, Gant would know, but I don't. It never came up in conversation. But if he's white, yeah, that could make a big difference in how it's perceived. I don't like to pull the race card but in this instance, it could definitely work in her favor, especially if he was perceived to feel he could harass and verbally abuse her because she's a minority *and* a woman."

"Oh. Yeah, that makes sense."

"You need to go to the sheriff's department and talk to Jack. I'll talk to him too. But ultimately, she's the one who'll have to ask for the order. Neither you nor I can do that for her. It has to come from her."

"Gotcha." There was a lapse in the conversation and then she heard him say, "Thanks for coming out. I knew if anybody would know what to do, it would be you."

"You're welcome. I love her like she's my own. Don't tell Gant about this. He'll go find him and whup his ass."

"Yeah, Gant behind bars won't help anybody, especially her."

Lorna laughed. "Won't help my bank account either!"

She heard them open the door and it closed behind them. Their voices were muffled as they talked outside, so she lay there and thought about what Lorna had said. She needed to go ask for a restraining order against Craven. That would stop him, she was sure. She didn't want him and she didn't need him. Her baby would be fine without him, and she'd be better off without him too. She was still lying there, thinking about all of it, when the bedroom door opened. "Hey, you're awake."

"Yeah. I'm okay. Just tired."

Jackson sat down on the side of the bed and took her hand. "Don't give that another thought. You're going to be fine. I know having somebody basically put a price tag on your child's life upset you, but don't let it. I promise you, if he thinks that's all the baby's worth, he thinks that's all he's worth too. By the way, is he some kind of trust fund baby or something?"

"No." A deep sigh slipped out before she could stop it. "You know the company that makes auto parts? Bradshaw Unlimited?"

Jackson nodded. "Yeah. Guy that owns it … Morton Bradshaw. His dad was some kind of big oil guy or something."

She sighed. "That's his family."

Something passed across Jackson's face, something Amethyst didn't recognize, but it was gone as quickly as it came. "Don't worry about any of that. Just let me take care of you, and you take care of yourself and that baby, okay? It'll be fine. I promise. Dinner's about an hour out. Need anything?"

"Nah, but thanks. Can I go out and see the goats?"

"Sure. Get your boots though. Might be the only thing that keeps you from having goat shit between your toes." Amethyst laughed. "You think I'm kidding, but I'm not," he said with a lopsided grin.

As she petted the goats a few minutes later, Amethyst took a deep, cleansing breath. Jackson would take care of her. She and the baby would be fine. There were a lot of things she didn't know, but there was one she did.

With Jackson around, she felt safe.

THE SAUCE IN THE POT WAS BOILING, AND SO WAS Jackson. The *nerve* of that entitled little twit, calling Amethyst and saying something like that! He couldn't believe it, although he wasn't sure why. Everything he'd heard about Craven told him the guy was a piece of shit and Amethyst was definitely better off without him. Unfortunately, he was a well-to-do piece of shit, and money like that could cause problems.

While he waited for the water to boil, Jackson took out his laptop and started looking up Texas law on harassment, what constituted a hate crime, restraining orders, anything that might help. All he knew for sure was that it was going to stop. He'd find a way to stop it. Then he heard her voice and rose from his chair.

From the window over the sink, he could see her out there, playing with the goats. One of the kids had butted her in the knee, and she was chasing the little thing, clapping her hands and watching it bounce around. A minute or two later, she pulled out her phone, and he knew she was making a video of the lot of them as they played. They scampered here and there, and she laughed at them as they butted each other playfully. That smile … It was all he wanted, to see her smile, to know she was happy and enjoying life. She deserved every sweet and wonderful thing he could give to her.

She was laughing when he called her in to eat. "Did you see them out there? Those goats are crazy!"

"You looked like you were having a good time with them."

"I was! They're so cute. Wouldn't it be nice if they could stay that small?"

"I guess, although they wouldn't be much use, and when you live on a ranch, anything that isn't of use doesn't make much sense. What would you think about a dog?"

"Oh! I'd love to have a dog! Could we get a dog?"

"I'd been thinking about getting a border collie, something that could help me herd the cattle, so yeah. We can definitely get a dog."

"I've never had a dog."

That made Jackson horribly sad. She'd never had a dog. When you lived like a gypsy in a small camper with two kids and a wife, having a dog probably wasn't something to even consider. "Well, you'll have one now. I told you I planned to make sure you were happy here, and I wasn't kidding. I'll start looking around and see what I find."

"Okay. I'll look too." He knew she had absolutely no idea what to look for, but that was okay.

They chatted all through dinner and when they were finished, Amethyst insisted on cleaning up, since he'd cooked. "I'm going down the hallway to pay some bills and stuff. I'll be back in a little bit."

"Take your time. I'll just turn on the TV."

He could hear her from his little office at the end of the hallway, and she was humming and singing to herself. *I'm doing a good job so far*, he told himself and smiled. When he'd finished paying the bills, he checked his bank account and then his investments. It looked good, plenty good enough for everything they'd need. All those years of being in the military and having no one to spend money on had really paid off in a big way. If things worked out, they'd be looking for a car for her in the next couple of weeks …

If things worked out. He sure hoped they would. Amethyst was like a breath of fresh air in his home and his life. She couldn't possibly know how lonely he'd been, or how many nights he'd lain awake, wishing somebody, anybody, cared something about him. Sure, he had friends, but he didn't think any of them knew how alone he'd felt, especially when thoughts of Cassidy kept him awake at night. And then there were the nightmares …

No. I'm not going to think about them. Maybe with Amethyst here, they'll go away. That was his greatest wish. Long periods of time would go by and he didn't have one. And then it would rain. Or someone would say, "Let's go fishing!" It had taken him months to get to the point that he didn't hold his breath when he drove across Williams Creek, but he'd finally managed. Of course, every time it rained a lot and the creek swelled, he got nervous again. It had been all those years ago and it still wouldn't go away. He supposed it never would. Experiencing something like that … It stayed with you and wouldn't turn loose.

No. With Amethyst beside him, he was sure they'd go away. She didn't know what he'd endured, and he didn't want to ever have to tell her. He didn't want *anyone* to know. The only ones who did were the guys with him and … No. He wasn't giving those monsters another square inch of real estate in his head. They'd had too much of it. They didn't deserve it.

When he'd finished in the office, he made his way back to the living room to find her sitting on the sofa with a small tablet on her lap. "Oh, you're a reader?"

"Yeah, but I was looking on the internet. By the way, what's the wifi password?"

"Oh. It's capital-J-a-b-b-e-r-w-o-c-k-y."

"What the hell is that?"

He shook his head and chuckled. "Spoken like the generation who watches reality TV! I'll read it to you sometime."

"Okay." She poked around a little bit more—he figured she was logging into his wifi—and then said, "I found something. Look." She turned the screen toward him.

He squinted and then leaned back, wide-eyed. "What is he?"

"He's half Shetland Sheep Dog and half Australian Heeler. Says they're both good herding breeds and so he should be good."

"He looks like he's at least a year old."

"Two. His owners surrendered him when they lost their farm. They couldn't keep him, so they turned him over to the rescue. Says they used him for their goats. His foster mom says he's a great herding dog."

"Where did you find him?"

"It's a website. It's called Getapet dot com. They have all kinds of pets—dogs, cats, rabbits, birds, fish, lizards, snakes—"

"Snakes aren't pets. They're hawk food."

"Nuh-uh. My mom used to have a reticulated python. I loved him. His name was Barry."

Jackson side-eyed her. "I have no idea what a reticulated python is, and why the hell was his name Barry?"

"Hell if I know. He was about, oh, I dunno, probably fifteen feet long and—"

"Oh *HELL* no. Nope. Uh-uh."

"Weighed about a hundred and eighty—"

"Stop. No. Don't want to hear this."

"She had to find a home for him because he ate somebody's bird on the circuit."

"Jesus!"

"No, not Jesus. His name was Conroy." Jackson

rolled his eyes and Amethyst laughed at him. "I thought you were all adventurous and stuff."

"I'm adventurous, not ridiculous. And that's ridiculous. What did she feed it? Small children?"

"No. Big rats. Or rabbits. Or squirrels. Or whatever we could kill."

"You killed food for it?"

"How else were we gonna get it to him? 'Oh, come here, little rabbit. My big snake wants to eat you.' Yeah, that's a winner." That set Jackson laughing. "I mean, really, you got a snake, you gotta feed it or it starts eyeing you." That made him laugh even harder, and in no time, she was laughing too.

He wiped tears from his eyes and kept chuckling on, but he took her hand and kissed the back of it as he did. "You know, I love having you here."

"I love being here. When I'm here, I feel like I'm … home."

Every fiery question in Jackson's mind, every smoldering doubt, turned to smoke and ashes with her words. It was all he'd ever wanted, someone to share a home and a family with, and there she was, a beautiful, smart, loving young woman carrying the promise of a family straight into his heart. "I don't believe in tiptoeing around stuff." She quirked an eyebrow up as she looked at him. "I'm … There's love in my heart for you, angel, if you want it."

"I want it. I want it more than anything."

"Then it's yours."

"Can I ask you something?"

He turned sideways with a knee up on the sofa and smiled. "Sure. Anything."

"Does it not bother you that I'm black?"

He shrugged. "Why would it bother me?"

"Because you're in Texas and that's still not very accepted here."

"In case you haven't noticed, I really don't give a shit what other people think."

"I know, but doesn't it worry you? You know, that somebody might target you for being with a black woman?"

"No. I'm not worried about that at all."

"Because it's a very real possibility."

"I told you, I'm not worried about it."

"Well, I'm worried about it. I'm also worried about my half-black kid going to school in a public school in Texas."

That was something Jackson hadn't even considered. He'd hate to have to snap someone in half, but he'd do it for his kid. "They bully my kid, they'll only do it once."

She grinned. "You really do feel that way, don't you?"

"Damn straight. I won't put up with that shit, not for one minute."

"Well, okay then."

"I mean, I suppose if you wanted to, you could home school them."

"What about socialization?"

"You know what? We've got at least five years before we really have to worry about that, so let's don't. Let's just hope that in five years, things have changed."

"You obviously weren't brought up as a black child in America."

"No. I wasn't, so I can't even imagine. All I can promise you is that I'll take care of you and that little boy or girl, and I'll protect you with everything I have. Whatever it takes." When the last word was breathed out, he leaned over and kissed her.

It took less than ten seconds for her to crawl up into his lap, and he wrapped himself around her like a vine. If she needed shelter, he'd build it. Food, he'd grow it, buy it, cook it. Medicine, he'd get it if he had to steal it. He'd go naked and cold before he'd let her do the same. It didn't matter what he had to do, he'd take care of her and that precious child, *his* precious child. When he pulled back to look into her eyes, she yawned. "Wow. Am I that boring?" he asked with a laugh.

"No. I'm that tired. Today was good, but parts of it were … stressful."

"It's almost eleven. Let's get ready for bed and we can read or watch TV or something."

"That sounds good. Do we need snacks?"

"Might want 'em. Whatcha want? We've got some chips in here, and some popcorn, and—"

"I like popcorn."

"I bought truffle popcorn last week."

"Ooooo, that sounds good! I'll go change. And can you make me—"

"One of those potions? You bet, babe."

She stood, then leaned down, pressed her hands to the tops of his knees, and gave him a little kiss. "Thank you." At the head of the hallway, she stopped and turned. "I know you guys have nicknames, like Tank's. What's yours?"

"Boss."

"Oh. I thought that was just something Dad said to you."

"No. That's my call name. Boss."

"Why?"

He shrugged. "I have no idea."

"Well, you ain't my boss!" she said, laughing.

"Oh, I'm not? Well, then, what am I?"

"Yo my Papa-boo." With that, she disappeared into the bedroom.

I'm her Papa-boo. He liked it. It was sweet.

He gave her a couple of minutes, then wandered down the hallway to the bedroom and knocked. "What you knocking for? I thought we were gonna be all open and stuff."

"Just didn't want to startle you." He opened the door and almost gasped. Amethyst stood there in nothing but her panties, and he truly believed those were the most beautiful tits he'd ever seen in his life. "Well, hello to me," he said with a grin.

"Yeah, they're yours. Might as well get used to seeing them."

"Ain't nothin' wrong with that." Jackson reached into a drawer and pulled out a pair of lounge pants.

Amethyst frowned. "They're too big."

"No, darlin'. They're perfect for you."

"Butt's too big too."

"No it's not! You're gorgeous! Stop it!" He leaned over and gave her ass a smack.

"Oh, you one-a them, huh?" she asked, laughing.

"I might be."

"I don't mind if my Papa-boo spanks me," she said with a naughty wink, then pulled a tee shirt on.

"And I will if you keep talking about yourself that way."

She chuckled, a deep, dark chuckle that sent a shiver of anticipation up his spine. "Oooo, promise, promises."

I can see now that we're gonna get into all kinds of

mischief, he told himself. He hadn't expected it, but he had a feeling she was a hellcat in the sack, and that would suit him just fine. "You made that appointment yet?"

"No, but I'm going to Monday."

"Do you want me to go with you?"

She stood there for a bit before she said, "Yeah. Yeah, I think I do. If we're gonna be a couple, that's what couples do, so you should go with me."

"You won't mind me being in the room for your exam?"

"You're gonna see it anyway. What difference does it make?"

"Got a point there."

"Are we watching TV in there or in here?"

Jackson laughed. "I'd really rather not sleep on popcorn!"

"I agree with that!"

She liked a show that Jackson had never heard of and after watching the next episode in her queue, he decided she had very good taste in shows. It was some kind of British murder mystery with a quirky police sergeant, and that was right up his alley. "You watch much stuff like this?"

"Yeah. I don't watch that stupid stuff most college students do. And I only watch one show at a time and binge through them."

"Makes sense to me." As they sat there, munching on popcorn and watching TV, Jackson's arm was around her shoulders and he pulled her up against him. She cuddled into him as they watched, and he couldn't believe he was sitting there with her. If only she knew how much hope she represented to him, she'd never doubt his feelings for her.

The show was over and it was late. "I have to get up early tomorrow and get to town for some wormer for the cattle. You coming with me?"

"I can if you want."

He smiled. "I want."

"Okay. Bedtime." She hopped up and headed toward the bedroom, so Jackson picked up the glasses and popcorn bowl and deposited them in the kitchen before he followed her.

She was already in bed. Even better, her tee and panties were lying in the floor, and she lay on her side, waiting for him. There was a real question in his mind about his ability to control himself, and he wasn't sure he could. When he slid into the bed with her, she smiled. "You keeping those on?"

He grinned. "You want me to take them off?"

"Yeah. I do."

"Okay." Instead of just slipping off his lounge pants and boxer briefs, he stood, took them off, and crawled back under the sheets. "Better?"

"I don't know. You tell me." Before he had a chance to say anything, she pressed herself against him and kissed him, and everything inside him went on red alert, including the blood rushing to his dick. There was no chance of hiding that, and he didn't want to. There were so many possibilities for satisfying her without penetrating her that he couldn't decide what to do, but he instinctively reached for a nipple and she moaned into his mouth as soon as he'd tweaked it. "God, Jackson, I want you."

"I want you too, angel, but you know—"

"Yeah, yeah. I know. But there are a lot of other things we can do."

"I'm well aware, and you will be too in a few minutes." He trailed kisses down her neck until he reached her breast and sucked a large, hardened nipple into his mouth. Teasing, nipping, and sucking, he tormented the other with his finger and thumb and watched her squirm. It didn't take much—she was very sensitive, and every time he tugged just a bit, her hips tipped forward. After that had happened a few times, he let his free hand wander and when it reached her hip, he whispered against her lips, "I'm going to satisfy you. Always. You come first. After that, you can do whatever you want with me, or nothing at all. Up to you." She didn't get to answer before he stroked up her slit and slipped a finger under her hood.

Her back arched and she let out a long moan. He stroked insistently, watching her, listening to her cry out, enjoying the way she writhed against his hand. Screaming. He wanted her screaming and begging him to stop. "Come on, angel. Give it up for me, babe. You know you want to."

"Oh, god damn, Papa-boo, I want you to fuck me."

"Nope. But I'll give you all you can stand of this until you're too weak to want more." He picked up the pace of his stroking just a bit and listened to her whimper. "Come on and do it. You're soaking wet, girl. I know you want it."

"Fuck, Jackson, oh my god. Ohhhh, yeah, I want it. You know how it's done, baby. You know how. You're making me feel so good. So damn good." That only made him stroke her faster. "Fuck, fuck, fuck. Oh, god, yeah. Make me come, babe. Come on. Drive me crazy, Jackson. I want it."

"Then turn loose." He stroked a little faster and she

squealed. “You’re holding back, angel. Stop it. Give it to me. I want it right now. Come on, girl, let go.”

Amethyst’s legs stiffened and she let out an unholy shriek as the orgasm swallowed her. “Shit! Shit, fuck, damn! Oh fuck, please … Oh, fuck, fuck, fuck! Stop! Oh, god, no more!”

He didn’t stop immediately, and she swore and writhed, but when he finally quit, her hips were still pumping, and when he pinched a nipple, her pelvis bucked forward. Instead of waiting, he ran his finger back down and started again.

“Oh, damn! No, I can’t. Oh, god, please …”

“Oh, yeah, you can. And you will. I wanna watch those hips pump, girl. Come on. Do it.”

“Shit! Jackson, please! Oh, god! I, I, I, *fuuuucckkkkk*!” The second one took her so fast that he didn’t have time to do anything but hang on, and she screamed and swore as he refused to stop. When he did, she lay there, panting, and that time when he twisted a nipple, she didn’t move.

With one arm under her and the other draped across her belly, Jackson moved in and pressed his lips to hers. Her arms wound around his neck and she met the kiss with her own, her tongue searching out his, sliding like a serpent in a frenzy. He was in heaven. When he broke the kiss, he pressed his lips to her neck, then nipped her earlobe before he whispered, “I’m falling in love with you, angel. You’re precious, you know that? So fucking precious.”

The words hadn’t even evaporated in the air when he felt her fingers wrap around his hardness. “I want your stickiness all over my hand, Papa-boo. It’s your turn.” She pressed him onto his back and worked his shaft with a firm hand. “Yeah. I see you like that, huh? Oh, yeah.”

“Yeah, I do.” She leaned in and kissed him again, then trailed her tongue down his neck and nipped one of his nipples. “Jesus, girl, do you want me to shoot off right now?”

“Hell no. I wanna torture you like you tortured me. Does that feel good?” She worked a little harder, then ran her finger across the crown and used his precum to lube his shaft.

“Oh, god, yeah. Feels amazing. Oh, hell, careful there,” he whispered as she fondled his balls and kept stroking him. “Oh, yeah. That’s good. Very, very good.” That time when she kissed him, he pulled her in and held her lips against his, stroking into her mouth with his tongue, exploring it, tasting her and enjoying the sensation of her fingers tightening even more around him. “Oh, damn, babe, that’s it. Oh, yeah, just like that.” The hand that had cradled his balls stroked the crown of his cock with a soft palm, and he thought he’d come undone right that second, but she stopped that almost immediately and went back to his jewels.

“Am I enough for you, Papa-boo?”

“God, yeah, baby, you’re more than enough. Jesus, kiss me, Amethyst.” She’d barely pressed her lips to his when he stiffened even more and sent a stream of pearlescent cum onto his belly. “Oh, god … Jesus, you know what you’re doing.”

Instead of answering him, she bent down and kissed the head of his manhood. Jackson tipped his head back and groaned. The mattress shifted when she stood and he wondered what she was doing until she reappeared and wiped up his offering with a warm washcloth. He heard it make a *smack!* as it hit the floor of the shower where she tossed it, and it made him smile to think she'd do something so simple but so loving for him. When she stretched out on top of him, he wrapped his arms around her. Her cheek rested on his shoulder, her lips against his neck, and she whispered, "I'm falling in love with you too."

"Get that exam, babe. I want to be inside you."

"I want you inside me. God, you've worn me out! I don't think I can move."

"Here we go." Rolling just enough that he could dump her onto the mattress, he pulled her into him and smiled as she rested her cheek on his chest. With his arms wrapped protectively around her, he kissed her forehead and sighed. "You're mine now, angel."

"Good. I want to be yours."

"And tomorrow you need to call your sister and talk to her, tell her what's going on. Then we need to get Tank, Callie, Bree, and Slade out here and have a talk with them. They're your step-brother and step-sister and in the interest of being part of the family, they need to know where we are with this."

Her voice was a whisper when she asked, "Where are we?"

"Well …" He pulled back enough that he could look down into her eyes in the dim lamplight. "Are you one of those women who doesn't ever want to get married?"

"No. I'm not."

"So you're saying you wouldn't be opposed to it?"

"I would not."

"So is that the direction you want to go?"

There was silence for a bit before she said, "You know, I think so. I always thought I'd get married when I found the right person. Just living with somebody for the rest of my life never crossed my mind. And I'll say that for my mom. She might be flighty and flaky, but she was faithful to Dad. They didn't mess around on each other. Of course, as soon as they split, she had a guy twenty years younger than her in her bed, but while they were together, they were *together*. There was no fooling around. They believed in that commitment. Dad obviously still does. And I guess I do too, especially if there's a child involved. I think knowing their parents are committed to each other makes them feel more secure."

"I'd have to agree. My parents had been happily married all those years, and I think that's why it's been so hard for me to be alone. I never dreamed I'd be this age and have no one."

"You're not alone anymore."

"Yeah, and I thank God for you, babe. I really do."

"So yeah. I'd be interested in getting married."

"Okay. I'll take that under advisement." When he kissed her that time, it was a tender, sweet thing intended to make her understand what she meant to him. "But I'm very interested in making you mine."

Amethyst snuggled into his side and Jackson held her as tightly as he could. He wanted to wake up just like that the next morning, her cheek on his chest and his arms around her. They were together, safe and healthy, awaiting the birth of their child in the home he'd thought would always be empty save for his own lonely rattling around. Now it would be filled with happiness and laughter. He'd always dreaded morning.

For the first time in years, he'd be glad to see the sun rise so he could look into her beautiful face.

CHAPTER 5

"WHAT THE HELL?" she muttered as the sound echoed in the bedroom.

"That's the alarm." Jackson was out of bed and dragging clothes on in seconds.

"Alarm? Why do you have to get up this early?"

He glanced at the clock and knew she already had. "It's the VFD. I've gotta go. Don't know when I'll be back, but I'll lock the door behind me."

He was running out the door when she yelled out, "Be careful!"

"I will! I promise!" Then the door slammed shut and he was gone.

Amethyst lay there in the bed, wondering if that was going to happen often. It was a little scary, not knowing what was going on, and she wondered if Gant had gotten the same alarm. She supposed he would if it was a fire, but if it was a car accident or a slip and fall accident, did he get called out too? She had no idea. Lying there alone, thinking about what Jackson might be walking into in minutes, her mind spun out of control, imagining all the horrible things that could be happening. Then her phone rang. "Hello?"

"Honey, you okay?"

Lorna's voice was what she really needed in that moment. "I guess this means Dad got called out too?"

"Yeah. It doesn't happen often, but it does happen. I knew this was a first time for you, so I thought I'd check on you."

She lay there, her heart hammering. "Do you ever manage to go back to sleep while he's out?"

There was laughter on the other end of the phone. "Lawd, no, hon! If I knew Tank was out, I couldn't go back to sleep either. I'm awake until your dad gets back, and I always hope it's before I have to go to work. The idea of having to get up, get ready, and leave before he gets back just tears me up, but at least I work here in town. He'll come by the office to see me as soon as he gets finished so I know he's okay. Jackson will be fine. It's part of being a VFD member."

"I don't want anything to happen to him."

"Sweetie, he could get out of bed, trip on the way to the bathroom, and fall and break his neck. Anything can happen. I don't like it when your dad has to go on these jobs, but what if no one wanted to? And our house caught on fire? Who would fight the fire? There'd be no one." Amethyst remembered Gant saying almost those exact words to her before. "These guys, they want to do this. This is their community, their home. This is where they raise their families and build houses and eat at Mama and Daddy's after church on Sunday. It's all about community. I don't like it, but I'm proud of Gant. He's very dedicated to the fire department. Jackson is too. It'll always be scary, but it won't be as scary down the road as it is the first few times."

"If you say so."

"I know so. My late husband died in a fire. Do you really think I'm comfortable when your dad runs out of here and heads to the station? I like to think if Gant had been a member of the department back then, he could've saved Otto. Of course, Gant would've been just a kid when Otto died, but you get my point, right?"

"Yeah. I still don't like it."

"You don't have to. You just have to support him. That's all you can do." Amethyst sighed at Lorna's words. "Now, turn off the light and try to go back to sleep. I know you won't, but at least try. Bless your heart, this is a helluva way to spend your first night together."

"Guess I'll have to get used to it somehow. Thanks for calling me."

"Do you feel a little better?"

Amethyst laughed nervously. "No!"

"Okay! My work here is done! Love you, honey."

"Love you too. See you later. Bye." She ended the call and lay there before rolling over and snuggling into her pillow. In seconds, she was on his side of the bed, her face pressed into his pillow. It smelled like him, that shampoo he used. What was that? It had some kind of sandalwood or cinnamon fragrance to it, and it made her smile.

Everything about Jackson made her smile. At first, she'd wondered how he'd managed to keep some busty blond from grabbing him up, but she knew exactly why that hadn't happened. He'd stayed to himself for years, never putting himself out there, never meeting anyone.

Connecting with her had been a total fluke, first at the hospital, and then on the side of the road. He wasn't looking for anyone when he found her. They just stumbled across each other. She certainly hadn't been looking for anyone.

Going back to sleep wasn't an option, so she got up and wandered down the hallway. There were two other bedrooms, so she opened the door to the first one. It was nicely decorated and had a queen bed in it, along with some pretty furniture that was an older style. After she'd checked out the closet space, she opened the door to the second room and gasped.

Everything in that room screamed "nursery." The best part was the outside wall. There was a window in the middle of it, and the walls to either side were tall bookcases. Between them and under the window was a beautiful little window seat with a cushion, matching bolsters on either end, and a bevy of colorful toss pillows. There wasn't much on the shelves, just a box here and a couple of books there, and she assumed he'd just never really used the room. The only furniture was a recliner that looked completely out of place and wouldn't have fit in anywhere else in the house either, and right beside it, a small table with a lamp.

But it was perfect. The bookcases were a light wood of some sort and looked whitewashed against the pale green walls. It was cheerful and bright even in the incandescent ceiling lighting. Would he let her fix it up as a nursery? She couldn't imagine he'd say no.

The only other room was the office, and she'd never been in there. It surprised her that the door wasn't locked when she turned the knob, and it swung open effortlessly. Nothing unexpected there—a large desk strewn with all kinds of papers. A quick glance told her there were bills, bank statements, and investment portfolio reports. Even though she knew Gant wanted to know about those things, she couldn't bring herself to look. That was something she and Jackson hadn't talked about, and she decided immediately that she wouldn't invade his privacy. She wasn't with him for money, and she didn't ever want to give him any reason to think that. As she sat down in the leather desk chair, she was overwhelmed with the sensation of him, the hours he spent sitting there, the decisions he made on the desk's gleaming surface, the Bluetooth speaker on the shelf nearby where he surely listened to music from his phone as he worked quietly to take care of everything there, deciding what needed to be done for the ranch, the animals, and the house. Looking around, she was impressed with the neatness and the way things were displayed. The man certainly had a flair for making his surroundings look warm and inviting. On the walls were pictures of him in his uniform, him with guys in his unit, certificates that had been awarded to him, and a case with a glass front.

Amethyst made her way over to it and looked down into it. Lying on the velvet surface of the base were medals attached to ribbons. She didn't know what a lot of them were, but there were quite a few. There were several stars among them, and she didn't know what the differences were, but some were different kinds of metals, and at least two had some kind of leaf pinned to the ribbon. One she recognized instantly—the Purple Heart. She'd seen pictures of it her whole life. There was another one, and it was round with an eagle on the front and some kind of wreath around it. She picked up the Purple Heart and turned it over. On the back was a name, but it wasn't Jackson's, and it was tiny and very hard to read. Once she'd replaced it, she picked up the round medal and turned it over. In raised letters, it read, "AWARDED TO," and farther down, "FOR HONORABLE SERVICE WHILE A PRISONER OF WAR," and those words had a shield underneath them. Directly below that were the words, "UNITED STATES OF AMERICA." But under the first line was an engraved area and, faint as it was, she could still make out, "MSG JACKSON L FRAME." That was the moment it hit her.

Jackson had been a prisoner of war.

A million thoughts tumbled through her head, and tears poured down her cheeks. Where? When? What had they done to him? How long did they have him? And who was it? She wasn't sure why the Purple Heart had someone else's name on it, but the POW medal was most certainly Jackson's. Her heart broke as she thought about his quiet demeanor, his deliberate ways, and his penchant for being alone. He'd let her into his world. That appeared to be more than he did with most people.

That was the moment she spotted it. Placing the medal carefully back into the box and closing the lid, she crossed to the shelves on the wall. There was a picture displayed, and when she reached it, she discovered that it was a photo album thick enough to stand on its own. The photo in the front made her cry even harder. It was a tiny baby, wrapped in a standard hospital blanket, and she knew instantly who it was.

Sure enough, they were all pictures of Cassidy. She didn't have to wonder. The baby's face had Jackson's in it, and she knew whose eyes she was looking into. There were pictures of Jackson holding her, and in some of them he had a buzzed haircut and was wearing fatigues. There were many, all in stages leading up to her third birthday, and it appeared his ex-wife had sent them to him while he was away. The very last picture in the book made her chest ache. It was the same little girl, lying in a woman's arms, and she was limp, her eyes vacant and pupils dilated, a nasal cannula in her nose and an IV line coming from her little arm. There was no question that it was taken right before she died.

Amethyst closed the album, clutched it to her chest, and wept. The pain had to be enormous for him, the agony, the grief, the aloneness, the uncertainty and fear, only to find that doing what he was told left him without a memory of her in her last days. She longed to find a way to comfort him, to take away that mind-numbing, stomach-turning grief and give him something to make him glad he was alive.

She'd give it to him. He'd hold another baby in his arms. Of course it would be her responsibility to care for the child, but she wanted to take care of *him.* He needed someone who'd put him first, who'd see to his needs, to hold his hand when things were too unspeakable to utter them. Jackson was a man filled with pain and grief, sadness and longing, and she wanted to replace all of that with love and laughter and happy days.

When no more tears would come, Amethyst placed the album back on the shelf, then stepped out of the room and closed the door behind her. By the time she got back to the bedroom, she was crying again. There was no denying it—she loved Jackson, not in that starry-eyed, infatuated way that most people thought of love, but in a way that was solid and stable, that transcended houses and cars and clothes and money and all the other things people often married for. She was embarking on a relationship with an adult, something she'd never had before.

He made all the other guys she'd dated look like little kids. That seriousness about him was what had attracted her to him because in many ways he reminded her of her dad. Gant could be funny and silly and weird sometimes, but most of the time he was quiet and deliberate, and she knew the stories of the things he'd gotten involved in before he met her mother. They were horrifying. Jackson was the same way. Gant's service had been to a club, but Jackson's had been to his country. She couldn't think of anything more honorable than that.

Peace had finally been made with the idea of staying up when she heard the front door open and he stepped inside. "What are you doing up?"

"I couldn't sleep. Lorna called me and we talked."

He let out a deep sigh. "Good."

"Was it bad?"

"Not too. House is a loss, but the people are okay. That's what really matters."

"Yep. Want me to make some coffee?"

"That would be awesome. I'm gonna go rinse off and put my lounge pants back on." He kissed her on his way past, and her heart finally stopped hammering from fear.

By the time he'd returned, she had a mug of hot, steaming coffee sitting on the coffee table for him. He dropped onto the sofa, picked up the mug, and took a big swig. "Ahhh. That's more like it."

Amethyst took a deep breath before she spoke. "I saw your medals." Jackson didn't respond. "You have a lot." She waited, but he still said nothing. "You've got a Purple Heart, but it has somebody else's name on it."

"I didn't steal it."

Amethyst bristled and glared at him. "I didn't say you did! I just thought it was odd! Wow. Sorry."

He sighed, but it sounded more like frustration than anything else. "I'm sorry too. I shouldn't have snapped at you. I just don't like talking about any of that."

"Why not? You were a hero."

He shook his head slowly. "I'm a lot of things, but I'm not a hero."

"Those medals say otherwise. And you had one as a prisoner of war. What's that about?"

There was a shift in his demeanor that was almost visible. "That I'm *not* going to talk about."

"Why not? If we're going to have a relationship, I should—"

"That's not relevant to our relationship. At all."

"If it's something you went through, then I think I—"

"No. It's not something you need to know about. It's not something we need to talk about. Just drop it." He'd never been quite so curt with her, and she was a little shocked.

"Well, fine."

"Good."

"You don't have to be nasty about it," she added.

"I'm not! I'm … Look, I'm tired. I just want to get some sleep."

Amethyst stood and held out a hand to him. When he took it, she helped him up to standing. "Go. Want me to bring more coffee?"

"No. I'd really like some juice."

"We've got pomegranate. I'll bring you some."

"Could I have half and half, tea and juice?"

"Yes. Now go!" she barked and pointed down the hallway.

"Yes, ma'am." Without another word, he shuffled off

toward the bedroom and Amethyst watched him go, the tightness in her chest refusing to abate.

By the time she got to the bedroom with the juice and tea mixture, he was sound asleep. She slid into bed beside him but she didn't try to touch him for fear she'd wake him up.

Instead, she pulled up her browser on her tablet and started poking around. That name on the back of the Purple Heart medal … Maybe she could find the guy on the internet. She tried different spellings of his name, but there were dozens, so she tried one more time and added *purple heart* to the keyword search.

Local man receives Purple Heart, the headline of the newspaper read, a little twelve-page weekly publication from some miniscule town in the middle of nowhere. After she read about him for a bit, something else puzzled her, so she went back to the search and scrolled down.

Sure enough, there it was. Tobias Rodgers was dead. How had Jackson come by his medal? She'd ask her dad, but she was pretty sure he wouldn't have any answers for her. He probably didn't know much about that part of Jackson's life either.

There was a little sound from his side of the bed, and Amethyst glanced over to see his lips moving. He was saying something, but she wasn't sure what. Every instinct inside her told her to reach out to him and touch him, calm him, but she didn't want to wake him. Whatever was in his dream, she hoped it wasn't something that would keep his sleep from being restful, because he really needed to rest.

THEIR FACES. THEY WERE ALWAYS THERE, TAUNTING HIM. HE couldn't get away from them. Down the corridor, the sounds of others prisoners were loud and terrifying. Would he ever get out of there? Would anyone ever come for them?

A voice snapped him back to the room where he was held. "Tell us where. Where, dog? Where they will be? You tell us now."

"Jackson Lewis Frame, Master Sergeant, United States Army, Social Security number ..." He'd recited it until he didn't even have to think about it anymore. Name, rank, and Social Security number. They didn't care about his blood type, and they sure as hell didn't care about his religious preference.

"I say, you tell us!" the bearded man screamed into his face.

"Jackson Lewis Frame, Master Sergeant, United States Army ..." Over and over they asked him where the next encampment would be set up, how many soldiers would be present, who the commanders were, how many weapons they'd have and what kind. Truth was, he didn't know. He was a medic, and he didn't care about any of that, just saving lives. He'd tried to tell them that, but they weren't interested in anything else he had to say, just information he could give, and that was none.

"You will tell us!" The board he was strapped to was tilted until his head was lower than his feet, and when they threw the filthy towel over his face, he knew what was coming. Over and over, all day and all night, they kept it up. Sometimes he wished they'd just go ahead and kill him so he didn't have to endure it anymore.

But somewhere down the hallway, he was sure there were enlisted men, and he was a superior. He was respon-

sible for them, even though he didn't know who or where they were. Afterward, he'd be left in the dark until they came back and started again. His terror grew by the hour, and he had no idea how many days he'd been there or what time of day it was. Twice a day he was given stale bread and some broth, but nothing to drink. There was no point. He was getting more than his share of water.

And when they'd start again, he'd yell, "STOP!" just like he did every time. And just like every time before, they'd ignore him and keep going until he lost consciousness. He knew he'd lose consciousness at some point and never wake up, and that was fine.

Anything was better than the hell he was living in.

There was movement somewhere near him, and his eyes flew open. A voice to his left asked quietly, "Babe, you okay?"

Home. He was home in his own bed. The voice … That was Amethyst. "Uh, yeah. Yeah, I'm okay."

"You didn't sound okay. You were mumbling something. Sounded like 'stop.'"

"I dunno. Maybe. Probably some stupid dream." *It's no stupid dream. It's a nightmare*, he wanted to say, but he wasn't about to drag anyone else into his hell. He'd managed it for several years on his own and he'd just keep doing it.

It was late morning by then, and he groaned when he realized the cattle hadn't been seen to, or the hog, or the goats. "I need to get up."

"You probably need to stay in bed," Amethyst told him.

"I can't. Cattle and hog and goats …"

"Can't you tell me how to take care of them? Because I will if you'll just tell me."

He shook his head. "No. But I'll show you so you can do it another time if you need to."

"Okay. But take it slow, all right? You don't look too good."

Ten minutes later and in dark sunglasses, he stepped out the back door with her and headed toward the barn. It only took a few minutes for him to show her how much to feed the hog and what and how much to feed the goats. The cows were a different story. It was harder to take the grain and hay out to them, and he had to hitch the wagon to the four-wheeler and show her how to feed them. That only took about half an hour, and by then, he was exhausted. She said something, but he wasn't paying attention. "I'm sorry, angel. What did you say?"

"I asked, are we done? You need to go lie down." He turned and froze.

She had the water hose in her hand and it was pointed right at him. Everything inside him screamed and he wanted to run, but he managed to mumble, "Um, can you put water in the troughs? I'm just going to … I've got to …" He threw a thumb toward the house.

"Go on. I've got this. Be careful!" she called after him as he hot-footed it across the back yard and dragged himself up the steps.

The inside of the house was darker than outside, and cooler too, as he headed straight for the bedroom. It took him all of two seconds to strip off all his clothes, and he crawled back under the sheet and curled up into a ball, his heart still pounding. He hated hoses. He hated water. Creeks scared him. Rivers terrified him. And he couldn't think of anything worse than being at the beach.

When you'd been drown more times than you could count, water wasn't your friend.

It was late afternoon before he woke again and by that time, Amethyst had found some frozen chicken breasts, baked them, and made chicken salad. Gant had taught her and Sapphire how to make it with few ingredients, and even though she had a lot more stuff at her disposal those days, she still liked it the simple way. The food processor in Jackson's pantry was really nice, and she tinkered with it for a few minutes before she figured out how she wanted to pulverize the chicken. Once that was done, the rest was simple enough.

"Feel any better?" she asked as he wandered into the kitchen in just his jeans, his feet bare.

"A little. Did we feed the animals?"

"Yeah. You don't remember?"

He shrugged. "I wasn't sure if I was remembering or I dreamed it."

She leaned over and gave him a kiss on the cheek, then went back to spreading chicken salad on the bread. "Hungry?"

"Yeah, and that smells good."

"Good. I'm making you two sandwiches and I want you to eat them and then go lie down." Then she remembered something she'd been intending to ask him. "Hey, when do I get to meet your family?"

He shrugged. "I really don't have any. Parents have passed."

"When?"

"My dad, right before I left the military. My mom, about four years ago."

"And that's it? No one else?"

He scowled. "Well, yeah. My brother lives down on

the Gulf. Wyman. That's about it except for some cousins I haven't seen in years. When do I get to meet your mother?"

"Whenever you can find her and get her still long enough to talk to her, I guess. That's not always easy. She flits around like a damn dragonfly. I never know where she is, and I sure as hell don't know who she's with. I know who she *was* with, but she may not be with him anymore."

"Gotcha. Tell you what. Give me a few minutes to shower and then I'll call him and you can at least talk to him on the phone. How's that?"

There was a question she had to ask, and she figured she might as well jump in. "So he's not going to have a problem with me not being white?"

He pursed his lips and then frowned. "No. Why would he?"

"Because a lot of people do."

"His wife is Asian. Thai."

"Oh!"

"Her name is Chimlin, and she's a very sweet person."

"They have kids?"

"Yeah. Their daughter is fourteen. She's like captain of the debate team and won some science fair and I dunno—really smart. Their son is autistic but highly functioning. And he's brilliant too. He can, like, add long lists of numbers and spell unusual words. They must've gotten it from her, because my brother's a dumbass," he said and laughed.

"Younger?"

"Yeah. Not by much. About twenty-two months."

"No other siblings?"

"Nope. Second marriage for my dad, only one for my mom. His first wife was killed in a car accident when they'd only been married for a few weeks. He was a lot of support to me when we lost Cassidy."

"I can imagine. Is that good?" she asked and pointed toward the sandwich.

"Yeah, it really is. You're pretty handy in the kitchen, woman," he said with a grin.

"Thanks!" They ate the rest of the meal quietly, sometimes talking, sometimes not, and Amethyst was struck by how comfortable she felt in silence around him. It was as though no one had to fill the dead air space. Saying nothing was fine.

An hour later, he yelled, "Hey, do whatever you need to do to be presentable and come on in here."

When she entered the living room, he was sitting on the sofa with his laptop in his lap. "What's going on?"

"Doing a video chat with Wyman. Sit over there until I tell him about you, and then I want you to move over here with me so he can see you and talk to you."

"Okay." Amethyst took a seat in the chair adjacent to the sofa and waited, surprised at how *not* nervous she was.

There was a ringing sound on the computer and then it stopped. From the speakers, someone asked, "Can you hear me?"

"Yeah! I hear you fine! Can you hear me?"

"Oh, yeah. Great. Hey, bro, how's everything?" the male voice asked.

"Good. You guys doing okay?"

"Yes, we're fine. You doing okay?"

"I am. Very okay. There's something I want to tell you."

"Oh! You met somebody!" his brother said with a laugh.

"Actually, you're right!"

"No! You've found somebody who'll have you? That's amazing!"

Jackson's face was one huge smile. "Yep. You are. Remember me telling you about my friend? The one we had to cut down out of the tree?"

"I thought he was straight," his brother said, and Jackson burst out laughing.

"He is! It's not him! He's married! Dear god, you say the craziest damn things sometimes. And no, I'm not gay, and you know that, so why the hell would you ask me that?"

"Hey, I'm open-minded. You know that," his brother answered.

"Yes, and I'm glad. So when he was in the hospital, I met his family. He has two daughters, and the oldest one and I kind of embarked on this relationship, not knowing what would happen."

"And?"

"And we're together. And ..." Amethyst watched him take a deep breath and straighten his spine. "And we're pregnant."

His brother's jaw dropped. "You're joking."

"Nope."

"So when do we get to meet her?"

"You can meet her right now. She's right here. Amethyst, this is my brother, Wyman. My sweetie, Amethyst Meadows."

Amethyst sat down beside him and smiled. There, on the screen, was a man who looked remarkably like Jackson, especially his smile and his eyes. "Hi. I'm Amethyst.

This is kinda weird," she said and glanced over at Jackson.

"It's nice to meet you! Hey, brother, you've found a beautiful woman!"

"Yeah. I have."

Wyman laughed and pointed at Amethyst. "Can you get him to behave?"

"It's an hourly challenge, but I'm trying," she said with a sneer at the man sitting beside her.

"He's always been a handful."

Jackson barked back, "Hey! I was a good kid!"

"Let's see, ask Mrs. Baker about that. It was her cat you tied the can to and turned it loose. Damn thing ran around for two days, scared to death," Wyman said, and Amethyst laughed.

"Yeah, but it was inside her privacy fence, so it's not like it ran out into traffic or anything," Jackson pointed out.

"Yeah? What about that time I fell asleep in the tub and you poured two bottles of blue food coloring in there with me?"

Amethyst was laughing so hard that she couldn't breathe. "Hey, you shouldn't have fallen asleep!" Jackson barked. "Bathtubs aren't for sleeping. They're for bathing and getting the hell out of there so somebody else can take a shit!"

Amethyst was gasping for breath. "Y'all are killin' me."

"Oh, he was such a good kid," Wyman repeated mockingly. "He only got in trouble, what, every third day or something like that?"

"Wow. I'm not sure I want my girlfriend knowing about all that stuff."

"So when is this baby due?" Wyman asked.

"She hasn't been able to get an appointment with an obstetrician yet, but I think about seven and a half month? Maybe seven months? Maybe less?" Amethyst nodded. "So it won't be terribly long. Probably around Thanksgiving?"

"A Christmas baby! That'll be nice. Everybody loves having a baby around at Christmas. So, you have family there?"

Amethyst nodded. "My dad and stepmother. They're awesome."

"What about your mom?"

"My mom … My mom travels the Renaissance faire circuit and god only knows where she is. She's still living in the sixties, if you know what I mean."

"Hey, the sixties were groovy!" Wyman cooed, and they all laughed. "Could I get your phone number, Amethyst? You know, in case there's an emergency? I mean, seeing as how my brother is wholly unreliable when it comes to staying in touch."

Amethyst could tell he wasn't trying to be nosy. He was sincere, and that made her feel like he wasn't just doing it lip service—maybe he really did like her.

"Sure. I'll have Jackson text it to you."

There was a sound from somewhere on the other end of the connection and a face came into view. "Who is it? Jackson?

"Yeah, babe. It's Jackson."

"Hi, Jackson! It is Chimlin."

"Hey, honey! Good to see you! You doing okay?"

"I am fine. You sick? Something wrong?"

Jackson chuckled. "No. I just wanted you guys to meet my girlfriend, Amethyst."

Amethyst leaned in and waved. "Hi."

"Oh! Real girlfriend! I thought maybe she was one of those computer people. You got real girlfriend? How you get real girlfriend?"

Jackson, Amethyst, and Wyman were all howling. "They were out of inflatable ones at the store, and she took pity on me!" Jackson gasped out.

"Oh, honey, you get new man. That one is broken," Chimlin said with a grin.

"So I've heard! But he's good to me, so there's that."

"He better be. I send his brother to pow-pow on his butt!" Chimlin barked out, and that set everyone laughing again.

"I'll call you if he needs it."

"Probably not long. Week. Two weeks. He's rotten, that one," the beautiful young woman answered.

"Wow. So we should probably go, since you're threatening to send my brother to pow-pow on my butt," Jackson said, still laughing.

"You come here. You have vacation and you stay with us. It will be fun," Chimlin said, and he was smiling. "You good guy, Jackson. You need to see our children. You their only uncle."

Jackson nodded. "That I am. Give them hugs for me. Maybe we can get down to see you before the baby comes."

"Wish you would, big brother. You're my only sibling, and hers all still live in Thailand. Our kids don't have relatives. It would be nice for them to see you."

"Yeah. I'd like that. Well, I guess we'd better get off here. Love you, brother."

"You too."

"Love you, Chimlin!"

"Love you, Jackson. Nice to meet you, Amethyst," Chimlin called out.

"Yeah, nice to meet you, sweetie. Take care of my big brother," Wyman said.

"I'll try if he'll let me! Nice meeting you guys too."

"Bye," Jackson said and reached for the touchpad on the laptop.

"Later, bro."

With that, the screen went dark, then snapped back to the app. "Well, they seem nice," Amethyst said.

Jackson snorted. "She is. He's a dumbass."

"Yeah. You said that before." Amethyst sank back into the sofa. "So, Mr. Frame, what are we doing for the rest of the day?"

"I think we should watch some TV and relax. God knows things have been upside down today."

Amethyst nodded. "I agree with that!" An evening sitting beside Jackson, his arm around her, her legs across his lap, watching some sappy old movie and cuddling?

It sounded perfect.

WHAT THE HELL IS THE NAME OF THAT STUPID LITTLE town? Craven had heard Amethyst mention it several times, but he couldn't remember what it was. Her dad was some kind of pretend firefighter or something there. He poked through the internet and typed in "Grant Meadows," but he got nothing. She'd blocked him on social media, so he couldn't see her posts. Then he remembered a different platform and checked there.

Apparently she'd forgotten that he followed her there, because he accessed her profile easily. Running down through the list of people following her, he found several of their college friends, plus her sister, but he still couldn't find her dad. He couldn't remember her stepmother's name either. He typed in "volunteer fire departments texas" and groaned—there were hundreds.

Over against the wall was a box of things that had been in the drawers of the desk by the front door of the apartment, so he started going through that. He'd just about given up when he saw an envelope and opened it. Inside was a beautiful birthday card, and the handwriting read, "Hey, baby, wish I was there to take you to dinner. I love you and miss you. Study hard. I'm so proud of you. Love, Dad." Craven turned it over and … *bingo!* The return address was for Gant Meadows in Tarpley, Texas. *That* was the name of that shit hole her dad lived in.

Based on his internet search, there were no hotels there. Matter of fact, it seemed that Tarpley wasn't much of anything, just part of a network of small towns in Bandera County, little pockets of residents here and there with not much of anything in between. He checked his navigation app and groaned. It would take hours to get there, and the nearest place to stay in a decent hotel was in San Antonio, but that was over an hour out.

Horrible as it would be, he didn't see any other way to take care of the situation. He'd have to go there. And once he got there, he'd have to figure out what to do. One way or another, there could be no baby, no matter what he had to do.

Whatever it took, he'd get it done.

CHAPTER 6

THE WEEKEND HAD BEEN GLORIOUS. With a bit of sleep, Jackson's was a little livelier, and they managed to get some things done toward moving her in. She hadn't worked up the courage to ask him about the nursery, though, but it could wait. There was plenty of time to worry about that and besides, she'd probably find out the gender and be able to decorate better.

"So, is this the right move?" Jackson asked as they ate turkey submarine sandwiches and chips on Sunday evening.

Amethyst wiped a dribble of mayo from the corner of her mouth. "Does it seem right to you?"

The smile he gave her was gentle, even wistful. "I love having you here. I think we get along really well. I mean, we could have some kind of blow-up next week, but for now, things seem fine."

"Yeah. I like being here. I especially like being here with you," she said and winked. They'd tumbled around in the bed for two hours the night before, kissing, touching, stroking, licking, sucking, and generally driving each other crazy. She'd gotten more satisfaction from him than she ever had from any man, and she couldn't wait to see what he could do with … Thinking about it almost made her giggle.

"I like being with you too." He leaned over and gave her a kiss on the cheek, and Amethyst felt like a princess. Didn't matter that they were eating subs instead of filet mignon, or drinking tea with pineapple juice instead of some very expensive wine. Jackson made her feel special almost constantly, and she really loved it. She hoped she was doing the same for him.

"So I guess I'll go to Dad and Lorna's and get the little bit of stuff I've got over there." Paper plate in her hand, she reached for his and took everything to the trash. "If that's okay."

"Oh, sure. Need some help?"

"I'd take it, but I really don't have that much."

He sat for a few seconds before he said, "I've got a few things I should probably do around here. That bathroom door is still sticking, and I need to put some of that grippy stuff under the throw rug at the front door before one of us goes sliding and gets hurt."

She nodded. "Yeah, I almost fell yesterday."

"Nope. Can't have that! Okay, you run on over there and I'll see if I can get a few little things done. If you discover you have something that you can't handle by yourself, just call me."

"Dad will be there. He can help me get it in the car and you can help me get it out."

"Would it help if you took the truck?"

"That's great idea! I can get it all in one trip if I do that."

"Keys are by the door, and I think it's still got a good

bit of gas in it." As she turned to leave the kitchen, he called out, "Hey! Aren't you forgetting something?"

What did he mean? She spun back to face him and found him grinning. "Oh!" Almost skipping back to him, she leaned down and gave him a soft, firm kiss. "I'll be careful, I promise."

He patted her butt and grinned. "You'd better be. I don't wanna lose my angel."

Amethyst laughed aloud. "I'm coming back home to my Papa-boo!" She was still laughing as she headed back to the door.

"Oh, lawd, girl, you're gonna drive me crazy! See you in a little bit. Love ya."

"You too." Still smiling, she slipped behind the truck's steering wheel, adjusted everything, and headed out.

Her life had been condensed down into about eight boxes of stuff, and Gant helped her get it loaded. "Sure this is what you want?" her dad asked her as he slid the last box into the truck's bed.

"He's an amazing person, Dad. Kind, thoughtful, sweet, charming, sexy as hell …" she said without thinking.

"NO! I do *not* want to hear that!" Gant bellowed.

"Sorry. Just slipped out."

"Well, keep it in. I'm glad you feel that comfortable with me, but I really don't need details."

"Oh, I'm not giving you those. That ain't none-a yo business," she pointed out.

"Agreed." Gant pushed the tailgate upward and slammed it shut. "Is that everything?"

Should I? It only took her a couple of seconds to decide. "Can we go sit on the edge of the porch?"

Gant's eyebrows rocketed upward. "Uh, sure. Something going on?"

Once they were settled, she turned to her father. "Do you know anything about Jackson's past?"

"Only what I know from just being around him and from the things you said. I know he was military. I know he was married before. I know he had a child who died. Is there something else I'm *supposed* to know?"

She shrugged. "I dunno. I was in his office and I saw this case. It had all these medals in it. Some of them were really pretty, but I don't know what they were, just military stuff. One of them was a Purple Heart, but there was something weird about it." One of Gant's eyebrows cocked up. "It had somebody else's name on the back."

His brow dropped as he thought. "That *is* kinda weird."

"Yeah, and that's not all. Did he ever say anything about being a prisoner of war?"

"No! He was a POW?"

She shrugged again. "I guess. He had a medal that's only given to people who were POWs, so I guess that means he was."

"Wow. No, I had no idea."

"I thought I should ask. He was mumbling something in his sleep the other night, and I swear it sounded like he was saying, 'Stop!' I dunno. Just thought you might have some insight."

"No. Did you ask him?"

"Oh, yeah, and he clammed up. Told me he wasn't going to talk about it and to drop it. It's the first time he's ever gotten kinda short with me. So now I feel like I can't ask him about it, but I'm really curious."

"I can see why. I don't know of anyone else to ask."

The minute the words came out of his mouth, Amethyst realized what she needed to do. “Well, anyway, I’ve got all my stuff.” Lorna had stepped out onto the porch and Amethyst smiled up at her. “I appreciate you guys letting me stay here.”

“You didn’t stay long!” Lorna replied, laughing. “Things going okay with you and Jackson?”

“More than okay. I feel like I’m where I’m supposed to be. We get along great, enjoy each other’s company, have fun. I mean, it’s pretty much perfect.” The conversation between Lorna and Jackson flashed through her mind, but she shut it down immediately.

“Well, that’s great! I’ve gotta go check on the roast, but I’m sure we’ll see you sometime in the next few days. Drive safely, honey,” Lorna said as she turned and disappeared into the house.

Gant followed her to the truck, opened the door for her, and closed it as soon as she was in. The window was down, and he reached up and stroked a knuckle down her cheek. “I love you, baby.”

“I love you too, Daddy.”

“Do you want me to ask Jackson about—”

“No. No, please don’t. He’ll get mad if he finds out I’ve talked to you about it.”

“Okay. I won’t say anything, but if I hear something, I’ll let you know.”

“Thanks. Bye, Dad. See you soon.”

“Bye, punkin. Be careful.”

Amethyst drove back toward town from her dad’s farm and stopped in the parking lot of an abandoned gas station. Flipping through her text messages, she found the one from Jackson that had Wyman’s phone numbers in it. She warred with her own thoughts as she stared at the message. Maybe she shouldn't pry. But if it were her, he'd want to know more. It wasn't like she was asking so she could go talk about him around town. If there was something she needed to know to help him, she wanted to find out what it was so she could do exactly that. Every detail of his life wasn't necessary, but she wanted to know enough to understand him.

It took her five minute to work up the courage before she touched the number he'd sent her for Wyman and it started to ring. "Hello?"

"Um, Wyman?"

"Yes?"

"It's Amethyst. Jackson's girlfriend?"

"Yeah! Hi, honey! What's up? Is Jackson okay?"

"Yeah, but something's not right."

"How so?"

"He was mumbling something in his sleep the other night and when I asked him, he just passed it off as nothing."

"What was he mumbling."

"He was saying, 'Stop!' over and over." Wyman said nothing. "I mean, is there something I should know?" When she didn't answer, Amethyst tried again. "I asked him about the medals in his office, especially the Purple Heart with somebody else's name on it, and he shut me down."

"I was afraid of this."

Fear gripped Amethyst. What the hell was going on? Why wouldn't anybody tell her anything? "Please, if there's something I need to know … I want to help him. Please?"

"Please don't tell him I told you about this."

"I wouldn't do that. I called you asking for information he obviously doesn't want me to have. I'm not going to say a word." Then she waited.

"It's about Jackson's military service. And he told you nothing?"

"I asked, and he shut down like a car with no engine."

"What *do* you know?"

"I saw his medals. I saw the Purple Heart with someone else's name on it. And I saw his POW medal."

She heard Wyman sigh. "I can explain the Purple Heart. There was a young man in Jackson's unit who lost a leg and an arm in an explosion. Jackson saved his life. After he got out, he was awarded the medal, but he wound up killing himself because of PTSD and depression. His mother gave it to Jackson, said she wanted him to have it because at least she got a few more months with her son."

What did one say to something like that? "That was very nice of her."

"She used to send Jackson a Christmas card every year. He didn't get one a couple of years back and found out she died of cancer. That sent him into a tailspin for a couple of months." That would've been before he moved to Tarpley. "So he was talking in his sleep? God, I don't want him to accidentally hit you."

"No, but he was mumbling 'Stop!' in his sleep."

"Yeah. Sounds right." He hesitated, then asked, "And you asked him about all this?"

"Yes."

"I feel like I have to tell you for your own safety." *Well, that doesn't sound too good*, Amethyst told herself. "He was a POW while he was in Afghanistan."

"For how long?"

"Eight months."

"*Eight months*?" Amethyst thought surely he meant eight weeks.

"Yes. Eight months. They were traveling in a convoy to another location when they were ambushed. Most everybody was killed. Jackson and about twenty other soldiers were rounded up and taken to a facility." He fell quiet and Amethyst was about to ask if he was still there when he said, "He was tortured."

"What?" Something in her chest constricted and her eyes blurred with tears.

"Daily. Several times a day. For eight months."

"Dear god!"

"They were trying to get information from him, but he was a medic and he really didn't know anything. They thought because he was a master sergeant, he knew everything. But he'd only been with that particular unit for about five days and hadn't heard what their true mission or destination were. Didn't matter. He had to go, so he hadn't asked. When the animals holding him and the others kept asking him for details, he really had none, but they didn't believe him, so they just kept tormenting him."

Her face felt like it was on fire, and the air around her was still and thick. "What did they do to him?"

"They waterboarded him. Tipped him back and slid his head into a bucket over and over too. Drown him several times, but they brought him back and just kept torturing him. He prayed for death so they'd at least leave him alone and he'd have some peace."

"How'd he get out? Soldiers went in and got them?"

"No. The military tried, but it was too risky and they were afraid the prisoners would be killed before they could get them out. One of the guys had parents who had a lot of money, so they hired a black ops team to go in and extract them. By the time they got there, only ten of the twenty were alive. During the extraction, one of the captives and one of the team members were both killed."

"Why didn't he just make up something? Anything? Tell them *something* so they'd let him go?"

"Well, first, because they wouldn't have. They would've just killed him when they got what they thought he knew. But also because he was a master sergeant. There were enlisted men being held there and he felt responsible for them. As long as he was there, they were pretty much leaving the enlisted men alone. He just repeated his name, rank, and Social Security number to them over and over, and it infuriated them, so they beat him, starved him, left him in filth." There was silence for a few seconds before Wyman started again. "Amethyst, when they got him to the field hospital, he had sores and rat bites all over him. Some of his hair had fallen out, and they'd torn some out too. All he was wearing was his pants—no underwear, no shoes, and they'd taken his dog tags as trophies. And he only weighed about a hundred and forty pounds.

A hundred and forty pounds? Jackson was tall and broad-shouldered, and she'd guess him to be about two hundred and twenty-five pounds or more. All she could squeak out was, "My god."

"We thought we were going to lose him. He wouldn't talk to anybody, wouldn't eat, wouldn't drink. He didn't sleep—just stared at the wall. If anybody stepped up to him and touched him without him knowing they were there, they got a fist in the face. He hit Mom one day. Didn't mean to, but she startled him, and he just rounded on her. Busted her nose. She told him she was sorry she'd startled him, but he cried for three days. It wasn't until Tobias's mother gave him that Purple Heart that we started to see him heal a bit. He's so much better now, but the Jackson you know? That's not the Jackson we knew. That Jackson, he's gone. Sometimes it's hard to handle I'm we're around him. Makes me sad. But he's got a good life there, he likes the place, likes the people, plus he's removed from all of that, and now he's got you. Believe me, I'm thankful for you. I know you haven't been together very long, but if anybody can help him, it'll be you."

That was a huge responsibility, and Amethyst was terrified. "What should I do? What can I do?"

Wyman let out a soft little chuckle. "Oh, honey, just love him. That's what he really needs, somebody who'll love him and accept him just like he is. You didn't know him before, so he doesn't feel like he's disappointing you."

"I can definitely do that."

"I have a secret I need to tell you."

"Yeah?" She couldn't imagine what else it could be.

"You know how he and Georgie talk from time to time?"

"Yeah?"

"That's because of me. I was so desperate that I called her and asked her if she could at least be kind to him. After the first time she talked to him, she called me crying. Said the guy she'd talked to on the phone wasn't the same Jackson she'd known, and I told her that's why I'd asked her to do it. I'm just thankful that she would call him. I think it makes him feel better, to talk to somebody who knew Cassidy well. He has told you about her, right?"

"Oh, yeah."

"Good. This baby? This is exactly what he needs."

Amethyst didn't know what to say. There had been times when she'd questioned herself, wondering if it was fair to Jackson to let him take on her and a child, thinking maybe she was being selfish, and hoping she'd fall madly and deeply in love with him because he was a good man with a good heart. All she managed to come out with was, "I'm glad."

"Me too. Honey, you take care of yourself, okay? And let Jackson take care of you. He was born to do that. Taking care of people is his whole purpose in life. He's convinced of that. He'll do it for you if you let him."

"And I will."

"By the way, how are you talking to me without him knowing it?"

She sighed. "I went to pick up the rest of my things from my Dad's and talked to him about all this. I've been sitting in a parking lot talking to you. I should probably get going. If Jackson knows I was supposed to be on my way home and I'm not there by now, he's going to worry."

"Don't want him to worry! Okay, well, you take care, honey, and thank you."

"For what?"

"For loving my brother. Talk to you soon."

"Thank you, Wyman. Please tell Chimlin I said hello. Talk to you soon. Bye." Amethyst sat there for a minute, and then she smiled. He'd thanked her for loving his brother.

And she did.

By the time she got there, he was completely flustered. He didn't give her time to even come in, just met her on the porch. "Where have you been?"

She smiled up at him. "What? What's wrong?"

"Your dad called and said you were on your way back, but you didn't show up and I was getting kinda worried."

"I'm sorry." As soon as her feet hit the porch, he reached for her and clutched her to him. "I'm okay. There's this farm down the way, the one with the green barn, and I pulled off to watch their goats. They're so cute."

Jackson breathed in her scent and willed his heart to calm before it beat a hole in his chest. "It's okay. I just didn't know where you were and I was a little afraid."

"I'm fine!" She pressed a soft hand to his cheek and smiled. "I didn't realize I'd been there that long. I didn't mean to upset you."

"It's okay. I just don't want anything to happen to you."

"Jackson, until a few weeks ago, you didn't know where I was or what I was doing, or even really know me, and look—I survived and made it here. I'm fine, Papa-boo. Don't worry." She dropped a soft little kiss on his lips and Jackson melted. If anything happened to her, he'd never forgive himself.

"Yeah, but you weren't mine back then. And you're mine now." His eyes fixed hers with a serious glare. "Are you mine?"

"All yours. Absolutely, positively all yours. But this girl needs to eat pretty soon. What are we doing for dinner?"

"We're going to Mac & Ernie's."

"Sounds good. I probably need to freshen up a bit and maybe lie down. I'm a little tired."

"Go for it. I'll get the boxes out of the truck and put them in the back bedroom."

She kissed him again, then headed into the house. "That sounds good. I won't be long. Maybe a thirty minute nap?"

"Works for me. I might join you."

He heard her laugh. "I'd like that!"

Thirty minutes later, they were both stretched out in the bed, him in nothing but his underwear and her in a tee and her panties. She was almost snoring, but not Jackson. Her face was soft and relaxed and her breathing gentle. He loved to watch her while she slept, her features peaceful and glowing. She was a beautiful girl, and what she'd want with a washed-up old guy like him was a mystery, except that she needed a place to be and someone to love her and her child. *Their* child. He had to stop thinking of the baby as just hers. It was theirs. He'd started out thinking that she only wanted to be with him for the baby and what he could offer her, but she said she loved him, and he wanted to believe her.

As they sat at Mac & Ernie's, they talked about the day, and he asked her about the goats. "So those are the goats you thought we were getting when I bought ours?"

"Yeah. They're so cute! I saw those videos on Your-Videos with the goats in pajamas. So adorable!"

"What? Goats in pajamas?"

"Yeah! They put little baby goats in pajamas! It's the cutest thing!"

"Oh good lord. Please tell me you don't want to do that. They're *goats*, for the love of god."

"Maybe once?" Jackson laughed loudly. "Or twice. Or maybe make a video of them in their pajamas."

"Pajamas on goats. What is the world coming to? I didn't get dwarf goats because, I mean, milking dwarf goats? That can't be a good thing." The idea left him shaking his head.

"Hey, did you check on that dog I showed you?"

Jackson grinned. "We're going to meet him tomorrow."

Amethyst almost knocked her chair over as she rocketed out of it and kissed him, laughing the whole time. "Thank you, Papa-boo! I can't wait!"

Jesus, everybody in the whole place is staring at us! Then another voice in Jackson's brain whispered, *Because they're so fucking jealous they can't stand it!* Yep. They were bound to be. "You're welcome, angel. We'll go check him out. I emailed them and they answered right away. They said we can meet him at the shelter, so I told them maybe two o'clock. Sound good?"

"Sounds great! Oh, I'm so excited!" She took her seat again and tied into the ribs she'd ordered, and as he watched her eat, his heart was full. They could have a good home for them and the baby, and a very good life.

"Your first job tomorrow is to make yourself an appointment with a doctor, so do it first thing in the morning. Then we can get some work done before we go meet the dog. And listen to me. If he's not the one, we'll just wait. There are plenty of dogs out there, and if this one isn't perfect for us, we'll find another."

"I know, but I just have this feeling he's going to be great." She dropped the bone she'd been holding, sat back in her chair, and smiled. "I have something I need to ask you."

"Okay."

"That extra room in the house? Can I—"

"Fix it up as a nursery?" He'd figured out that she'd been thinking about it. More than once he'd caught her opening the door and looking around, then closing it again. "I don't see why not. But we need to talk first."

"Okay. Something bad?"

"No. Just clarify some things." He could tell she didn't understand, but he had some questions he had to ask.

They chatted on the way home but as soon as they stepped into the house, she wheeled and pinned him with her gaze. "Okay, what are these things we need to talk about?"

He pulled her down to sit beside him on the sofa. "I just want to make things clear. You want to fix up a nursery?" She nodded. "What happens if you have a miscarriage?"

Those beautiful eyes widened. "God, I hope that doesn't happen!"

"But what if it does?"

She shrugged. "I'm not sure what you're trying to ask me."

"I'm trying to ask you …" He had to know, but damn, the answer could be pretty painful. "If you lose this baby, is that it for us? Are we over?"

The same eyes that had stared at him a few seconds before filled with tears. "Would you not want me here anymore?"

"Would you still want to be here?"

"Of course! I mean, if that happened, I'd probably want to at least finish school, but wouldn't you want to try again? I mean, would you still want a family with me? If you wouldn't, then I … I mean, I thought …"

"Yes. I'd still want a family with you. I just wanted to know if you'd still want a family with me."

Those sweet hands took his and she sobbed. "I love you, Jackson. I know how this started out, but I want to be here with you. We've said it over and over, but you're right. This needs to be clear. And I want to be here. Or wherever. I don't care where, as long as I'm with you. You've given me more love in this teeny little bit of time we've been together than I've had in years from anybody except my dad. The only thing better than having this baby would be having *your* baby, and we can do that after this one is born for all I care. You're gonna be the most amazing dad."

"You're going to be the most amazing mom, angel. I'm sorry I keep questioning, but I'm … I'm a little scared, you know? I've been out here by myself and I've made a life for myself, and then suddenly I find a beautiful woman in the middle of it, and I'm a little nervous. Does that make sense?"

"I get it. I do. But baby or no baby, I want to be with you. I don't see having the baby and being here with you as being the same thing. They're two very different things, and one isn't dependent on the other."

"That's all I needed to know. Tomorrow morning we get up and we start building a life together. You go to the doctor. We get a dog. We get you a bigger car. Whatever we do, we're going to do it together. Right?"

"Right!"

"And I do love you, Amethyst. It's kind of like a seed, but it's going to grow. I know it will."

"I feel the same way. You're not the kind of guy I'd

want a one night stand with. You're an all-in kinda guy, and that's what I need. No more kids pretending to be super studs. Spoiled brats. Assholes."

"I can be an asshole," Jackson said with a snicker.

Amethyst snorted. "I can be an asshole too."

Jackson squeezed her hands. "So tomorrow morning, call the doctor while I'm taking care of the livestock. Then we'll go look at some cars, eat some lunch, and meet the dog. And if we like him, I guess we'll be going to the pet store!"

"I love pet stores!"

"We're not bringing home any more pets. Just getting supplies."

"Because they don't have dwarf goats?"

Jackson laughed aloud. "Because they don't have dwarf goats. Thank god!

"JESUS, GIRL, YOU'RE GONNA KILL ME!"

Amethyst laughed as she climbed over Jackson's leg and scooted up in the bed beside him. "You didn't think you could do that, did you?"

"Hell no! I thought I'd gotten way too old. I think you're some kind of witch."

"No, I'm fae." He stared at her. "Fae. You know, fairie people."

"What?"

She giggled. "Never mind. If you'd ever been to a Renaissance faire, you'd know what I was talking about."

"Oh. Corsets and herbs and mead and weird musical instruments," he offered.

She snarled, "Boy, you've got a lot to learn."

"Is there one around here?"

Amethyst shrugged. "I'm not sure. I don't remember ever doing one anywhere near here, but I could be wrong."

"I'd be open to going to one sometime. Might be fun."

She rolled toward him and propped her chin up with her fist. "I could find out which ones Mom's doing this year and we could go to one of those. Probably the only way you'll ever get to meet her."

"We could do that." Jackson dragged a twist of hair out of her face and stroked her cheek. "We can do whatever you want."

"What I want right now is to go to sleep. It's been a long day." Thoughts of her phone call with Wyman had made it hard for her to concentrate all evening, but she didn't want Jackson to think anything was wrong. He could never know she'd had that conversation with his brother.

"I'm tired too." He held out an arm and Amethyst scooted up against him, and as he curled it around her, she felt calm and peaceful. The little kiss he feathered onto her forehead comforted her racing mind. "I love you, angel."

"I love you too, Papa-boo. Get some sleep." With her arm draped across him, she rested her face on his chest and let herself drift off.

It was the wee hours of the morning when she woke to the sound of him mumbling something, and it broke her heart. "Stop. Stop! Stop. Please stop. Please? Please stop. I don't know. I don't know." He'd rolled to the other side of the bed, his back to her, and she didn't know what to do. If she reached out to touch him, he might strike out at her, but if she didn't, the torment would just go on and on for him. She wondered how many nights he'd lived through that horror over and over and how she could make it stop, at least for that moment.

Instead of touching him, Amethyst wiggled over to get as close as she could without touching him, and then she remembered something. Ever so softly, she began to sing a song Emerald had sung to her when she was little. It was Brahms Lullaby, and she knew every word by heart. Her mother might've been flighty and flaky but, by god, she'd read with her girls and sung them to sleep every night until they were old enough to tell her to just stop it, and they'd laughed the whole time they said it. There'd been plenty of times when things were going wrong or she was scared and alone and she wished she was still that little girl, listening to her mother's voice. She wasn't sure what would happen—he might roll over and punch her—but it was the only thing she knew to do, and it was worth a shot.

As she sang, his mumbling slowed, and eventually it stopped, but she kept singing. Almost like magic, he rolled toward her, facing her, and she moved back to give him room so she still wouldn't be touching him. The words slipped from her lips one by one and she marveled as his facial features softened, his breathing evened out, and he calmed. By the time she'd finished the song, he was resting peacefully, lips barely parted, and he wasn't making a sound.

Amethyst sobbed silently. They'd started that journey because she needed him, but it was obvious to her that he needed her too. She could help him heal. Sure, she'd have to be careful to not let him know how much she was aware of, but that was okay. She could do that. Whatever it took to get him back to the Jackson his family had known, that's what she'd do, even if it meant he didn't need or want her anymore.

The peaceful silence in the room hung there like the scent of roses on a summer night, and she carefully got out of bed and padded barefoot down the hallway. When she got to his little office, she sat down behind the desk, turned on the low light there, and pulled out a sheet of paper. Things were tumbling around in her head so wildly that she hoped she could slow her thoughts enough to gather them and get them on paper. There was a nice pen sitting in a holder, so she took it out and started.

Dear Jackson,

I just want you to know how much I appreciate everything you do around here. I'm not just talking about for me. I'm talking about everything you do, for me, for the house, for the animals, and for the people in this community. You're the finest man I've ever met, and I'm fortunate to call you my friend.

But you're so much more to me than that. You're my hero, Papa-boo. I've never been loved the way you love me, and I feel blessed to know you. If this baby is a boy, I want him to grow up to be the honorable, decent man his dad is. And if it's a girl, I know she'll be the apple of her daddy's eye and the most cherished princess on the planet.

Thank you for opening your heart and home to me, for introducing me to your family, and for trusting me and loving me. I'd die before I'd hurt you. Between you and my dad, this child will have the best role models ever because of the two of you.

I love you, Jackson. That will never change. You're everything I could ever want in a father for my child, in a

CHAPTER 7

AMETHYST WAS sound asleep when Jackson cracked open an eye, so he was careful not to disturb her as he got up and slipped on his boxer briefs. Every evening he left work clothes in the laundry room so he could dress there before he went outside, and it was a system that worked pretty well for him. He'd strip them off as soon as he came in, and none of that funk ever had to come into the rest of the house.

But his first order of business was always to make a pot of coffee, so he headed straight to the counter in his underwear and went about getting it started. He'd grabbed the bag of coffee grounds when he turned and saw the envelope.

A million thoughts went through his mind, and none of them were good. Of course, he reasoned, if she wanted to leave, she would be gone. She wouldn't leave a note saying she was leaving and then go back to bed, would she? And when had she done that? It wasn't there at bedtime, so he couldn't imagine. If she'd gotten up in the night, he never knew it. The envelope got moved to the side so he didn't drip anything on it while he was getting the coffeemaker loaded up, and as soon as he turned it on, he made his way straight to the laundry room and put on his work clothes. It didn't take long for the pot to start filling up, and he poured a travel mug full, snapped the lid on, picked up the envelope and stuffed it in his shirt pocket, and headed out.

Two of the cattle were already kicking up a fuss and one of the goats was acting like an idiot, but they'd live. The little storage room in the barn had an old metal folding chair sitting in it, so he sat down and pulled out the envelope. His hands shook as he opened it, fearful of what she'd written there, afraid it was all over before it ever really started. The first paragraph began with "I," so that wasn't too bad, but he noticed the second began with "but." In his experience, that usually meant a complete turn in whatever was above, and all he could hope was that the first part was bad and the second part was good.

As he read, the writing got harder and harder to read, and he realized his eyes were full of tears. No one had ever written anything like that to him. Georgie had written notes in greeting cards she'd given him while they were married, but she'd never penned anything that gave him hope like the letter he held in his hand. Dragging his sleeve across his face, he wiped the tears and his nose at the same time, then folded the letter, put it back in the envelope, and stood there, wondering what to do with it. There was a safe in his office, and he decided that was the place to put it. Losing that letter was something he never wanted to have happen. There was no way that young woman could've imagined what it meant to him. The tear stains he saw on the paper, surely shed as she was writing it, were all he needed to know about how their relationship should progress.

As he fed the cattle, fed the goats, and fed the ornery, smelly old hog, Jackson thought about what his future was going to look like. Along with those thoughts were the ones of the ring in the bottom drawer of his desk. "Shit, I hope she didn't find it while she was looking for paper and an envelope," he muttered aloud to himself. It wasn't a traditional ring with a big honkin' diamond. When he'd asked the jeweler about it, he'd envisioned it as something very, very personal, something other women wouldn't be given. The fellow had assured Jackson they could get a wedding band that would match the band of the engagement ring, and he hoped that was true. There were advantages to not getting married before the baby was born, but he'd already thought about them and they weren't important enough to wait, not if she was ready. He'd plan something special, maybe take her on a little trip, and propose. He wanted them to be alone. It was a private moment, something he didn't want to share with a crowd as so many other people did.

Some kind of aroma was coming from the kitchen when he stepped in the back door, and he could see her at the stove. She twisted just enough to see him and smiled. "Hey, babe. Breakfast's almost ready."

"Whatcha got?"

"You like pancakes?"

Jackson walked up behind her and wrapped his arms around her waist. "I like pancakes. I love you."

"I hope you know I love you too."

His lips brushed her neck and he whispered, "I do now."

"Good. Get us some plates and we'll eat."

It only took him a few seconds to change in the laundry room, and he grabbed two plates on his way back. As soon as they sat down, he looked up and just took in the sight of her. Really looked. The shape of her face, the color of her skin, the color of her hair, the way she wore it. And those gorgeous eyes. She grinned at him. "What?"

"Nothing. Just appreciating the woman across the table from me. Thank you."

"You're welcome. They're just pancakes!" she said and laughed.

"No. Not just the pancakes. Thank you for cooking them. Thank you for being here. Thank you for giving us a shot. And thank you for giving me hope." A lump formed in his throat and he had trouble speaking when he said, "Thank you for loving me."

"Thank *you* for loving *me*. I'm the luckiest woman in the world to have you and be here with you. I haven't told you this, but the very first time I set foot in this house, I felt like I was home. It was like you'd done everything in here for me, picked out stuff you knew I'd like, set up the kitchen the way I'd want it, everything. Dad's always said he doesn't believe in coincidence, and I think I feel the same way." He reached a hand across the table and she took it. "When I'm with you, I feel safe. So thank you. Thanks for being you."

"So I guess today's agenda is getting a doctor's appointment, lunch, and meet the dog, with browsing car lots in between. The rescue is in San Antonio. Want to go to one of those baby stores where they sell furniture and stuff?"

"Sure! That would be fun! I have no idea what I want for a nursery. Maybe I could get some ideas that way."

He cleaned up the dishes while she made the call. In seconds, she was back. "We've got to hustle. They made me an appointment for next week, but they asked me to come by and do one of their pregnancy tests before the appointment. I just walk in and they'll let me know in a couple of hours. Apparently they don't trust the drugstore tests."

"Sounds good. Let's get on the road." Jackson smiled as he placed the last plate in the dishwasher. It was going to be a great day.

SHE MADE ABOUT TWO HUNDRED PICTURES AT THE BABY goods store. When one of the employees noticed her looking at everything, they offered her a catalog of the furniture collections. That would help a lot. It had the dimensions, choices of colors, everything she'd need to do some planning.

Jackson took her for a nice lunch at the Riverwalk, and she loved the restaurant. They had wonderful seafood and chicken dishes, and the dessert was amazing. "So, are you excited about the dog?" he asked as he finished off his cake.

"Yeah. I hope he's what you need. He's so cute, and he sounds perfect."

"If he's not, we'll find another one."

She didn't want to tell him, but she'd pretty much fallen for the pooch as soon as she'd seen his picture. Sure, they could find another dog, but Jackson needed one who'd work for him, and this dog seemed to be the right choice. When they pulled up in front of the building, she could see dogs in the runs on the side where they'd parked, and there weren't that many. She was about to say something when her phone rang. "Hello?"

"Miss Meadows?"

"Yes?"

"This is Dr. Everett's office. Your test did indeed come back positive, so we'll see you next week at the appointment you scheduled."

"Thank you! I'll be there. Bye." She hung up and grinned. "That was the doctor's office. Their test was positive, so it's a go."

"Good. Now we know for sure. Let's go meet this mutt! Does he have a name?"

"Yeah. It's Buck."

As soon as they stepped through the doorway, Amethyst felt good about the place. It was clean. There were no horrible odors, and the main room was decorated very nicely. There were pictures all over the walls of dogs who'd been adopted and their new pet parents. Most were really cute. Some were so ugly they were cute. Others were disabled. There was a dog with three legs, and one with only one eye, and one with its face all misshapen. Under the picture it said, "Rastus was shot three times, but he lived and has a great life with the Wilsons." That made her smile.

The door opened and a woman stood there. "Hi! You here about Buck?"

Jackson nodded. "Yes, ma'am."

The woman let out a low whistle and a dog appeared. As soon as he reached her, he sat down beside her left foot. "So this is Buck. He's a very good boy. The folks who had him did a super great job of training him. Is there a particular reason why you chose him out of all the others?"

"Yes, ma'am. I have cattle and goats, and I wanted a dog she could play with, one that would keep her safe and be a good companion for us, but that could help me with the livestock."

"I think Buck would do great. They left us a list of his commands, so you should be able to figure them out pretty quickly.

"That's great!" Amethyst stooped to look into his face, and he gave her a steady look for about four seconds before he looked away. "Can I pet him?"

"Of course! Why don't you take him over there and have a seat. Sit there with him, pet him, talk to him, talk to each other about him. If you have any questions, I'll be right over here at the desk." With that, she clipped a leash onto his collar, then handed it to Amethyst and walked away.

He followed obediently as they crossed the room and sat down, and once they were seated, he turned with his back to them and sat on top of Amethyst's feet. "Okay, this is funny," she said with a giggle.

"He's very well behaved." Jackson reached out and scratched behind the dogs ear. That made Buck turn to look at him, and he gave the little fellow a scratch under the chin. "You're a handsome boy too. Very handsome."

"He is, isn't he? His markings are really pretty."

Jackson stood. "Give me the leash. We had a couple of K-9s in a unit I was assigned to once. Let me see if he knows some basic commands." Buck rose and followed Jackson across the room, walking right beside Jackson's left knee. When he stopped, he looked down at the dog. "Buck, sit." The dog's butt dropped immediately. "Buck, down." In less than a second, the dog was lying down, back feet drawn up under him and front legs flat on the floor, his eyes alert and his ears rigid. "Buck, heel." As Jackson stepped out, the dog rose and walked right beside him again.

"Wow. He's good," Amethyst whispered.

"He sure is. If they did this good with his obedience, I have to believe his herding skills are on track too. What was his adoption fee?"

"Four hundred?"

"Do you like him?"

Amethyst nodded. "I really do."

"Okay. Here." He passed the leash off to her and the dog immediately sat down on her feet again. "I'll take care of it."

Ten minutes later, Jackson had filled out all the paperwork, including an agreement to have the dog seen by his vet within forty-eight hours. They stopped by the pet store and even though it was crazy busy, the dog was perfectly behaved the whole time, and they were both impressed. Armed with dog food, a new collar and leash, and some shampoo and deodorizing spray, they headed home with Buck in the seat between them.

They hadn't been home thirty minutes before Jackson announced, "I'm taking him out to work him. Be back in a few minutes." He and the dog disappeared out the door before she had a chance to say anything and they were gone. Seconds later, she could hear various kinds of whistles from that direction, and she knew Jackson was putting Buck through his paces.

She sneaked down the hallway and into the office, then opened the drawer and pulled the box out. The ring sat there gleaming in the beam of sunlight shining through the window, and she almost gasped aloud. Everything inside her wanted to put that ring on and announce to the world, "I'm marrying Jackson Frame and he's so awesome!" Wasn't there someone she could call and gush to about everything that had happened?

The call was answered with, "Hey, Am!"

"Hey. What's up with you?"

"Nothing much. How 'bout you?"

She chuckled. "Sure you want to know?"

Her sister laughed back. "If I didn't, I wouldn't ask!"

"Well, okay then. Craven and I broke up."

"*What*? Are you serious?"

"Yeah. And I'm pregnant."

There was silence for a few seconds before Sapphire whispered, "No."

"Yeah. And I'm in Tarpley."

"Jeez, Am, does Dad know?"

"Of course. And I'm getting married."

"WHAT? What the hell are you talking about? Wait. Whose baby is this?"

"Biologically, it's Craven's. But that's not the name that'll be on its birth certificate."

"Oh, yeah? And what will that be?"

"It's last name will be Frame."

She'd begun to think the call had dropped when Sapphire asked, "Jackson? You're marrying Jackson? Hot Jackson?"

"What?"

"Am, Jackson's fucking *hot*. The guy is ... He's hot, Am. You're not marrying hot Jackson."

"I am."

"How the hell did this happen?"

Amethyst cranked up the storytelling and in fifteen minutes, she'd given Sapphire every detail she could think of, short of the information she'd gotten from

Wyman. Then she remembered something. "By the way, Craven called me and tried to pay me to have an abortion."

"He *what*? I never liked that asshole. I like him a lot less now."

"Jackson said if he calls again, he wants to talk to Craven. God only knows what he'll say. He was really pissed off because it upset me."

"Good. Somebody needs to look out for you. That's low—really, really low. I hope you told him to go to hell."

"I just hung up on him." Amethyst wished she'd said something to him, called him a name, but at the time she didn't think about that. She just wanted to get off the phone. "He won't call back, I'm sure. But I overheard Jackson and Lorna talking, and Lorna wants him to get me to file charges against him for harassment. I just want him to leave me alone."

"Asshole. I hope he shows up there and Jackson and Dad beat his ass."

"No. I don't want him here, and I sure don't want them going to jail because of his sorry ass."

"True. So when is the baby due?"

"Not sure. I've got an appointment next week to start my prenatal care, so I'll know more after that. Want me to call you?"

Her sister laughed through the phone, and it was like music to Amethyst. "Of course! I always want you to call me, even if you don't have shit to say!"

"This is the same girl who told me she was going to kill me because I dipped her pigtails in wax!" Amethyst remembered that. They were at a faire booth where candles were being made and when Sapphire hadn't been paying attention, Amethyst pushed her head sideways so her pigtail would go down into the wax. Lord, Emerald had been furious!

"Yeah. I remember. You just wait. I'm going to come to visit and put your kid up to all kinds of meanness."

"I bet you will." The sound of the back door opening caught her ear. "Oh, Jackson's done with the dog. I need to go see how he did. Catch up with you later?"

"Wait. There's a dog? What—"

"That'll give us something to talk about next time! Love you, Saph. Bye!"

"Who was that on the phone?" Jackson asked as he reached into the refrigerator for a bottle of water.

"Sapphire. I hadn't talked to her and I figured I should."

"And what did she have to say?"

"She said, 'You're marrying hot Jackson?'"

He stared at her for a few seconds, then burst out laughing. "Hot Jackson? I'm hot Jackson? Holy shit! That's the damn funniest thing I've ever heard in my life! I'm a lot of things, but I'm not hot!"

She planted her hands on her hips. "Yes you are."

"Okay, beautiful, whatever you say!" He was still laughing when he disappeared down the hallway, and she heard the bathroom door close.

There was movement, and she looked down to see Buck sitting at her feet. "Looks like you passed the test. He's not saying we've got to take you back." The dog looked up at her and opened his mouth to pant, which made him look like he was grinning. "Seems like you're pretty happy too."

Jackson appeared in the kitchen doorway and nodded. "I'm pretty happy with him. Took him out and tried him with the goats. The only mistakes he made were my fault. I've got to learn the signals. Otherwise, he did great."

"Good. Is it time to feed all the animals again?"

"Yep. Want to help?"

Amethyst nodded. "Yeah, if I'm gonna be a rancher's wife, I'd better learn how!"

THE BACK SEAT OF THE CAR WAS PRETTY WELL FULL. OF course, when someone was driving a car like a Camaro, they didn't expect a lot of cargo room.

He stopped by the dealership and had the vehicle serviced, then filled up the gas tank and hit the road. There was a room waiting for him in San Antonio, and he wanted to be there before bedtime. After that, he'd have to find a way to look around Tarpley and see if he could find her. And when he did, he had every intention of making sure his troubles were over.

It was a boring drive. God, he hated the south! His dad had done some research and found that it was easier to get a law degree at Bama than anywhere else in the country, so off he'd gone, straight into hell. The people were hicks. The food was greasy. The weather was hot and muggy with a one hundred percent chance of mosquitos. He'd be glad when he finished school so he never had to be down there again.

He crossed over into Texas on I-10 just east of Pinehurst and kept driving. He'd be in Houston by dinnertime, and he'd stop and eat there. After that, it wasn't very far to San Antonio, and he'd be able to get a good night's sleep. There had to be a way to get a car that no one would recognize—the Camaro wasn't exactly invisible. Maybe there would be a rental place around somewhere.

The sound of his Bluetooth connection in the car rang, and he looked at his phone's screen: Hardin. "What's up, man?"

"Some of the guys were asking about you. I told them you went to see your parents."

"Good. That'll work."

"Where are you?"

"Almost to Houston."

"Craven, what are you going to do when you get down there?"

"I told you before, I'm gonna fix this once and for all."

"Don't go doing something stupid, man."

"I won't." *Nope*, he thought. *Whatever I do, it'll be the smartest thing I've ever done.*

THE REGULAR TUESDAY NIGHT BUNCH WAS THERE, AND Pops went over some of the things they needed to do training on in the next month or two. It sounded doable to everyone, and there was a discussion about who'd do what training and when. Jackson had noticed a guy sitting off to the side, someone he'd never seen before, and he wondered what was going on.

As soon as the discussion on trainings had come to a close, Pops looked over at the man, then back at the group. "Now I'd like to introduce you to someone who's going to be around for a bit. This is Conor Paxton. He's a Texas Parks & Wildlife officer from San Antonio, and he's going to need our help. Officer Paxton, why don't you come on up and tell everyone what's going on?"

The tall man rose and stepped to the front of the group. "Sure thing. So, like Pops said, I'm Conor. We have biologists who work for the department, and they've been noticing a trend of some of the species, both plant and animal, below certain areas beginning to dwindle. When they started checking, it seems they're near rivers and creeks that aren't as rich in natural resources as they used to be. After doing more studies, they discovered that there are invasive species upriver from many of these places that are affecting drainage and the river and creek channels, blocking the flow of the water and leaving areas downstream with much less water than their ecosystems had in the past. We're here to try to figure out which areas are flooding and where the blockages are so we know where to concentrate our work. We spoke to the county engineer and found out that there's been some increased flooding of Williams Creek in recent years."

"Boy, that's sure true. It's made a mess of my property!" a guy they all called Monster griped.

"Exactly. We think the problem is nutria. They disturb the earth in their burrowing and that's causing dirt to wash into the river and creek beds when there's been a lot of rain. If those blockages are addressed, the flooding can stop and the downstream damage from lower water levels can be managed. When a body of water floods like that, some of that water never makes it back into the channel. And that's when the problems surface."

"What about javelinas?" Tank asked.

"They may be culprits too. We also haven't ruled out the role armadillos might play. It could be significant. I need some people who'll help with some surveys of the creeks around here. We're going to be doing things like measuring elevations and silt shifting, and since we're headed into the rainy season, we're hoping the data will come up fast. If you can help with any of it, please see me afterward and I'll get your information. Thanks."

When Conor sat down, Pops stood up again. "I hope a few of you will sign on to help. Since this affects both land that's flooded and unusable, as well as the downstream effects, we need to get involved in this."

Gant was sitting next to Jackson, and he leaned over to his friend and whispered, "You're right there close to Williams Creek. Be sure to sign up."

Not a chance in hell, Jackson wanted to yell. "I dunno if I'll have time to help. I'm going to be pretty damn busy over the next few months."

Gant gave him a puzzled look. "You've got more help now than you had two months ago. That should free up some time."

"I dunno. I'll think about it." *When hell freezes over*, he thought. He wasn't going anywhere near flood water, especially not in the rainy season. It was too damn scary for words, at least for him.

The meeting was winding down when the door to the building opened and in walked Lorna and Amethyst carrying containers of goodies. *This is our opportunity*, Jackson thought, so he waited until everyone was in the kitchen area and walked in, right up to Amethyst, and wrapped his arms around her waist. "You girls fix up something good?" He could see in his peripheral vision that some of the movement in the room had stopped.

"Yeah, Lorna made blond brownies with pecans and I made a dump cake!"

"Mmmm. Sounds good." He kissed the side of her neck and she giggled.

From somewhere in the room, he heard Pops' voice. "What the hell?"

The room quieted and another voice muttered, "Anything you two would like to tell us?" Jackson glanced up and saw Short Shit glaring at him.

"Oh! I thought everybody knew. Amethyst and I started seeing each other right after Gant's accident, and that long-distance relationship thing just wasn't working for us anymore. So she's here full time now."

Something in Tank's face told Jackson that Amethyst's stepbrother wasn't surprised. That meant Lorna or Gant had told him, and that meant Bree and Slade most likely knew, and probably Carly and Ross too, plus Tank had surely told Callie. Before Jackson got a chance to say anything, Gant chimed in. "And we couldn't be happier." One glance told him Lorna was beaming.

"So this has been going on for a while now?" Dirty-D asked.

With a grin, Jackson answered, "Yeah. Long enough that we're expecting."

"Well, hot damn! Congratulations, both of you!" Pops called out and rushed to the front of the room to hug Amethyst and shake Jackson's hand. In seconds, there was back-slapping and hand-shaking and neck-hugging going on everywhere in the room, and he laughed to himself when he thought about how that fish and game officer probably thought they were all crazy.

"So, when's the happy occasion?" Buff asked.

"Which one?" Amethyst asked and everyone laughed.

"Patience, everybody. We don't have a due date yet.

She's got a doctor's appointment next week and we'll know more. As for the other happy occasion, give us a bit. We're still trying to settle into day-to-day life and get our feet under us. It's a big adjustment, going from sneaking around to seeing each other every day, all the time." Jackson gave her a little squeeze from behind and felt her hands fall on top of his as they rested around her waist. "We weren't going to say anything just yet, but damn, when you've got good news for a change, you really want to share it!"

"I'm glad you did! Now, eat up, everybody!" Pops called out, and a line formed as the VFD members waited to get some of the goodies Lorna and Amethyst had brought.

"Did you drive?" Jackson asked Amethyst as he stepped up to get another brownie.

"No. Lorna came and got me, so I can ride home with you."

"Perfect. I hope it was okay that I did that."

She smiled and pressed a finger under his chin. "It was perfectly okay. I'm glad everybody knows. But did you get the feeling Tank—"

"Already knew?" Amethyst nodded. "Yeah, I'm guessing your dad or Lorna told him. That means they all probably know by now."

"That's okay too. Doesn't matter. It doesn't change anything." The lips she pressed to his were soft and warm, and he wanted to squeeze her to him and deepen it, but not there in front of everyone. When she pulled back, she smiled. "Help us clean up so we can go?"

"Sure thing, angel." Jackson set about gathering up paper cups and plates and wiping down the countertops. Everyone knew. No more hiding.

Everything was going to be fine.

HE GRABBED A RIDESHARE AND HEADED TO THE AIRPORT. That would be the easiest place to find a rental car. The credit card would do the trick, and in an hour and wearing a ball cap so security cameras couldn't identify him, he had a non-descript sedan with Texas plates, both things he'd specifically asked for when he'd reserved the rental.

By the time he got back to the hotel, it was late and he was tired. It was tempting to drive on into Tarpley, but he could do that in the morning. He had every intention of finding out where she was and getting to work. It wouldn't take long once he found her. It was one thing to hear about the money on the phone. It was entirely something else to see it in person, and he had the crisp dollars bundled in the duffel in the Camaro's trunk. Talking the people at the bank into letting him take out that much money without his dad's consent hadn't been easy, but he'd pointed out that in a year, he'd be free to do whatever he wanted and if they didn't help him out at the moment, he'd pull his money then and take it elsewhere. That lit a fire under them, and they'd packed the bills into the bag in record time.

Back in the room, he undressed, took a shower, and laid out a game plan. The front end of the plan was the money, but the back end … That was going to be a good bit messier. The only person who knew where he was wouldn't say anything, and no one would guess that he'd come all the way there to do what he was doing. He'd borrowed Hardin's brother's credit card and driver's license—they looked a lot alike—and if anything was said, Barrett could claim both had been stolen. Craven made it worth the guy's while. A few thousand to use a driver's license and credit card? Nice way to make a buck.

He ordered a decent meal, a big one, and had the delivery people bring it to the front desk. If he went down, picked it up, and ate in his room, few people would see him. Once he'd gotten a good night's sleep, he'd start looking for her. How hard could finding her possibly be? After all, it wasn't like the was in New York City.

She was in a nowhere little town called Tarpley.

"COULD WE HAVE DAD AND LORNA OVER? MAYBE tomorrow night?" It was Friday evening, and the week had gone incredibly well. Buck was doing his job better than Jackson could've ever hoped for, the breeding of six of his heifers had resulted in calves on the way, and two of the horses were trained well enough that they were about ready to sell. Plus she'd almost nailed down the baby furniture she wanted, which was pretty much all she'd talked about all week. Not that he minded. He absolutely loved how excited she was about all of it, and it made him excited too.

Jackson grinned as he answered her. "Sure. Anybody else? Tank and Callie? Bree and Slade?"

"I'd really rather keep it small." She was fussing with a bouquet of sunflowers that he'd picked up for her on his way back from the feed store. "I just feel kinda … I dunno. Unsettled, I guess."

As he slipped the last dish into the dishwasher, he

turned toward her and couldn't help noticing the strain in her face, that beautiful brow creased and the corners of her mouth turning downward. "What's so unsettling?"

"I'm not exactly sure. I've just felt that way since …" And she stopped.

"Since when?"

"Nothing."

"Uh-uh." Jackson crossed the kitchen in two steps and slid his arms around her from behind. "Talk to me. What's going on?"

She spun and clasped her hands behind his neck. "Ever since Craven called me. It just really … I dunno. I can't shake it."

"You're here with me and you're fine. There's nothing to be worried about."

"You don't know Craven. He's used to getting his way. So are his parents. I don't know if he's told them about the baby or not, but if he has, I can expect some pressure for sure."

"Do you know them well enough to call them?"

She shook her head. "No. Barely. I think I met them twice. He never invited me for holidays or anything."

"Wait. He never invited you for holidays? Didn't you think that was odd?"

Amethyst stared at him, her brow dipping toward the bridge of her nose. "No. Why would that be odd?"

"Because most of the time, couples invite each other to their family gatherings."

The shrug she gave him almost seemed to be one of embarrassment as she went back to the flowers. "I dunno. We didn't have family gatherings, so I don't know anything about that stuff."

Jackson was beyond floored. He knew Gant had tried

to do his best by the girls after he came on the scene, but she'd never been to a family gathering? "What about your grandparents?"

"I don't know them. I'm not sure Mom knows where they are. They weren't around us, or maybe I should say, we weren't around them. She didn't mention them very often and when she did, it wasn't very nice. I think she was abused when she was growing up."

Oh god. No wonder her mom is the way she is, Jackson thought. It sounded like the woman hadn't known how to raise kids because she hadn't had much in the way of raising herself. "You do realize you're going to be expected to come to my brother's from time to time, right?"

The eyes that turned back to him were filled with tears. "I'll be really hurt if I'm not invited."

"Invited? Angel, you'll be part of our family. And Wyman and Chimlin may be all I've got, but I could do a lot worse."

"I really like them. They seem super nice."

"They are. You'll fit right in." Every time she was the least little bit upset, it cut through him like a knife. One single tear shed was too much to suit him. He wanted her happy and smiling. Of course, life couldn't always be like that, but that was his goal, and he thought it was a pretty damn good one.

"We did go to Dad's family's place sometimes, but most of the time, we were out on the road and too far away. There wasn't money for airfare, and he said his parents considered him an enormous screw-up and not worth their time. Of course, now that I've spent more time around them, I know that's not true. I mean,

Grandma Juju and Grandpy Jeffy treat us just like they do Aunt Constance's kids."

"Don't you have another aunt?"

"Yeah. Elizabeth. They don't have any kids."

"Oh." He wondered how Mr. and Mrs. Meadows were going to feel about having a great-grandchild. "Have you called them to tell them about the baby?"

"No. I suppose I should do that. I'd rather tell them than have Daddy tell them."

Jackson passed her on his way to the refrigerator and kissed the side of her neck as he walked by. "I think that would be good."

"So, about having Dad and Lorna over, could we …" He listened as she grew more excited, talking about things she could cook for them and how she could use the pretty dishes Jackson had in one of the cabinets. She wanted to play hostess, and that was good. It meant she was starting to feel like the house was her home, and that was exactly what he wanted. Of course, he said yes to everything she wanted to do. None of it was extravagant, and the idea of having a beautiful woman cooking in his kitchen and serving guests in his dining room appealed to him. *Our dining room*, he reminded himself. He made up his mind right then—the first thing he'd do after they got married would be to put her name on the deed to the property. That way, if he died, she and the baby would be protected, and that was his first priority. It would be for the rest of his life.

"That all sounds perfect, babe. Sounds like you've got it all planned. Anything you want me to do?"

"Could you do some bread? And rolls? You said you like to do that stuff."

"I'd love to! How 'bout a loaf of garlic wheat bread and some cross buns?"

"Oh, yum! I'd love that! Thanks, Papa-boo! That's one thing I won't have to worry about. And can we go to the grocery tomorrow morning?"

"How 'bout if we go this evening and go to dinner in town? That way you won't feel rushed tomorrow."

"Sure you have time to do that?"

He grabbed an apple out of the basket on the counter and kissed her cheek on his way past her. "For you, angel? Every second of my time is yours anyway." It thrilled him to hear her giggle as he winked at her on his way out the door.

Dinner and the supermarket. He couldn't imagine a better date.

CHAPTER 8

"YOU OKAY?"

Amethyst sat there for a few seconds before she slid out of the truck's cab. "Yeah. I'm so full I can barely walk."

"I know what you mean. I'm stuffed, but it was good."

"I'll say. The quiche was delicious."

"I loved it. And yes—real men do eat quiche."

She wrinkled her nose. "What?"

"Oh. Before your time. Never mind. What's on your list?"

"Hmmm." She pulled out her phone and tapped the list app's icon. "Let's see … Garbanzo beans, spaghetti sauce, noodles, ricotta cheese, fresh basil, shredded mozzarella …"

"So I'm guessing we're having lasagna?"

"Yeah. Is that okay?" She hadn't thought to ask him first.

"Oh, yeah. That's more than okay. I love lasagna.

Hey, instead of garlic wheat bread, maybe I should make some focaccia."

"That would be great. Do you know what you need for it?"

"Yep. I'll just go round all of that up while you're getting the rest of the stuff. How's that?"

"That sounds perfect." She grabbed a cart and handed him one of the shopping baskets provided next to them. "Here ya go. Come find me when you're done."

"I will, angel. See you in a minute." He gave her a light kiss on the lips and headed off into the store.

Amethyst had only been in that particular store twice before, so most of her shopping would be searching for things. Everything that was canned was easy to find, but the noodles were a bit of a mystery. It took her a little while to find those, and then she went to search for the dairy products. Glancing down the aisles, she saw Jackson in front of some jars and wasn't sure what that was about, but at least he knew where things were. It was a sure bet that the dairy stuff was on an outside wall, but she glanced down each aisle as she passed, hoping she could familiarize herself with the store a bit as she went. *The next aisle has to be chips*, she thought, hoping for some kind of snack to eat later. She rounded the corner and glanced down the racks of shiny bags until her heart thudded to a stop.

There was a man at the other end of the aisle, and he had two bags of chips in his hands. Yes, he was walking away, but she'd know that gait anywhere. It was Craven. She just knew it. Her hands started to shake and she felt a little faint. It occurred to her to pull out her phone and call Jackson when she heard a voice say, "Angel, you okay?"

"Uh, um, yeah. I mean, no. Did you see that guy?"

Jackson looked around. "What guy?"

"The guy in the khaki pants and ball cap."

"Uh, no. I don't think so."

"Will you please go look down the aisles and see if you see him again? Don't say anything to him or act like you know him. Just find him. Please?"

He shrugged and frowned. "Uh, okay. Sure. Be right back." As soon as he disappeared down the rear aisle, she wished she hadn't sent him. It was terrifying to be standing there alone. What if it was Craven? What if he was in the next aisle, listening? *Oh, god, stop it, Amethyst*, she chided herself. *You're being ridiculous.*

The thought wasn't finished before Jackson stepped up to her, and he was huffing just a little. "Nope, babe. I didn't see anybody dressed like that."

"But he was right there," she said and pointed.

"Maybe he checked out and left."

"He didn't have time to! I saw …"

"Amethyst, what's going on?" Jackson asked, his voice very no-nonsense.

It felt like everything inside her was deflating. "It was Craven. I just know it was."

"Babe, I think your mind is playing tricks on you."

"No. It was him."

"So you saw his face?"

"No, but I'd know that walk anywhere. I mean, we dated—"

"You didn't see his face?"

She shook her head. "No. But I know it was him."

"Let's get our shopping finished and go home, okay?" He dropped his basket into her cart and smiled.

"You don't believe me."

"I didn't say that."

"You don't have to!" She was beyond frustrated. "I wouldn't make something like that up!"

"I'm not saying you made it up, angel. I'm just saying I think you just … I mean, maybe the way the guy walked reminded you of him, but I don't think—"

"You don't believe me." That pissed her off royally. She'd never lied to him about anything!

"I believe you *think* you saw him," Jackson answered.

"Jackson, if I say I—"

"Okay! I'm not going to argue with you about it! If you saw him, you saw him. I believe you. Now, let's get finished and get out of here so if he really is here, you won't be able to see him and he won't see you. Come on." He didn't really sound angry, but he sure didn't sound happy.

That was okay. She wasn't happy either.

The conversation on the way back to the house was almost non-existent. She was irritated as hell, and she knew he could tell. As soon as the truck rolled to a stop in the driveway, she hopped out, not waiting for him to open her door. By the time he reached her, she'd grabbed two bags of groceries and was storming toward the house. "Amethyst?" he called after her, but she just kept going.

She slid the ricotta and mozzarella into the refrigerator and was about to turn around when he wrapped his arms around her from behind. "I'm sorry, baby. I know you think you saw—"

"I *did*! It was him! I know it was!"

"Then why didn't I see him anywhere?"

"Because if he saw me before I saw him, he'd go hide somewhere."

Jackson rested his chin on her shoulder, his lips right

beside her ear. "Don't you think if he came all this way to talk to you, he'd try to do so?"

"What if he's not here to talk?"

She felt him step away from her, so she turned to find him glaring down at her. "And what exactly do you think he'd be doing, other than talking?"

"I dunno! Trying to get me to have an abortion! Trying to hurt me! Trying to hurt the baby! You just don't know him, Jackson! He always gets his way! And if he's here—"

"STOP!" She bit back the next word and waited. "Stop it. He's not going to hurt you, not while I have breath. I told you I'd protect you and this baby, and I will. You don't have anything to be afraid of—*anything*. He comes near you, he'll find himself in a pine box. Do you understand?"

"I don't want you to get in trouble because—"

"You let me worry about that. Now, I don't want you worrying another minute about that asshole. You're fine. The baby's fine. Everybody's safe. So let's put up the groceries, get dressed for bed, and sit down to some chips and a TV show, okay? Please?" She'd thought he was angry, but he wasn't. She could tell from his face that he was tired. "It's been a long day and we just need to sit down and relax."

"Yeah. Okay. I'm sorry."

He reached out, pulled her head toward him, and kissed her forehead. "Don't apologize. If you're afraid, then your fear is valid. And I'm sorry if I made it sound like I don't believe you. But I don't want you worrying about this kind of shit, angel. It's not an issue. *He's* not an issue."

"Okay." Everything inside her felt wrung out.

Thinking about Craven exhausted her. Maybe Jackson was right. Maybe he could keep them safe. She sure hoped he was right.

Anything less would be disastrous.

HE SAT IN THE RENTAL OUT IN THE STORE'S PARKING LOT, over in the area where the employees parked. It was a pretty sure thing she couldn't see him, but he could see the front doors of the store. He'd see her when she came out, and he might just have to go over and have a conversation with her.

But when the doors opened and she stepped out, he got a big surprise. There was a guy behind her, and a pretty good sized guy at that. Who the hell was that? Didn't look like her dad, at least not from the distance between them. In a split second, he saw the man wrap an arm around her waist, and he knew it wasn't her dad. So who was it?

After they'd loaded up their groceries, they climbed into the big truck and the lights snapped on as it started. He watched them pull out of the parking lot and followed at a good distance. At one point, there was enough light from the street lights to see well, so he flipped his headlights off. As soon as he saw them turn a corner, he switched them back on, spun around the corner, and kept following them. They headed out of Hondo and, sure enough, toward Tarpley.

The houses got farther apart and the road was much darker, thanks to the absence of any kind of street lights. They were, after all, on a state highway and moving away from town. He kept his distance, watching and waiting, until he saw the truck turn right and disappear.

There can't be more than a couple of houses on that road, he thought as he passed the end of it and saw the truck's taillights disappear over a rise. Back in there somewhere was the house where she was staying. But who was the guy? She'd only been there a short while. Had she been seeing someone in Tarpley all along? He knew that wasn't the case. Between classes and him, she hadn't had a spare moment to go to Texas, much less strike up a relationship with someone.

No, whatever it was, it was a recent development, but he had to know more. He wasn't sure how to find out, but he would. The thing had to be done.

The sooner, the better.

Saturday evening had been glorious. The dinner Amethyst made for them was delicious, and he was more than proud of the focaccia he'd made. It was decorated with flowers made from sundried tomatoes, sundried bell peppers, and strips of onion, and both women went on and on about how pretty it was. Tasted pretty damn fine too.

"Your doctor's appointment is Tuesday, right?" he asked as they put away laundry on Sunday.

"Yep. Two o'clock. You're coming with me, right?"

"Wouldn't miss it. While we're out, I think I found an SUV for you to look at."

"Yeah? What kind?"

"A GMC. Big one—Acadia. My mom had one and

she loved that thing. This is a newer one, but I think you'll like it."

"I want to see it. What color is it?"

"Champagne, I think."

She laughed. "Ooooo, fancy!"

"Only the best for my angel!" The words had barely escaped his lips when the sound of tires on the gravel sounded. "Who the hell is that?" He caught a glimpse of her face and smiled, hoping that would reassure her. "Doesn't matter. You'll be fine. I'm right here. Let me go see who it is."

A man climbed down out of the cab of the pickup truck and Jackson recognized the emblem on the side: Texas Parks & Wildlife. "Hey! Conor, right?"

Holding out a hand, the man came toward Jackson. His handshake was firm, and Jackson instantly liked him. "Yeah. Conor Paxton. How are you? Jackson, right?"

"Yep! I'm great, and you?"

"Couldn't be better! Actually, that's a lie. Tank and G-man told me to come talk to you about something."

Oh, shit. Here it comes. "Yeah? What might that be?"

"So you know we're going to start doing this work on the surveys of the creeks around here, and you're right here at Williams Creek. I was wondering if you'd be able to help us at all."

"I'm not sure. I've got a lot of responsibility around here."

The man smiled. "Yeah, I heard you say you've got a little one on the way! Congratulations!"

"Yeah, thank you. But like I said—"

"Oh, this wouldn't be a big, heavy-duty commitment. I'd just need help when it was raining hard. You know, watching the creek to see how it's draining, calling me if it looks like it's coming up out of its banks, things like that."

Watching it? I can barely stand to look as I drive over it, he thought, his head swimming. "Um, I'm not sure I'm the right guy for the job. I mean, I'd like to help and all, but I'm not usually—"

"Just when it's raining hard. No other time." Conor stopped and then gave Jackson a sad smile. "Had a run-in with F and G in the past?"

"Oh, no. Nothing like that. It's just that ..." *Lie like a dog, Frame,* he told himself. "It's just that I lost a friend to drowning when I was younger, and I really don't like water." *That's good. Stick with that,* his brain told him.

"Oh. Well, you wouldn't have to go near it at all, just keep an eye on it. Does any of the creek lie on your property?"

"Yeah." Jackson pointed out toward the ridge a mile behind the house. "On the other side of that rise."

"Gotcha. Mind if I go back there and take a look?"

"Of course not. Knock yourself out. I've got a four-wheeler you're welcome to use."

"Great! Don't mind if I do! I'll only be out there as long as it takes to take a few shots of it with my phone."

Jackson nodded. "You can probably do that from the ridge itself. Better picture. You'll be able to see it plainly and get a better feel for the lay of the land."

"You spend any time back there?" Conor asked.

"Nah. I'm too busy with my herd." *Of a little over a dozen cattle. I'm a real big rancher,* he heard his inner critic mumble.

"Oh. Well, I'll just run out there and run back, if that's okay."

"Sure, sure." Jackson handed him a key. "It's right there in the barn. Feel free."

"Thanks! Back in a few." Conor wandered off toward the barn and Jackson felt better, but only a little. He had the distinct feeling he wasn't off the hook yet.

About an hour and a half later, he realized Conor wasn't back. He was about to saddle one of the horses and go looking for him when he heard the growl of the four-wheeler's motor in the distance, so he stepped out onto the back porch and watched the TFG officer roll up to the barn. "Hope you don't mind that I was gone a little longer," he heard Conor yell from the barn.

"Nah. I was just getting a little concerned. I was about to grab a horse and go looking for you!"

"Thanks!" a laughing Conor said as he strode out of the barn and handed Jackson the key. "I got a little carried away looking around."

"Yeah?"

"Yeah. Went on down the creek and drove in a measuring rod. It's showing some signs of erosion and flooding. That's bad. And it's because there's not enough flow until there's a hard rain, and then the flooding makes everything worse. We really need to monitor it. I'm thinking I should be starting at the bridge up there on the highway. Thoughts?"

Jackson shrugged. "I have no idea. I'm not very well-versed on that kind of thing, so I really don't know. I could look at it and not know what I was looking at, frankly."

"I understand. But we can show you what to look for. You can monitor the upper creek from up there." Conor stopped for a second and seemed to be studying Jackson's face, which made him hugely uncomfortable. He was even more uncomfortable when Conor asked, "Is there anything you need to tell me?"

"Nah. Nothing you'd want to hear."

"Yeah? Try me."

Jackson studied the man's face. He could tell Conor was sincere, and he would probably be sympathetic, but Jackson just wasn't inclined to share. "It's history. Just not something I want to ever have to deal with again."

"Gotcha. Well, if you change your mind, let me know. And if I need somebody to run up to the highway and check the water level, it would really help if I could give you a call."

"You can, and if I can do it, I will." *No, I won't, but he doesn't have to know that*, Jackson thought. "Let me give you my number." He rattled it off and watched as Conor tapped it into his phone.

"Thanks. I'd better be getting on. Got some of the guys waiting for me for dinner. You should come with us some night. We're just going to Mac & Ernie's."

Jackson thought about how panicked Amethyst had been when they'd been at the store. "I'll try, but my sweetie likes having me around." Maybe that would get him off the hook. He didn't want to go to dinner with the guys. Making friends with Conor would make the officer think Jackson would help. But there was one thing Jackson Frame knew for certain.

He wasn't going anywhere near that creek.

THEY'D BEEN ON THE ROAD FOR A LITTLE WHILE BEFORE Amethyst asked, "Hey, do you think I could go to a salon while we're in town? If I can find one that takes walk-ins?"

"Sure! I can find something to do until you're done. There's a new western store I've been wanting to poke around in. That'll kill some time."

"Okay." That made her happy. A doctor's appointment, then a trim. If she liked the person, maybe she'd schedule something else, like nails or a pedi, or maybe a weave or something. Maybe she'd just cut it close, since she'd be busy with a baby. Working with her hair could be tedious and time-consuming, and she might not have time for it anymore. "Would you mind if I had my nails done sometime?"

"Baby, you do whatever you want. We've got the money for it, and I'll gladly chauffeur you around all over the place if it makes you happy!" Jackson was smiling and stealing glances at her as he spoke, and it made her feel like the luckiest woman on the planet.

And if she was really lucky, the doctor would give a green light to sex. That was right at the top of her "things to ask the doctor" list!

She filled out all the paperwork and only had to wait about fifteen minutes before they called her back. "It's okay if he comes, right?" she asked when she reached the door.

"Of course! If a dad wants to be involved, we definitely want that!" the pretty nurse told her. "Come on, Dad!" the woman said and motioned for Jackson, and Amethyst smiled as he hopped up and followed her down the hallway.

They weighed her—she'd only gained about five pounds—and measured her, both for height and for her waist size. Then the nurse took them to an exam room, gave her a paper gown and sheet, and told her to undress and get on the exam table. "The doctor will be with you in a couple of minutes," she said as she stepped out and closed the door.

They chatted quietly until the door opened and a ruddy-complected woman of about fifty appeared in the doorway. "Hey there! I'm Dr. Everett! How are you today?"

"I'm fine!" Amethyst answered. The woman looked pleasant and friendly, and she instantly felt better. "I'm Amethyst, and this is my boyfriend, Jackson."

The doctor shook their hands and grinned. "So, are you guys excited?"

"Very! Can't wait!" Amethyst answered.

"I'm very, very excited," Jackson chirped, and it was obvious he meant it. He was grinning so hard that Amethyst was sure his cheeks were aching. She wanted to tell the doctor about Cassidy, but she didn't think that would be appropriate. Still, it would be nice if she could let the physician know how much the pregnancy meant to Jackson.

The exam was finished, the questions asked, and the doctor slipped off her exam gloves and tossed them into the trash. "You're plenty healthy enough. From your timeline and the answers to my questions, I'd say you're about ten weeks along. Having a lot of trouble with morning sickness?"

"Only a few times. I'm glad for that."

Dr. Everett chuckled. "You should be! Want to do an ultrasound to see if we can see it?"

"Could we?" Amethyst was ridiculously excited.

"Sure! Let me get a tech in here with the machine and we'll take a peek." She flipped a switch by the door and in seconds, it opened to a tech pushing a cart. "I think she's about nine or ten weeks," the doctor told the young woman as she plugged in the ultrasound machine.

"Okie dokie! Let's see what we have here." The tech pulled up Amethyst's gown, squirted some lube on her tummy, and pressed the ultrasound transducer into her skin.

The screen looked weird, with all kinds of splotchy and stripey things showing up, and then there was a large dark area. Right in the middle of it was something that looked like a bean—with stubs. "Is that it?" Amethyst whispered, not really sure.

"Yep. Sure is. See that?" the tech asked and pointed to a flashing spot. "That's its heartbeat."

"Oh my god! Jackson, look!"

"I see, angel! I guess it's too early to—"

The doctor laughed loudly. "Yeah! It's a bit early for that! Probably won't be able to tell until at least week sixteen. But I like to guess. And I'm going to guess that it's a boy."

Amethyst chuckled. "Why?"

"I dunno. I just think so."

"How often are you right?"

Dr. Everett laughed. "Oh, about a third of the time, but it's fun to guess!" The doctor stopped and smiled at Jackson. "This is the time in the appointment when I talk to the mommy by herself. Nothing personal. And you," she said, pointing at Jackson, "take care of her."

"Yes, ma'am. She's my priority number one," he assured the physician.

"Good. Thank you. Now, this is just something I like to do. If that's okay," she tacked on.

Jackson shrugged. "Sure. I'll just, um, wait out front. See you in a minute." Before he left the room, he leaned in and kissed Amethyst lightly on the lips, then disappeared out the door. Amethyst turned toward her, curious what was going on.

The doctor pulled up the rolling stool and sat down. "Now I get to ask the hard questions, and I ask every one of my patients, so don't think I'm singling you out, okay?" Amethyst nodded. "Are you feeling okay?"

"Yeah. A little tired sometimes, but that's all."

"And your boyfriend, is he helpful?"

Amethyst nodded. "Oh, yeah."

"Do you feel safe at home?"

"I don't understand …"

"Has he ever been violent toward you, or threatened you in any way?"

"Jackson? God, no! He's amazing! And he's super excited about this baby."

"Is the baby his?"

The question took Amethyst a little by surprise. "Um, I—"

"There's a reason I ask. So? Is it his?"

"No. It's my ex-boyfriend's."

"And Jackson's aware of this?"

Amethyst nodded. "Absolutely. And it's perfectly okay with him. He's divorced, and they had a little girl who died when she was around three. So he's really, really happy about this."

"And the biological father knows about this?"

Should she say anything? If there was anyone she

could talk to, it would be the doctor. "He's actually been threatening me. He wanted to pay me to have an abortion."

"Is your boyfriend aware of this?"

"Yes. And my dad. He lives in Tarpley too."

"Do you feel safe from him?"

"Not really, but I trust Jackson to take care of me and watch out for me. He's a veteran and he doesn't have a job away from home. He has a ranch, and he has cattle and a few horses. And goats, because I like them."

Dr. Everett smiled. "It sounds like he really cares about you."

"He says he loves me, and I love him too. I mean, we're in the beginning of it all, and we're really getting to know each other now that I've moved here, but he saved my dad's life a while back, and if there's anybody I'd trust, it would be Jackson."

"That's great. It sounds like you're in excellent hands there, so you go get your maternity vitamins, be thinking about going over to the hospital to do some preregistration kind of things, and I'll see you in a month unless you have problems or questions. You can get dressed and go out front when you're ready. Take care."

"Thank you so much." The doctor stepped out, but Amethyst remembered. "Wait!" The door snapped open and Dr. Everett's face appeared in the opening again. "What about sex?"

"Oh, you can't get pregnant. You already are," the doctor answered, grinning.

"I mean, is it—"

"Okay? Yeah. As long as it's not some kind of extreme insanity, it'll be fine. Go have fun." And she disappeared again.

Amethyst got dressed and looked in the mirror. When she saw her reflection, she saw the same face she'd always seen. Would she look different in a few months? Fatter? Swollen? Would Jackson still think she was pretty?

She wandered down the hallway and opened the door. Jackson was standing at the check-out desk, writing something, so she sat down in a chair and waited, her eyes closed. A hand touched her shoulder softly and she looked up. The man who gazed down at her gave her a gentle smile. "Ready to go, angel?"

"Yeah." As soon as she stood, he took her hand, and in seconds, they were in the truck and headed down the road.

She'd asked the only employee of color in the office if there was a good walk-in salon around, and the woman had given her a name and address. When they pulled up, there were big colorful posters sporting all kinds of ethnic hairstyles on the windows and a big sign that read, "OPEN! Walk-ins welcome! Wait possible." She waited while he got out, rounded the front end of the truck, and opened the door for her.

Before she got a chance to kiss him goodbye, he grabbed her wrist and pressed something into her palm. "Here. This will take care of it. Do whatever you want." She glanced down to see his debit card pressed into her hand.

"But what if you want to—"

"I've got a credit card. If I find something I want, I can just charge it. No biggie. Now, go have fun and relax. Call me when you're about done and I'll come back."

"Okay." Leaning toward him, she waited until he

pressed his lips to hers and she smiled against them. "I love you."

"I love you too. See you in a little while." When she opened the door, she turned to look over her shoulder and found him there, leaning against the truck, hands shoved down in his front pockets and a silly grin on his face. She understood that grin because she felt exactly the same way.

Jackson picked her up two hours later and proclaimed her the most gorgeous woman in the world. That made her laugh, but it was okay. She enjoyed the attention, and when he said things like that to her, she wanted to believe they were true.

They'd been home about two hours when he announced, "I'm gonna go put some gas in the truck. Want to come?"

"Nah. I'll just stay here. You going anywhere else?"

"Thought I might run past the station, see if there's anybody there or if Pops needs me to do anything."

"Okay. Don't be long."

He kissed her and chucked her under the chin. "I won't, angel. It'll be like no time at all."

She listened to the sound of the truck's engine receding until it was gone, so she wandered back into the kitchen to unload the dishwasher from earlier. After that, she started another load of laundry. It occurred to her that she should probably check the watering troughs, since that was one of her jobs, and she put her boots on. She'd gotten one of them on when she heard the knock on the door.

There'd been no sound of a vehicle, so she glanced out the kitchen window. She could see the drive from there, and there was no car. Nothing. Then she heard something else, something that made gooseflesh pop up on her arms.

Buck was standing between her and the front door, and the growl deep in his throat told her that the person on the other side of the door was a stranger, at least to him. Waiting in silence, she listened. Sure enough, there was another knock. There were no neighbors close enough to walk to the house. She reached into her pocket and pulled out her phone to call Jackson, but when she touched the button to unlock the screen, an icon of a battery with a red slash through it lit up, and then nothing. No juice. The doors were locked—that much she knew—so she sat down in the kitchen floor, away from the door and the windows, and waited.

It only took another minute before a voice called out, "Amethyst, I know you're in there. I watched you come in. And I know you're alone. I want to talk to you."

Jesus! It's Craven! Oh, god, what do I do? She had no phone. But she did have Buck, and he was definitely in defensive mode. Shaking and sweating, she crawled through the kitchen, passed through the dining room, and skittered into their bedroom. The blinds were still drawn in there, so he couldn't see in if he was out there. She rummaged through the closet, wondering if there was anything she could use to defend herself, and her hand hit something.

A rifle. It was a huge, long thing, and firing it would probably knock her down, but she could do it. Gant had taught her to shoot when she was younger, and it only took her a second to figure out how to load it but … no ammo. Her hand immediately went to the shelf above where the gun had been leaning into a corner, and sure enough, there was a box there with a label that read ".358 WIN." She ratcheted the lever down, slipped one into the chamber, and left the lever open, then carried it to the living room and stood beside the door on the hinge side. "I know you're in there, Amethyst. Come out, damn it. Don't make me come in there."

Might as well do it because he's not going away. "You'd better not even *try* to come in here! What do you want?"

"I want to talk to you!"

"You can talk from right there."

"No. We need to talk face to face."

"The only face to face you're going to get is your face in the barrel end of my gun."

There was loud laughter. "Your gun? You don't have a fucking gun!"

"Would you like to put money on that? Oh, and by the way, the dog may get you first. Just sayin'. Now, go. Don't make me do something we'll both regret. Well, that you'll regret anyway." *Damn, I wish I had a pump action shotgun*, she told herself. The sound of the action ratcheting would've been perfect in that situation.

"Really? This is how you want this to go? Seriously?"

"I'm going to start shooting. I've got a whole box of ammo, and Dad taught me how to shoot, so if you don't want to get shot, I'd suggest you leave. Now. And don't come back."

"Look, just have the damn abortion and I'll leave you alone permanently. I told you, I'll—"

"Shut the fuck up and leave!" she screamed. Buck instantly started to bark. "Go away! I went to the doctor today, and I have every intention of having this baby! I don't want your fucking money!"

"Oh, yeah? How's your boyfriend gonna feel when he finds out this baby isn't his?"

"He already knows, asshole, and he doesn't care. His name is going on the birth certificate, so you shouldn't give a shit."

"Yeah, but DNA doesn't lie. And I don't want that nightmare in eighteen years. It's gotta go, Amethyst, one way or another."

"What the hell is that supposed to mean? You know what? I don't care. Get. Out. Of. Here. Or I'm going to open this door and start shooting." With that, she grasped the lever and yanked it upward. The *SNAP!* that sounded in the room was satisfying, and it was also apparently loud enough that he could hear it.

"Do you really have a gun in there, you bitch?"

"Do you really think I've been in here thinking of ways to lie to you all this time? Now get the hell out of here before I come out shooting!"

"You *will* talk to me, Amethyst! You can bet on that!" he yelled, but his voice seemed to be moving away. She wondered where he was parked, but she didn't dare move. If he came in the back, her line of sight was pretty much clear for taking a shot. If he came in the front, she was right there, and she'd get him before he could take three steps into the house. Instead, it got quiet. In about five minutes, Buck sidled up to her, leaned against her leg, and sighed. Her knees were weak, and she slid down the wall until she was sitting, back against the wallboard, with the rifle still in her hands.

She didn't know how long she'd been sitting there when she heard a vehicle, and her hands began to tremble. The engine shut down, and then it was quiet until she heard the back door knob. Still terrified, she leveled the barrel at it and waited. Buck perked up and headed that direction, but Amethyst didn't move. She couldn't. Every joint in her body was locked in fear, and her eyes couldn't leave the sight of that knob turning.

When the door swung open, she almost screamed—until she saw his face.

CHAPTER 9

HE HUSTLED to fill up the truck, then set out again and turned down the little lane. Only Gant's truck was there, which he'd expected, so he parked and hopped out. He was almost to the front door when he heard a voice call out, "Yeah? Who's there?"

"Jackson."

"I'm out in the shop. Come on out."

The forge was glowing and even though it was still cool out, it was hotter than Hades in Gant's metalworking shop. "Hey!"

"Hey there! What brings you here?" Gant asked his friend.

Jackson leaned back against a table. "I just needed to talk to you for a minute."

"Yeah? What's going on?"

"Well, first off, we went to the doctor today. Said she's probably about ten weeks along."

"And?"

"Oh. Perfectly healthy, both of them. Saw it on the

ultrasound. Cute little peanut," Jackson said, trying hard not to grin like a fool.

"And you're not excited at all, right?" Amethyst's dad asked and laughed.

"Oh, no. Not at all!"

"That's all you came to tell me?"

"No." How to ask? "Have you ever known Amethyst to, um, imagine things? You know, have a vivid imagination?"

Gant laid down his ball peen hammer and turned his full attention to Jackson. "Imagine things? What kind of things?"

"We were at the grocery store in Hondo and she was convinced she saw that damn Craven guy there. I went looking, based on what she said the man was wearing, but I didn't find anybody who looked like that. I told her I thought she was letting her mind run away with her, and she got all pissy."

"Yeah, I think she would get pissy. She's not inclined to stuff like that. She thinks she saw him?"

"She got all worked up. Insisted it was him. But I didn't find a guy dressed that way anywhere in the store."

Gant stood there for a full minute, staring at his workbench, while Jackson waited. Finally, he said, "Boss, if she says she saw him, I believe her."

Jackson sucked in a big breath and sighed it out. "Okay. Good enough for me. So now I go into protection mode."

"We both do. Don't leave her alone, not even for a minute. If you have to be away, either take her with you or bring her here."

"Will do. And that means I need to get home."

"Yep. And call me when you get there and let me know she's okay. Please?"

Jackson slapped Gant on the shoulder. "I absolutely will. Thanks."

"Thank you. Hey, wait!" Jackson spun to look back at the grinning grandfather-to-be. "Boy or girl?"

"We won't know for a while. Probably another seven weeks. What difference does it make?" he asked, laughing and walking backward toward the truck.

"Doesn't. I'm just not a fan of surprises," Gant said with a laugh of his own.

"I hear ya! Catch ya later." Jackson climbed into the truck, started it up, and headed out onto the highway. Gant believed that Amethyst had actually seen Craven. He'd known her a lot longer, and if he believed it, maybe she really had seen the scumbag.

The big truck rolled up into the drive, but Buck didn't meet him when he stepped out. That was odd. The dog was the first one out the door, always. Maybe he was taking a nap with Amethyst.

When he tried the knob, he was thankful to find it locked, so he pulled out his key and slipped it into the lock, then turned the knob and stepped inside. "Hey, babe, I'm—"

And found himself looking up the barrel of his own Browning Model 81 BLR, its scope like a piercing eye looking straight at him.

"Jesus, Amethyst! It's me! What the hell, baby? What's wrong? Don't point that thing at me!" Her eyes were as big as softballs and her hands were shaking, but otherwise, she was motionless. Buck moved toward him and cowered at his feet. "Babe! It's me! Put that thing down! Amethyst!"

It was as though he'd slapped her when she sucked in a huge gasp and let her arms fall. In an instant, he was beside her and prying the big weapon out of her fingers. "Angel! What the hell? What happened?"

"Oh, god, Jackson. Oh, god. He was here."

"Who was here?"

"Craven."

Either she's completely lost her mind or I'm gonna have to kill a sumbitch, Jackson told himself. "When?"

"I dunno. You hadn't been gone very long. He was banging on the door and yelling. Told me to come out. I got the gun. I didn't know what else to do."

"You should've called me!"

"I couldn't! My phone's battery was run down! I didn't know what to do!" And she fell apart.

"What kind of car was he driving?"

"I don't know. It wasn't here," she mumbled as she heaved in air.

He remembered in one blinding flash. There'd been a car parked at one of the abandoned mobile homes nearer to the highway, but he hadn't seen anyone around it. "Holy fuck. Give me that rifle and you stay here. Keep Buck with you. I'll be right back."

"Where are you going?" she screamed in terror.

"I'll be right back! Stay right there!" With the door locked behind him, he bolted to the truck and took off.

But when he got to the old mobile home, the car was gone, and he knew. She really had seen Craven. He was there somewhere, and he'd been watching them. As soon as he was back inside the house, he called out to her. "Amethyst? Get in here. We need to talk."

Her tear-stained face appeared in the entrance to the hallway. "Did I do something wrong?"

"No! Absolutely not!"

"I'm sorry I was pointing that gun at—"

"No. Don't apologize. Sit down." He patted the sofa and she sat next to him, her thigh against his. "I went to get gas, but I also went to talk to your dad. I asked him if you'd ever imagined stuff like this happening, and he said no—if you said you saw it, you saw it. And I believe you. I just went back toward the highway. When I came in, there was a car parked near one of those old mobile homes, but I didn't think anything about it. People come out here all the time to pick flowers, use metal detectors, collect rocks in the creek bed, all kinds of things. I've never minded anybody coming out here and enjoying the property. But when I got back out there, the car was gone. I think it was probably him."

Her voice was barely a whisper. "So you believe me?"

"Yes, angel. I do. Until we get rid of him somehow, you're not to be alone. Ever. Understand? I go somewhere, you go with me. If you can't, I take you to your dad's. Or Pops'. Or Tank's, or Bree's. Or somewhere. Hell, I'll drop you off at Lorna's office and you can sit there with her. But you can't stay here alone. Period."

He'd thought she'd argue with him, but she just whispered, "Okay."

He stroked a hand down her hair, then cupped her cheek. "It's gonna be okay. I'll keep you safe. You've got nothing to worry about, you hear me? As long as I'm in your field of vision, you'll be fine."

Amethyst curled up against his chest and his arms wound tightly around her. She was his future, she and that baby, and he'd protect them with his life. "I feel safe with you, Papa-boo."

"That's all I really want, for you to feel safe and loved."

"And I do."

That was his only true goal, his new purpose in life. She and her child, *their* child, would be safe, loved, and have the things they needed. Most importantly, they'd have *him*, a man who'd protect them, teach them, lead them, and be there for the ups and downs. There'd be plenty of those, he was sure. But at that moment, there was a huge down. Showing up again would be a massive mistake for Craven Bradshaw. Jackson was a fair, easy-going guy.

But he had a lot of property. The opportunities for hiding bodies were endless.

She didn't know how long she'd been asleep, but when she woke, she was still on his lap, her cheek pressed into his chest. Before she could speak, she felt him shift and that low, slow voice asked, "You okay?"

"Yeah. I'm okay. I was just so scared."

"I know. Scares me too. That's ballsy, coming out here like that. He'd better not try that again."

"Please don't do anything that'll land you in jail," she whispered.

"I would never do that. I wouldn't risk our future that way."

Amethyst sat up straight and looked into his eyes. "You really mean that."

A laugh bubbled up from his chest. "I've been telling you that! Did you not believe me?"

"I do now!" She leaned in, kissed him, and sat up

again. "Oh, I forgot to tell you what we talked about after you left the room today."

"Yeah?"

"She asked me if I felt safe with you, if you'd ever been violent with me, if I felt unsafe at home. Of course, I told her you'd never do anything like that."

"Damn straight."

"Then she asked me if the baby is yours. And I told her the truth. She wanted to know if you knew, and I told her you did and it didn't matter to you."

"Also correct." He waited, and she wondered how long it would take before he asked. "Anything else?"

"How 'bout I don't tell you. How 'bout I show you." Amethyst wiggled forward until her feet were on the floor and she stood, then reached for his hand. "Come on. I think it's bedtime."

Jackson sat there, his head tipped a bit, and stared at her. "Bedtime? It's not even … Oh. Bedtime. *Bedtime.*" He was on his feet in seconds. "Right. Bedtime. It's definitely bedtime." Instead of taking her hand, he threw a thumb toward the front door. "I'm just gonna check all the doors, make sure Buck's okay, and I'll be right there."

"Okay. Bring some water with you, wouldja? For if we get thirsty?"

Jackson chuckled, that deep rolling sound that made her stomach quiver. "Oh, yeah. We're gonna get thirsty. I can guarantee that."

She sighed as she made her way to the bedroom. After she'd brushed her teeth, she crawled under the covers and was lost in the softness of the sheets just as Jackson strode into the room. "You done in the bathroom?"

"Yeah."

He tossed his phone onto the bed. "I'll just be a sec."

Watching him was like something from a movie, the way he moved, the way his muscles bunched and released. He was male—solid, sturdy, and pure sex on legs. Much as she'd enjoyed their playing around since she'd been there, the longing for something long, hard, and all his inside her had consumed her repeatedly, forcing her to beg him, knowing he'd say no until that moment when the doctor gave the nod. And the moment was on them. The bathroom light snapped off and she gave him the sexiest smile she could manage. He gave her the side-eye and asked, "What?"

Her skin sizzled as she took in the sight of him again. "I wish you'd get over here in this bed, that's what."

"Oh, that's gonna happen, and it's gonna happen right now." He didn't make a show of it, just whipped his tee off over his head, unbuttoned and unzipped his jeans and stepped out of them, and hooked his fingers in the waistband elastic of his boxer briefs and pulled them right off without a moment's hesitation. Sitting down on the side of the bed, he grabbed his phone, plugged it in, and then pulled off his watch and laid it right beside the phone before lifting the covers and slipping under them.

"You're not the least bit shy, are you?"

He shrugged as his head pressed into the pillow. "I guess not. Why be shy? I mean, when I did get to shower, I sometimes was showering with fifteen or twenty other guys. We didn't give a shit because we knew it was the last shower we were going to get for maybe a very long time, so nobody cared. Nobody was looking. We were all just trying to get as clean as possible before somebody opened fire on our camp, or we ran out of water, or some other calamity took place. You do what you've gotta do in situations like that."

"Did you have any women in your unit?"

"Yeah, but nobody cared about that either. We weren't there to find girlfriends. We were there to find and eliminate targets. Anything that got in the way of that had the potential to get us killed." She was about to ask a question when he asked, "Can we talk about something else? Because talking and thinking about that shit makes my willy shift into dormancy, and I really don't think you want that.

"No. I don't."

"Then let's talk about something else."

"Like what?"

"Like how amazing and beautiful your tits are. How incredibly round and lush your ass is. How deliciously kissable those lips are. And those eyes, angel—those eyes slay me."

"Oh yeah? What about you?"

"What about me?"

"I love those big hands, and those big muscles, and that big ol' log between your legs. Lawd, Papa-boo, you're more man than I think I've ever seen."

"What about your dad?"

She sat bolt upright and frowned. "Wow. Talk about a way to make your willy go dormant. If I had one, it would be running for the door!"

"I didn't mean like … Oh, come on. You've been around a lot of maleness in your life. All those faires?"

She snorted. "You've obviously never been to one or you'd know how ridiculous that sounds. I mean, Mom used to have to fight the women off with a broom because they all wanted Dad. He was the only decent-looking manly-man on the circuit. The rest looked like they fell into a barrel of mead and then lay out in the sun too long. Way too long. Couldn't get near them for the flies," she added and snickered.

"You won't have that problem here." She scooted toward him and rested her chin on his chest, an arm thrown over his belly. "I take a bath once in a while."

"Yeah, I've noticed." She closed her eyes and sighed.

"Hey, angel." When she snapped her lids up, he was staring right into her eyes. "Everything's gonna be fine. That asshole will leave us alone, and we'll have a good life. We'll cook and eat and tend the animals, and you'll pack the baby around in one of those weird little sack things while we work outside, and everything will be sweet and peaceful. You'll see." The words had barely left his lips before he pressed her back and rolled his weight on top of her. "You're mine, and you're going to stay mine. That little shit isn't going to take you, or the peanut, or anything or anybody, away from me."

"The pea … Oh! I get it! Peanut!" Amethyst laughed. "I was thinking jumping bean."

"Then jumping bean it is!" The vibrations from his laughter reverberated through her own chest, and she felt herself relax. "You are my angel. That is my baby, my son or daughter. You belong here with me."

"I do." He gave her a light kiss and pulled back. "What?"

His gaze locked with hers. "I'm gonna give you a reason to say that again soon."

"Say what?"

"I do."

"You do what?"

"No. Say, 'I do.'"

There was no holding back the laughter. "I knew what you meant! I was messing with you!"

"Yeah, okay. So I'm gonna stop messing around right now. I'm dead serious about this, baby. You'd better hang on." He pressed her knees apart with his leg, then dropped between them. "I hope you're ready because if you're not, you'd better get that way fast."

"Oh, yeah, I'm ... Oh, holy shit," she whispered as he pressed himself inside her and filled her. She'd been with a couple of boys in her high school years, and one on the faire circuit, then Craven in college, and she realized something instantly.

She'd never been with a real man.

There was no stopping the gasp she sucked in when his finger touched her jewel and he stroked decisively. Never in her life had she felt that way, so wild and unfettered and yet so loved and protected. "Oh ... Oh, Jackson, baby, I'm gonna ... I'm gonna ..."

"I want you to come for me and then we're gonna consummate this relationship, baby girl. You'll be mine, I'll be yours, and ..." Amethyst groaned as her belly spasmed with the orgasm. "Yeah, just like that. You had enough, angel?"

"Ummm, ohhhh, uh, yeah. Please. No more." There was no time to even catch a breath before he rose up on his knees, gripped her hips, and drove himself into her.

She'd always loved roller coasters. Every chance she got, she'd ride one if they had the money, and she rated them all. Memories of one outside Atlanta in the big theme park there slipped through her mind, but that was replaced with the frantic clawing in her belly, a raw need that made her beg, just before she felt herself constrict around him and pulse madly. "Jackson, please. Oh, god, please, more? Please?"

"Angel," he gasped in her ear, "I don't think I can hold on. You are …" Then there was a groan. "Damn, girl," he muttered as he slowed. When he stopped, he pulled her with him as he fell to the mattress beside her, still buried in her warmth. Those big hands slid from her waist up her ribcage and cradled her breasts, his thumbs brushing across her nipples tenderly. "Amethyst Meadows, I love you, girl. Whatever you need, you tell me. I'll sell my soul to try to get it for you. I just …" His voice cracked ever so slightly when he finished. "I just waited so long to find you."

Her finger traced down his cheek, across his lips, and then pressed his face upward with a finger under his chin. "Papa-boo, I ain't no virgin. I been with a few boys but, damn, that's the first time I been made love to by a real man. You my man, baby—you my man." Her lips trapped his and he kissed her back with a hunger that surprised her. Everything about him tuned her up, turned her on, and satisfied her. She couldn't wait for her mom to meet him. The warmth of his palms on her cheeks made her pull back to stare into his face. "I love you, Jackson. Nobody else. Just you."

He chuckled. "You gonna love me again in about an hour?"

"I'll love you again in thirty minutes if you can manage it."

"Well, then," he said with a laugh, "looks like you'd better get busy!"

Her soft, rhythmic breathing sank into his soul and gave him a peace he couldn't remember ever experiencing, the warmth of her skin like a soothing salve. Holding her in his arms was the feeling of coming home after a long, long time away, the overwhelming sense of relief as you slide into your own bed and sigh. That was what it was like to be there with her, her scent, her touch, her smile. Even though he wanted her again, he wouldn't wake her. Rest was something she was going to need a lot of, and taking any of it away from her was unthinkable, matter how much he wanted to bury himself inside her until they were one.

But in the next second, he groaned deep in his soul. Their first time. Yeah, they'd been fooling around for weeks, but that had been their first time to … He wanted to kick himself. There should've been a fire in the fireplace, even though it was plenty warm enough outside. Wine—no, not wine, but something special. Good food. Soft music. They could've danced! Wasn't that what people did on a date? Sure, it wasn't a date, but he could've put *some* effort into it, and yet he hadn't bothered.

Amethyst would be missing out on so much by being with him. The baby she was carrying would probably be their only child. He wasn't young anymore, and it would be hard enough running after one, much less two or three when he was even older. She'd still be a young woman when he retired. She'd still be a young woman when he died so, yeah, there was a good possibility she'd be a young widow. They lived in the middle of nowhere, so she would miss out on shopping, friends, lunch dates, all of the things young women liked. Being with her was selfish on his part, even if he was filling a spot in a situation where he was needed. Wasn't it unfair of him to expect her to give up all that?

But when he looked at her, he saw a woman wise beyond her years, a woman who'd raised her little sister until an honorable, trustworthy, caring man had come along to at least help. He also saw a woman who'd be a good mother, one who'd love, care for, and protect her child. She'd watched her mom and her dad, then her dad and Lorna, and he was pretty sure she wasn't one who'd sneak around and cheat on him. That didn't seem to be something that would be in her character.

She roused just a little bit, and he drew her closer. Still mostly asleep, she whispered, "Jackson?"

"I'm right here, angel."

"Ummm. Okay." Instantly, she quieted and her breathing leveled out again. She was depending on him to keep her, to keep *them*, safe. He'd do that. He had to. So that was that. It made his next decision one of the surest he'd ever made.

If Craven Bradshaw came back, Jackson Frame had every intention of killing him.

SOUNDS ROUSED AMETHYST FROM HER SLEEP, ODD sounds, and Jackson wasn't there, but the smell of coffee permeated the air around her. Slipping her feet into her scuffs, she headed toward the noise coming from somewhere in front of the house and was shocked.

At the end of the long drive, there was some kind of piece of heavy equipment—she didn't know what those things were called—plus Jackson, Gant, Tank, and a couple of guys she recognized from the fire department.

At that distance from her, they looked like little ants, and she tried to figure out what they were doing. One glance off to the side and she understood.

They were installing a gate at the end of the drive. She'd never paid any attention before, but the fence came up to each side of it, so once they put the gate in, no one would be able to just drive up the driveway or onto the property. Problem was, Craven hadn't. He'd walked in. So what good would that do?

There was a huge tub of Greek yogurt in the refrigerator, plus a container of mixed berries, along with some cinnamon bread Jackson had made on Sunday afternoon, so Amethyst set about pulling it all together to make herself some breakfast. It wasn't quite nine o'clock and the guys had to have been working for a few hours, based on what they'd gotten done. She didn't know about the other two men, but Tank had obviously taken time away from the shop to help, and she needed to remember to thank them all.

A sound startled her and she looked up to see Jackson step inside the back door. "You're up! Everything okay?"

"Yeah. Why are you putting up a gate? He walked in last night. That's not going to help."

"It will. With a gate, I can post 'no trespassing' signs and if he comes around, I can have him arrested for trespassing."

"Oh! I never would've thought of that. Makes sense though." She poked around in the yogurt with her spoon a bit before she said, "I just want him to go away."

"I do too. So I just wanted to check on you, see if you were okay. I need to get back out there. We'll have it finished in just a little while and the weather man is saying rain's coming."

"Could I make lunch for everybody?"

He smiled. "If you want. I think they'd appreciate it." Instead of moving toward the door, he crossed to where she sat and kissed her forehead. "Love you, angel."

"Love you too, Papa-boo." She smiled up at him and watched as he made his way back outside. God, he was a good-looking man. Maybe someday she'd get a chance to show him off to her college friends. Boy, they'd be jealous as hell!

As soon as she'd had a shower and dressed, she set about making some kind of lunch. She had enough veggies for salad, and there was some ham that Jackson had smoked on Monday. He sure loved that big smoker. If he had his way, he'd use it every day. The only home-made bread she had was the cinnamon he'd made, but she had a loaf of multi-grain from the grocery. Everything was all laid out except for the refrigerated items, and she'd even pulled out a couple of bags of chips from the pantry. A glance out the window told her the guys had been joined by another man and from where she stood, she thought he was the fish and game officer who'd been at the station house during the meeting, so she hustled around to make him a sandwich too. It appeared the four working on the gate were finishing up, so she retrieved some drinks from the refrigerator in the laundry room and checked to make sure she had sweet tea ready. Their voices were filtering in through the windows when her phone rang and she picked it up without even looking at it. "Hello?"

"You should've come out to talk to me."

Amethyst hit END immediately. In the next second it rang again. She screamed into the phone, "LEAVE ME ALONE!" and hung up again.

The back door opened just as it started ringing the third time, and she glanced up at Jackson. She couldn't imagine what her expression must've looked like, but it had to be clear to him what was going on because he instantly barked, "Don't answer that!" and reached for the phone. He didn't bother with greeting. Instead, he hit the speaker function and growled out, "It would be in your best interest to back the fuck off."

"Says who?"

"Says me, asshole. Leave her alone."

"I just want this taken care of as simply as possible."

"I'm taking care of it, so it's no longer any of your concern."

"It *is* my concern! That kid grows up and comes after my family money, and you're telling me—"

Jackson's voice exploded, and all the other men stopped and stared. "You listen here, you low-life, dumbass piece of shit, you leave her and our baby alone. You've got no say in this. No say. Period. Don't call back." With that, he hung up.

Gant's face was a mass of fury. "Was that who I think it was?"

"Yeah. He comes around here again, he's a dead motherfucker. I've had it. Baby," he said as he turned to Amethyst, "don't answer the phone again when he calls. Hand it to me or if I'm not right beside you, just don't answer."

"Well, at least now we know what he's thinking," Tank muttered.

"Yeah. He's thinking the kid will eventually find out about him and come after his part of the family business." Jackson paced like a madman and Amethyst wondered if he might explode. "We need to talk to Jack. You need a restraining order against him and we need to know what our options are to keep him the hell away from you, angel."

She shook her head and felt the tears coursing down her cheeks. "You don't know Craven. If he wants something, he gets it. He always has. And he wants this baby dead. Trust me, he doesn't care how that happens as long as it does."

Jackson dropped to his knees in front of where she'd plopped down in a chair and took her hands in his. "That's not happening, so don't even think about it." Thunder rumbled in the distance, and an ominous sense of dread filled Amethyst's chest. Jackson just didn't understand. Craven Bradshaw was all about himself, and he always got what he wanted. He wanted to kill the baby. He'd kill her if he had to. But no matter what, one or both of them was going to die. It was just a matter of time.

The guys sat around the dining room table and chatted as they ate, but the threat of rain and Craven hung in the air, and she could feel the hair on her arms rise. Something bad was about to happen. She didn't know what or when.

But she knew it would.

"JESUS! THAT GATE MAY NOT BE STANDING WHEN THIS IS over. It hadn't had time for the concrete to set up before the rain started, and it's just not stopping." Jackson stood in the front door and peered through the storm door at the driveway. It was more like a small river. They'd warned him that there were years when it seemed like the rain would never end, and then years when there wasn't a drop of water to be had. Feast or famine. Hell, they'd had a huge ice storm that year. Nothing was certain about Texas weather.

He caught the evening news and shook his head. There didn't seem to be an end to the rain for at least a week, maybe longer. In the darkness, the stars normally would've been putting on a show. Instead, there was the occasional lightning bolt, followed by a jarring peal of thunder that shook the entire house and rattled the windows. "Everything okay out there?" a soft voice asked as her arms wrapped around him from behind.

"Yeah, just raining like a son of a bitch. Pouring. I don't know if we'll have cattle or horses or goats when this is over unless they know how to swim. But don't you worry yourself about it. It'll be fine. As long as the roof holds and the driveway doesn't wash out, I can handle everything else." He wished he was sure about that, but every time he thought of that asshole, he felt a shudder run through his whole being. Nothing could happen to her or the baby—not on his watch. He spun to face her and feathered a kiss onto her forehead. "We're safe, dry, and warm. We've got food and water. Trust me, I've been in situations where none of that was true for me, and this is nothing like that. It's a little depressing, but that's about it." She pressed her cheek to his chest and he stroked her hair, conscious of the texture as his palm slipped downward. She worked hard on her hair to keep it looking the way she wanted it, but he didn't care. She'd be beautiful if she was bald.

"Jackson?"

He turned in her embrace and his arms closed around her. "Um-hmm?"

"Last night. Did you like it? I mean …"

"What?"

"The sex."

He smiled and kissed her lips gently. "You mean the lovemaking."

"Yeah. Did you—"

"I can't believe you're asking me that, but yes. I did. Very much. Enough that I wanted to do it again, and again, and possibly again, and then—"

"I get it!" she said and giggled. "But I fell asleep."

"Baby, it's not gonna be long before an hour's sleep is a precious commodity around here, so you get it while you can. I'm not about to wake you up when you can get some rest. But about last night … I feel like I cheated you. We should've gone out, had dinner, wine—well, not for you—and chocolate. Soft music. A little swaying to the beat. And instead, I pulled off my dollar ninety-nine boxer briefs and crawled on top of you. Not very romantic."

She laughed aloud. "Where the hell can you still get underwear for a dollar ninety-nine?"

He rolled his eyes and smirked. "See? That's how old they are!"

"You looked pretty fine without anything, if you ask me." Her fingers walked from his belt buckle up his chest, and she dragged her nails through the dark hair there. "My Papa-boo is a handsome man, um-hmmm. Ain't no woman got a man finer. I'm a lucky girl."

"I'm the lucky one. And I promise you, as soon as this rain stops, we'll—" He was cut short by the sound of someone banging on the front door, and Amethyst's eyes flew open wide. What she was thinking … Yeah. He was thinking it too. "Come with me." His hand grabbed for hers and he half-ran with her in tow to the bedroom. "Get behind the bed over there. My pistol's in the second drawer. Get it out and make sure the safety's off. Know how to do that?" She nodded, terror on her face, and he spun to the closet, reached in, and pulled out his Standard Manufacturing DP-12. Above it were shells, and he grabbed the whole box, loading as he went. A double barrel pump action, it could spit out sixteen rounds in just seconds firing both barrels with one trigger, but he'd only need one pull. One glance at Amethyst told him she was frantic. "Angel, it's gonna be okay. Just breathe, hear me? It's fine." He crept up the hallway and heard footsteps outside again, then another knock. As soon as he stepped up behind the door's hinges, he racked the rounds into the chamber and yelled, "Who is it?"

"It's Conor!"

Jackson threw open the door and found the fish and game officer standing there, drenched. "What the hell are you doing out here?"

"Jesus! What are you doing with that? Gonna shoot me?"

"No. We thought it was that asshole … Don't worry about it. Amethyst, baby, it's just Conor!" he called down the hallway. When she didn't answer, he dashed into the bedroom and took the pistol from her hands. "You climb up on the bed and rest. I know you're scared, but it's okay." After he'd waited to see that she was safely on the bed, he headed back to the living room. "Sorry about that. She was behind the bed with my pistol."

"Holy hell. You guys mean business." Conor looked down. "Shit. I'm dripping water all over your floor."

"That's okay. It's seen worse. But what are you doing out in this?"

"I placed marking rods the other day to mark the elevations. I wanted to see what it looks like after this has started and your portion of the creek is upstream, but I didn't want to just go out there without you knowing I was there. Kinda wish I'd gone ahead," he said with a grin as he glanced at the shotgun again.

"Nah. You would've been fine."

"So could you come out there with me? I know it's raining pitchforks and pigs, but I'd really like to see it, and I'm not sure how to get there in the dark. Figured you knew the land a lot better."

I really don't want to go out in the rain, and I really don't want to leave her. But I'll just be over the rise. No big deal. "Yeah. Okay. Let me tell her where I'm going." Five minutes later, he was suited up and ready to go out.

His big ATV had seating for two and super-bright halogen headlamps, plus a canopy. As hard as it was raining, that wouldn't offer them much, but at least it was something. They climbed aboard and in a minute, they were headed up the back ridge. Jackson had only been out there once in the dark, and he hadn't liked it a bit. It had been dry too, not muddy and sloppy.

They crested the hill and when his headlamp beams tipped down, Jackson very nearly screamed. The creek was completely out of its banks. "Holy shit!" Conor yelled. "Yeah, we've definitely got some problems downstream!"

"Is this all you needed?" *Please, please, let him say yes!* his brain screamed.

"I need to find my marking pole. I've gotta have my …" Conor was rummaging around in a duffel, which only caused Jackson more anxiety. The longer he fumbled, the longer they were out there, and he could swear the water was creeping toward them too fast to get away from it. "Yeah. Okay." Conor lifted a pair of glasses, and Jackson recognized them—night vision. "Train this on the pole," he said and handed a big hand-held spotlight to Jackson.

"I don't even know where it is," Jackson barked back.

"That direction!" Pointing to the left, Jackson started sweeping the beam across until he heard Conor yell, "STOP! Right there!" The officer lifted the glasses and sat there. "Can you tip that just a little to the right? A little more … Perfect." There were a few moments of silence before Conor muttered, "Son of a bitch."

That didn't sound good to Jackson at all. "What?"

"That's rising at an alarming rate. The road will probably be underwater by morning. I've gotta get back. All my equipment is on the other side of the bridge, and I need to move it over on this side. Mind if I park it on your property?"

"Nah, man. That's fine. Ready to go?" All Jackson really wanted to do was get the hell out of there.

"Okay. Let's go. I gotta get moving." The tires spun just a little as Jackson wheeled the rig around and gunned it up the back side of the ridge. When they crested it, he could see some kind of vehicle in the driveway that wasn't one of theirs or Conor's. "Holy shit."

"Who's that?" Conor asked, pointing.

"I dunno, but I'm gonna find out right now." Gunning the engine, he powered down the front side of the ridge at an alarming speed, only one thought on his mind. *Amethyst. She'd better be okay or somebody's gonna have to die tonight.* He didn't even stop to put the ATV in the barn, just hit the ground running, slung the back door open, and dashed in. He slid to a stop in the doorway of the living room and his mouth dropped open.

"Well, don't you look like a drown jackalope?" Jack drawled, a wicked grin on his face.

Jackson was so out of breath he could barely speak. "What are you doing here?"

"I heard you had a visitor last night, so I came to talk to both of you, but you weren't here. Hope that's okay," he said and patted Amethyst's hand where it lay on the table.

"Of course. Scared me shitless, but yeah—I'm glad you're here."

"Um, I should probably …" a voice said from somewhere behind him and he spun.

"Okay. But you're welcome to park your rig in the drive here."

Conor nodded. "I'll just sleep in it, if that's okay."

Jackson shook his head. "You absolutely will not. You'll come in here to our guest room and get dry and warm. Get your shit and get back here."

"Aye-aye, captain!" Conor said with a laugh as he disappeared out the back door.

"Is that who I think it is?"

"Conor Paxton. Fish and game. They're doing some research on the flooding of Williams Creek. Hoping to find out what's causing problems. It's bloated feast on this end and parched famine farther downstream. They don't know what's going on." Jackson pulled out a chair and sat down, his pants making a squishing sound as he sat, so he stood up again. "Maybe I should change clothes."

Jack laughed. "Yeah, maybe you should! You sound like you've shit your pants!"

He has no idea how close he is to right, Jackson's mind whispered. "I'll just be a second."

An hour later, he didn't feel one bit better. Conor joined them at the table. There were two law enforcement officers there, and no one had anything to offer. "So there's *nothing* we can do?"

"No. He hasn't actually threatened her with bodily harm, so we've got no reason to get a protective order against him. No, let's back up. A *judge* will see no reason to issue one, and that's what I'd have to have in order to keep him away."

"So we just watch and wait. That's pretty unfair." Jackson was damn unhappy, but a look of total defeat spread across Amethyst's face. "It's gonna be okay, angel. You'll be safe with me."

"You can't be with me every minute of every day," she murmured.

"Yes, I can and I will. You'll be fine. But I wish we could do *something*."

Jack shook his head slowly. "Me too. If I think of something, I'll let you know. You've got the no trespassing signs up now, and if he violates those, we'll have something. Is this guy smart?" Jack asked Amethyst.

She rolled her eyes. "Like a fox."

"Yeah. Figures. Well, I'll leave y'all to it. If you need me, you know where to find me."

Jackson rose and followed the sheriff to the door. "Thanks, Jack. I appreciate you coming by."

"You're welcome. Anytime. You've been good to this community and good to her and her family. That means you're my brother, and brothers always look out for brothers." Jack reached out a hand, so Jackson took it. When he looked into the sheriff's eyes, a strange, primitive feeling passed over him. What the hell was that about? As soon as Jack dropped his hand, the feeling went away, and Jackson's chest felt warm. He'd never experienced that sensation before in his life. It was weird but not unpleasant, and he decided he'd have to give some thought to that, maybe talk to Gant. He didn't know Jack well, but the guy seemed genuine.

"Good to see you again, Jack," Conor said as he shook hands with the sheriff. Jackson had forgotten that Jack had been a Texas Ranger at one time. They'd probably known each other for quite a while.

"I'm tired. I think I'm going to bed," Amethyst said when Jackson returned to the table and sat down after he'd gotten Conor settled in the guest room. He stretched his arm out across the table and she took his hand. "I love you, Papa-boo."

"I love you too, my angel. If you're tired, go get dressed for bed. Wanna watch a movie or something? I think I've got *Forrest Gump* and *When Harry Met Sally* lined up on one of my streaming services. Those are just fun. Want to do that?"

She shrugged and stood. "I guess."

He rose too. "You get dressed for bed. I'll pull some things together for us. Go on." As she turned, he hopped toward her and slapped her on the butt, laughing when she jumped.

"You a bad, bad man, Papa-boo!" she called out, laughing as she shuffled off down the hallway.

"Oh, yeah. The worst!"

By the time she got back, he'd turned on the gas fireplace, the TV was on, and there were chips, chocolates, and some soft drinks on the coffee table. "Well, looky here! You've gone all out!" she said on a chuckle.

"Yeah, nothing's too good for my angel! Let's just try to relax, okay?" he said as he sat down and patted the sofa cushion beside him.

Two hours later, his feet were on the coffee table, her legs were across his lap, and she was sleeping soundly, his arm around her. Just a few months earlier, he'd been there alone in the silent house, drinking bourbon and waiting for bedtime so he could just forget everything. But she'd changed every moment of his life for the better. She'd never understand how thankful he was for her. She thought he'd saved her.

Instead, she'd saved him from drowning in loneliness, and she'd never know how thankful he was for that.

CHAPTER 10

IT RAINED. It poured. There weren't words strong enough to describe what was going on outside the cedar-sided house sitting on a plateau in front of the ridge. He'd lived there a good while and he'd never heard it rain like that. It was a good thing that ridge protected them from the creek or the water would be creeping toward the house. It stood in the dips in the gravel driveway, miniature lakes tapped constantly by raindrops, eventually connected like creeks and rivers as the deluge continued. He had to go out and take care of the animals, and he was pretty sure she'd be fine. Thinking a spoiled little rich boy like Craven Bradshaw would come out in those nightmarish conditions was most likely wrong. He wouldn't want to get his designer shoes wet.

His thoughts were interrupted as Conor strode into the room. "Mornin'. Mind if I take your ATV and go back over the ridge?" the fish and game officer asked as he poured himself a cup of coffee. There was no reason for an escort. The trail up there was clear, even in the downpour.

"Sure. Go right ahead. I've gotta make sure everybody has food." He let out a sour chuckle. "It's for damn sure they don't need anything to drink!"

"No shit. Okay, thanks. I won't be gone long, and I'll get my stuff and go back down to the site." Conor gave a backhanded wave as he finished up the cup of coffee and disappeared out the back door. A minute later, Jackson heard the ATV fire up and head out.

He brought down hay for the goats and cattle from the loft. A lot of the ranchers left their big bales in the pastures they weren't using so they'd be there when they moved their stock, but for reasons he couldn't understand, Jackson had insisted on square bales stacked in his loft. Boy, was he thankful for that odd little bit of insight. At least it wouldn't be molded and wet. Most of the time his livestock didn't give a shit about rain, but they'd all congregated in the barn. It wasn't hard to believe that even they were sick of it. He'd put a tin roof on the structure when he first moved there, and the sound of the raindrops pelting the roof was very nearly deafening. As soon as he finished, he slipped back into the truck, and it occurred to him that the mail needed to be picked up. God, he hated going down there for it. Why couldn't his mailbox be up by the house? Because the postal carrier would never go along with that, he was sure, but it would be nice in that kind of weather.

"Damn it, Margie," he mumbled under his breath. The mail carrier had left the door of the mailbox open, and Jackson reached in to find a pile of soggy, stuck-together mail. That would take a while to sort through. He tried to dry it off with his shirt, which was a practice in futility, seeing as how his shirt was almost as wet as the mail. That clearly wasn't going to work, so he started peeling everything apart and spreading it out on the truck seat to sort of dry. There were five or six pieces of junk mail, and those got tossed in the trash can he kept on the back floorboard of the truck. Two bills, power and water, a reminder card from his dentist in Hondo, and an envelope with no return address, addressed to Amethyst. Something about that envelope, its chicken-scratch handwriting smeared from the rainwater, sent a shiver through him. If he was right, he was going to do *something.* Sitting around waiting for trouble wouldn't happen.

Slipping his finger under one end of the flap, he ripped the top open to find a simple piece of blank paper inside. A fury blazed into existence inside him as he read the same handwriting on it.

You stupid bitch. You should've talked to me. Now I'll have to make sure this isn't an ongoing problem for me. I can't have this and I won't. You'd better change your mind or you'll be sorry beyond belief. Get to it—NOW!

Jackson's fury had turned into a finely-directed rage, and his thinking was crystal clear. He would stop it, and he had a pretty good idea how.

As soon as he stepped into the house, he yelled, "Amethyst!"

Her pale face appeared in the kitchen doorway. "Yeah?"

"You okay, angel?"

"No. Morning sickness. I haven't had much, but when I do, it's a doozie. Something wrong?"

Shit! I can't worry her with this! What could he do … "Do you have Craven's parents' phone number?"

"Uh, yeah, in my phone. Why?"

"Because I think I need to talk to them."

She shook her head. "No. Please, don't. It'll just make him madder than he already is."

"I can't believe they'd condone his behavior."

"I don't think they would, but they might cut him out of the family business and his inheritance. That's what this is all about, the money he thinks is coming from his family, and if I take that away … I don't know what he'll do, Jackson. He might set the house on fire in the night or something."

Jackson laughed. "Yeah? I don't think he'd have much luck! Wet wood doesn't burn! Now, get me the number, okay?"

He could see the fear in her face. "Papa-boo, please …"

"I told you, you've got nothing to be afraid of as long as you're here with me. Now, number. I need it. I want to end this, and I think this'll probably do it."

"Well, okay." She disappeared for a minute and came back with her phone and a towel. As soon as he'd taken the towel and started trying to dry his hair a little, he saw her poking through the phone. Then she picked up a pencil on the countertop, snatched a piece of notepaper off the pad on the refrigerator door, and wrote down a number. "This is Mrs. Bradshaw's number. I've never talked to Mr. Bradshaw, but I've talked to her. She's nice enough, but she didn't like me. They didn't approve."

"Of you, of your color, or of you and their son."

She shrugged. "Yes. All of it."

"Uh-huh. I see. Go lie down. I'll be there in just a few minutes."

"But Jackson—"

He pointed down the hallway. "Go. Let me take care of this. I told you I would, and I will. Go on now, baby.

It's fine." He waited until he heard her rustling around on the bed, then pulled his phone from his pocket, stepped into the laundry room, closed the door behind him, and dialed the number.

A feminine voice answered with a cheery, "Hello!"

"Yes, is this Mrs. Bradshaw? Craven's mother?"

There was a moment's hesitation before she asked, "Oh, lord. What's he done now?"

Yeah. Even his parents know he's a royal pain in the ass, Jackson thought. "Ma'am, my name is Jackson Frame. I live outside Tarpley, Texas. Medic with the volunteer fire department here."

"Oh, god! Is Craven down there? Is he hurt?"

"No, ma'am." *But he's gonna be*, Jackson wanted to growl. "He's fine as far as I know. Do you know his ex-girlfriend, Amethyst Meadows?"

There was a snort and a little laugh on the other end. "So she's finally his ex-girlfriend? It's about time. His father and I have been telling him for years now to cut that black gypsy trash off and get the hell—"

"Ma'am, that black gypsy trash is my fiancée. And I don't appreciate you talking about her that way."

"Your fiancée? My, my, my. She works fast! I'm sorry I offended you, but you know it's true."

Jackson was seething, but he had to keep going. "I'm a forty-three-year-old cattle rancher and friend of her family. I'm not sure when we're getting married, but we're expecting a baby."

"Well, congratulations. I hope you'll all be very happy. Now, if you'll excuse me—"

"You need to know that the child isn't mine biologically. It's your son's."

There was a choking sound on the other end of the phone. "What the … How do you know that?"

"Because she was pregnant when she came to her dad's house in Tarpley. We weren't even dating. I only knew her and her sister because her dad is a friend of mine. Fellow firefighter. So yes, it's your son's child."

"But she could've been sleeping around when she and Craven—"

"Ma'am, Amethyst is no slut. She hasn't been traipsing around all over the countryside, sleeping with one man and then another."

"But her mother—"

"Was married to her dad for years before they split up, and I've heard him say that regardless how flighty she is, he's sure she never fooled around on him while they were married. Amethyst isn't like that and, frankly, it kinda pisses me off that you'd say things like that. You obviously don't know her at all."

"I've only talked to her a couple of times. We made it clear to Craven that she wasn't welcome in our home." *Well, that explains why she didn't really know them*, Jackson thought. He was getting ready to say something when she said, "Tell that girl she won't get a penny of our family's money, DNA test be damned."

"She doesn't *want* any of your family's money, ma'am. She just wants to be left alone."

"If she's his ex, that shouldn't be a problem."

"That's just it, ma'am. He's here."

"In Texas?"

Jackson rolled his eyes. "Yes, ma'am. In Texas. Following her around, calling her, beating on the door. I've put up no trespassing signs, the sheriff has been out here, I've told him to leave her alone, and he just—"

"Oh, he will when I'm through with him! If my husband has our attorney draft documents for her to sign saying that she'll never ask us for money, I'll make him stay away from her—gladly."

"Ma'am, you just send all the papers you want. But I'm calling you to let you know ..." Jackson took a deep breath. "Let's just say this is a courtesy call. I'm divorced. Have been for years. I lost my toddler daughter to cancer years ago. Amethyst and this baby ... They're my whole future. If anything happens to them, I've got nothing left to live for. And if anything happens to them and your son has anything to do with it, god help him when I get my hands on him."

"Are you threatening him?"

"No, ma'am. That's no threat. That's a stone-cold promise that you can take to the bank just like all your high-falutin' money. You tell him to leave my girl alone, and you tell him if he doesn't, I have the ability to *make* him leave her alone. He won't like my methods, trust me."

"Well, I'll take that under advisement. If you hurt him, we'll—"

"Ma'am, if I hurt him, it'll be because one or both of my loves are seriously injured or dead and, trust me, it'll either be me or the guys on cell block B for bitch-boy. It doesn't have to happen, so make it not happen." There was a silence on the other end of the call as she hung up. "Well, guess she got the picture," he growled to himself as he stood there, hands still shaking with pent-up anger. That boy had better back the fuck off. If he hurt her or the baby, he wouldn't just be in trouble. Oh, no. If Craven hurt either of them, he hoped the asshole enjoyed it.

It would be the last thing he ever did before he saw eternity.

HIS PHONE RANG, BUT WHEN HE SAW WHO IT WAS, HE JUST sent it straight to voicemail. It rang again almost instantly, so he hit ACCEPT and barked out, "What?" in his most aggravated tone.

He hadn't even looked. If he had, he wouldn't have answered, because it wasn't his mother again. It was a male voice. "Are you in Texas?"

Craven sat up straight as a poker. "How did you know that?"

"Because your mother got a call from some guy who said that black girl is his girlfriend. Actually, I think the term he used was 'fiancée' or something as equally ridiculous."

That son of a bitch! "Yeah. Whatever."

"Is it true? Is that girl pregnant with your child?"

"Probably not. Probably somebody else she was fucking around with."

"The man your mother talked to seemed to think she hadn't done anything of the sort and that it was definitely your child. Don't you think you should've let us know about this so we could protect ourselves from any claims that might come along?"

"No. Because I'm down here trying to take care of it, okay? I've got this."

"No, you don't. What hairbrained, totally ignorant thing are you working toward, Craven? Because if you really, really screw something up, I've just about had enough of—"

"Of what? Bailing me out of trouble? Sweeping up my fuck-ups as I go? You've made that very clear, Father. Very, very clear."

"So why are we having this conversation? Have you ever heard of a condom, idiot?"

Idiot. Hairbrained. Fuck-up. Dumbass. Moron. Craven had heard them all. That was all he'd heard from his dad growing up. He'd heard Morton talking to other family members when he thought Craven wasn't around. "I'm worried what's going to happen to the company when Craven takes over." "Run the company? All Craven's ever managed to run was his mouth and himself and his reputation into the ground." "He could've gone to Yale or Harvard or Princeton, but there wasn't enough money in the world for me to buy that idiot into a school like that. At least a state school took him. I was afraid he wouldn't even be able to do that." He'd heard every word. And the sad part?

He'd actually loved Amethyst at some point. She was a good person. There was something else he was sure of —she'd never cheated on him. At times, he'd wished he had her character and upbringing. Every time she gave him a gift, he'd criticize it and acted like it wasn't worth his time to unwrap. But everything he'd ever to given to her she seemed to treasure, even the smallest things. He remembered sticking a quarter in one of those stupid machines at a pizza place and out popped a plastic container with a plastic ring in it. "Here ya go," he'd said and slipped it onto her finger. "Want an engagement ring? This should be about your taste level." The hurt look in her eyes had taken a couple of minutes to fade from his thoughts, and weeks later as she was getting dressed for school, he'd noticed that same stupid little ring on a chain around her neck. A plastic ring! What the hell kind of woman wore a plastic ring on a chain around her neck?

One who obviously cared more for the person who'd given it to her than they did for her. Being willing to take that kind of treatment had made it even easier to mistreat her, and it had escalated until … "Look," he blurted out. "I'm taking care of it. You don't have to worry about it."

"You do that, Craven. This is your last shot. Don't fuck it up." And the phone went dead.

He stared at the social media page again. There was a meeting of that stupid fire department on Tuesday night, and that could be a good time to make his move. *This is your last shot*, he told himself. By god, he'd figure out something.

IT WAS *STILL* RAINING. AMETHYST WAS SO DAMN TIRED OF rain! Jackson had ordered a load of gravel and spent all day in the downpour with a rake, spreading it at the end of the driveway in case the little culvert washed out. It had made an awful hump there, but if the thing collapsed, at least they'd only have to drive through a couple of inches of water to get out onto the road.

He kept promising her he'd take her on a real date, but neither of them wanted to get out in that mess, so they'd stayed at home except to go to the grocery a couple of times. Every time, they'd be soaked by the time they got the groceries in the truck. On more than one occasion the cell service had been down and they couldn't even call her dad or Lorna. At least one of those times, Tank had ventured out there to check on them and told them Gant had been trying to call. They invited him to stay for dinner, but he said Callie had cooked and he had to get back. It would've been nice if he'd stayed. The only other person they ever saw was Conor, and he spent all his time in rain gear, tromping up and down the banks of Williams Creek. They cooked every night and he ate with them, then showered to get warm, called his honey, and went to bed. He was the perfect house guest. Most of the time, they forgot he was there.

Tuesday night rolled around and she could tell Jackson was wrestling with something. When she couldn't stand it anymore, she finally asked him, "Papa-boo, something bothering you?"

"Yeah. It's meeting night for TVFD. I really need to be there. We've been having some talks, two or three of us at a time, about critical response during weather like this. Before I came here, they'd already been through a tornado and weren't as prepared as they wish they had been. This stuff doesn't seem to be letting up anytime soon, and we need to have a firm plan in place in case something horrible happens."

"That sounds like a good plan to me," she replied as she rinsed off a dish and put it in the drying rack.

"So I guess you should get dressed and get ready to go with me."

She turned and dropped her hands to her hips. "I'm not going out in this! It's awful out there!"

"I can't leave you here by yourself."

She chuckled. "Papa-boo, ain't nobody comin' out here to bother me in this. I'll be perfectly okay. You don't worry about me. Conor will probably be finished in a little while and he'll be here. So go on. I'm good."

"I really don't feel like—"

"Feel like I can take care of myself?" She stepped up

to him and pressed both palms to his chest. "Because. I. Can." The little kiss she gave him turned into a big kiss, a scorcher of a kiss, before she pulled back. "You go on. I'll be fine. I've got Buck and that big ol' shotgun thing of yours. I'm sure I can handle anything that comes up."

"Something's coming up right now that I know you can handle," he snarled as he nipped at her neck.

"And you ain't gonna make it to no meetin' if we're rollin' around on the bed! You go on, now, hear? Me and my honey pot will still be here when you get back."

"Lord, girl," Jackson sighed. "You make me crazy for you."

"Good. Then you'll get your ass right on back here when you're finished and not go runnin' around lookin' for women." When she kissed him that time, she chuckled against his lips and he squeezed her to him.

"Ain't no woman for me but you, angel. You get that through that pretty lil' head of yorn, you hear me?" There was a resounding *SMACK!* when he slapped her ass with his open palm, and she laughed. "I won't be gone long, I promise."

"Okay. I'll be right here. Run on now."

Ten minutes later, he was gone and she'd finished cleaning up the kitchen. She straightened up the living room, then did a load of Conor's clothes. He'd told her he'd wash them, but she didn't mind. When those were washing, she started folding the towels she'd washed earlier in the day. With all the rain, they sure were taking a lot of showers!

Jackson had been gone about thirty minutes when her phone rang. It was a number she'd never seen before, and she was a little afraid to answer it, but she hit ACCEPT and whispered, "Hello?"

"Yes, this is ..." There was a lot of static, and she couldn't understand the caller. A few seconds later, she understood "hospital" and "accident."

"I'm sorry. Our connection is horrible. Who? What?"

"This is Medina ... Hospital. There's ... accident. We ... Frame. You're showing ... emergency contact."

"Wait, what? Jackson's been in an accident?"

It was quiet before she heard the voice say, "... as soon as you ... urgent."

"Yes! Yes, I'm on my way! I'll be there as fast as I can get there! Tell him I love him and I'm on my way!" Amethyst grabbed her bag and keys. "Buck, stay here! I've gotta go see about your daddy." There was no time for a raincoat or even an umbrella. She had to get to the hospital!

The tires of the little Toyota slipped and spun as she headed out the drive, and she thought the bump at the end of the driveway would jar her teeth right out of her head. As she drove, she called Jackson's number, but there was no answer. *Oh, god, no. Don't let him be ... Jackson Frame, you can't leave me like this! Don't you dare leave me like this!* "Don't you dare leave me," she whispered aloud as she drove. The car sailed across the bridge at Williams Creek and she tore out toward Hondo as fast as she could go.

It was barely a thirty minute drive to Hondo, but it felt like hours. She was trying to be careful and still trying to drive as fast as she could. What if ... She couldn't even think like that. He'd be okay. He had to be.

Her little car slid up to the curb outside the emergency room and she didn't even care that she was parked in a no-parking zone. She just ran as fast as she could until she made it to the automatic doors of the ambulance bay, and they spit her out into the emergency department, right in front of a startled health unit coordinator and three nurses. "Can we help you, miss?"

"Yes! You guys called me! My boyfriend! Jackson Frame! He's here somewhere! He was in an accident. Please, can I—"

"Miss, we don't have anyone here by that name."

"But you have to! You called and said there'd been an accident, and I was listed as his emergency contact, and …" Amethyst couldn't figure out what was going on. He had to be there. The woman had said so!

"Honey, he's not here. There haven't been any accident victims brought in here tonight."

"Is there another Medina hospital?"

"No. This is it except for the VA hospital in Kerrville. I think somebody was playing games with you and on a night like this, I'd be especially angry about it if I were you," one of the nurses said.

Playing games with you. "Oh, no," Amethyst moaned. Craven. He was fucking with her. And then a paralyzing thought ran through her mind—maybe he'd done something to Jackson. If there was a hair on Jackson's head that jackass had harmed … "I'm sorry. I made a mistake. I'm sorry. Have a good evening."

She backed away from the desk and turned. Behind her somewhere a woman's voice said, "Honey? You sure you're okay to drive? You don't look …" She didn't wait to hear what the rest of the sentence was. Her feet were on the move and in seconds, she was in the car and headed back home.

She drove along, not as fast as before, and tried to call him again, but once more, the call didn't go through. She tried to call Gant, with the same results. Her third call was to Lorna. "Hello?"

"Lorna! Hey, it's—"

"Hello? Anybody there?"

"Lorna! It's Amethyst!"

"Amethyst? Honey, I ... The connection ... call you back." And the phone went dead.

"Shit. I wish I had Pop's number or somebody's. Tank's. Bree's. *Somebody's*." The phone rang once—Lorna's number—but when she answered it, she heard a bit of static and nothing else. "Oh, for god's sake. I'm going on to the fire station," she said aloud as she drove.

There was a house up ahead, and she recognized it. Jackson had always told her when she reached it, she was halfway home, so she only had about another fifteen minutes to get there. There was ponding on the highway and occasionally her little car would hydroplane, but she managed to hold it on the road. She was about another five minutes down the highway when a set of headlights shone in her rearview mirror. There'd been no one behind her just a couple of minutes before, so she wasn't sure where they'd come from. *Must've turned out of a driveway somewhere*, she told herself. As she drove along, they got closer and closer. The light reflecting from the mirror was almost blinding, and she wished they'd just go around her, so she slowed down. Instead of passing her, they stayed right behind her, so when she got to the abandoned gas station about three miles down the road, she pulled over to let them pass.

Instead, they pulled in right behind her.

A sickening wave of fear broke over Amethyst, and then she tried to calm herself. It was Texas Highway Patrol, stopping to make sure she was safe—that had to be it. She glanced in the rearview mirror on the door and looked back. A man got out, but he didn't have on a hat like the patrolmen wore, and that worried her. The car was still running, and she had it in gear, sitting there with her foot on the brake. As the man drew closer, she watched, and when he stepped up within five feet of her car door, she could finally see his face.

Craven.

Amethyst gunned the car and spun out onto the roadway, hands shaking and heart pounding. He'd been the one who'd called her! How had he done that? Paid some woman in a bar somewhere to call and pretend to be a nurse? Had somebody at a hotel do it? Didn't matter. He was behind her. No, he was *right* behind her. Right there. Feet away and getting closer.

Amethyst didn't know what to do. If she stopped, he'd have her. If she kept driving, he'd just follow her. *Just keep going and go straight to the fire station*, she told herself, using everything she had to try to calm herself. She thought of all the meditations and prayers her mom and dad had taught her over the years, but none of them would come. She was too terrified. *Where am I? Where am I?* she kept asking herself, scanning the dark horizon for a familiar landmark, and then she saw it up ahead. The bridge over Williams Creek. If she was there, she was almost home, but that wasn't where she was going, and fear threatened to swallow her. *I'll make it*, she told herself.

Before the thought had faded from her mind, she felt a jolt and her car fishtailed. "Oh my god! He's hitting me!" she screamed aloud as he slammed the car into the back of her little sedan again and again. It was getting harder and harder to keep it on the road, and she decided maybe she should just stop and take her chances. But when she tried, he rammed the car from behind and pushed it along the highway. Nothing was working. All she could do was try to hang onto the steering wheel and pray for the best.

But when she got near the bridge, one final *WHAM!* sent her car off the road. It slid and spun as she fought the wheel, and then there was the sensation of tipping, a *BANG!* as all four wheels landed again, and then a huge *WHOOSH!* Her head hit the steering wheel and everything got blurry …

THEY WERE ABOUT THIRTY MINUTES OR SO INTO THE meeting. Dirty-D was talking about the need for a rescue boat during times like that, and Jackson was trying to tune that out. No way was he getting in a boat. Never. Wasn't happening.

Pops was talking about funding for some emergency gear when the radio in the office squawked. That was unusual, but when the phones were as unreliable as they had been, sometimes that was the only way to reach anyone. "Hey, Tank, would you see what's going on?" Pops asked.

"Sure thing." Jackson watched through the open door as the big man fiddled with the dials on the radio, and then he heard the transmission.

"This is Texas Parks & Wildlife Officer Conor Paxton calling Tarpley Volunteer Fire Department. TVFD, respond. Over."

"Yeah, Conor, this is Tank Reardon, over."

"Tank, is Jackson there?"

"Yeah! Hang on." Jackson was on the move before Tank even turned. "He wants to talk to you," Tank said as he handed Jackson the mic.

"Yeah, Conor! What's up?"

"I'm not sure. I was down here beside the creek when I saw your girl go barreling past in that little Toyota of hers."

"What?"

"Yeah. She just flew by me. I mean, she was flying. Is something—"

"Which way was she going?"

"Toward Hondo."

Toward Hondo? That made zero sense. What in the hell would she be doing, heading off toward Hondo in that kind of weather? "Are you *sure* it was her?"

"Yeah. Left rear taillight broken out, am I right?"

Yep. That was definitely Amethyst's car. "Yeah. That's her."

"Okay. I'm somewhere behind her."

"What?"

"I tried to call you, but I couldn't get through, so I finally decided maybe I should get in the truck and try to catch up to her but, honestly, I haven't been able to. She's driving like a bat outta hell."

"How long have you been on the road?"

"Twenty minutes. Should be in Hondo just any minute."

"Do you see her yet?"

"No. I haven't and I don't. Any idea where she might be going?"

"No. None." Jackson sat there for a minute, thinking. What on earth could get her out of the house in that weather? She wouldn't go to the store. Hell, she didn't even want to come with him to the station. "I don't know—"

"I'll keep looking for her, but I think you need to head this direction."

"Me too. I don't know how we'll stay in touch …"

"Here." A voice beside him held out a handheld radio. "Take this and get on the road, son," Pops said with a slap on his shoulder. "Let us know if you need anything."

"I will. Thanks."

The streets were slick and his truck fishtailed a couple of times, but he kept going. He'd gotten about five miles past the bridge over the creek when the radio crackled to life. "TFG Officer Conor Paxton calling Jackson Frame, over."

"I'm here, Conor."

"Yeah, I'm on my way back. She's about a mile ahead of me and there's a car behind her. Where are you?"

"I can't be very far from where you are. I should be able to see …" A car appeared over a small rise in the road and sped past him. As soon as it got close, he could see the driver—Amethyst. And then the car behind her passed him.

It was Craven Bradshaw.

"Holy shit, Conor. I'm turning around. They just passed me, and that car behind her is that asshole who's been harassing us."

"Copy that. TVFD, this is TFG Officer Conor Paxton requesting assistance at the Williams Creek bridge or thereabouts. Copy?"

"We're already rolling, Conor," a familiar voice called out, and Jackson recognized it as Buff. "Jackson, you copy?"

"Roger that. I can almost see the bridge from where

we are so she should be …" The words froze in his throat.

Ahead of him, her car's taillights flashed on either side of the car behind her as it swerved all over the road. He saw the headlights of that car illuminate the side of her Toyota, and then saw the impact. As her car tipped up onto two wheels, it also veered off the roadway, plopped back down, and kept rolling.

Right into Williams Creek.

A million things raced through Jackson's mind. Faces, mostly covered in fabric, just their eyes showing, against a background of sand and brilliant sun. The same faces in a dark room, yelling questions at him that he didn't understand, his hands bound behind the chair he sat on. More faces above him as he lay on something long and rigid, a towel draped over his face as bucket after bucket of water was trickled or dumped on the towel. Nothingness as his head was slipped under water, his body tied fast to the board, and he could feel his life ebbing away as he fought to keep his mouth closed. Time after time of waking up to someone pumping his chest, and the memory of the foul water he spewed out as he caught a breath, only to have them drape the towel back over his head and start again. Over and over and over.

The truck slid to a stop and he threw it into park, then slammed the door open and bolted toward the dark colored sedan, but it jetted away just before he reached it, only one headlight still working. It didn't matter. He ran straight to the edge of the creek. Water rushed past, the roar deafening, and it was dark except for two things—her headlights. They still glowed under the surface, but the entire car was underwater.

Jackson stood there, paralyzed. He couldn't go into

the water. And yet, he couldn't *not* go in. That was his future buried under that torrent, the only two things in the world that mattered to him. It only took him a split second to decide, and he kicked off his boots, slipped off his shirt, ran to the bank, and waded into the icy water. With the surface three feet over the top of the car, he'd have to go under and pray he wasn't swept away. The car's presence would help deflect the water and make it easier to hang onto. If there was still an air pocket in the car, she could at least breathe for a few minutes, but time was definitely wasting. There was someone yelling at him, but he didn't care—he just dropped below the surface, hanging onto the car's door handle to keep the water from washing him away.

It took him a couple of seconds to get his bearings, and he opened his eyes. His hand was on the rear door handle, so he held on and reached for the front one, then thanked his lucky stars that it was the driver's door. He could barely see her inside, and she wasn't moving. Water wasn't quite up to her neck yet, but her seatbelt was still buckled, and he'd have to find a way to get that off. With a closed fist, he beat on the window, but got no response. *Dear God, what if she's ... No. I can't think like that. I've got to get her out.* Still holding onto the door latch, Jackson fumbled in his pocket for his keys, but they were still in the truck, so he didn't have his glass breakage tool. Bent over as far as he dared, his hand clawed along the creek bed and the first thing he turned up was a large, pointed rock. *Good enough*, he told himself as he dug it up with one hand and drew it back. If the rock didn't work, he didn't know what he'd do. The car would have to completely fill with water to equalize the pressure before he'd be able to open the door, and …

Jackson put everything he had into that strike, and the glass shattered. Water rushed into the car instantly, but once it had, the door popped open easily. Once he'd pushed her back into the seat, he reached across, unfastened her seatbelt, and grabbed her arm. It took every scrap of strength he had, but he tugged and pulled with all his might as he hauled her out through the doorway and struggled against the current to the surface.

The sky around him was brilliant red, lit by the emergency vehicles sitting everywhere. TVFD's trucks were there, their ambulance, all the guys with lights on their pickup trucks—everything in Tarpley was there. Jack's car was there too, and at least one highway patrol car. Conor was waist-deep in the frigid water, struggling toward him, reaching for her, and he dug his toes into the creek bed, pushing and fighting his way toward the bank. In what seemed like hours but was only seconds, Conor and Tank had grasped her under the arms and laid her on a backboard waiting there. Drained, he crawled up onto the bank and sat there, watching as they performed CPR on her with Buff barking orders.

Jackson dropped his forehead to the ground and pounded the gravel with his fists. Once again, he'd had a chance at happiness, a chance for a family with a woman who loved him and a child who'd adore him, one he'd love forever, and they'd been snatched away for. He couldn't keep one single good thing in his life. Why wasn't he allowed some happiness? Why was this beautiful, kind, loving young woman yanked from the happy world they were creating? Life was so fucking unfair! So fucking unfair. So fucking—

"There ya go! Roll her to the side, Tank. Got it. Get

me that oxygen mask. Hey, honey, let me put this on you, okay."

Then he heard the only thing that mattered to him. "Jackson? Where's Jackson? Is he okay?" her weak voice coughed out.

"I'm here! I'm right here, angel! I'm right here." Scrambling up from the dirt and gravel, he ran-crawled toward her and dropped beside her. "I'm right here, angel! Oh, god, you scared me so bad, baby! You're gonna be okay, please? You're gonna be okay." Those kisses he was pressing onto her forehead weren't enough. He wanted to take her in his arms and squeeze her to him as tightly as he could, but that thought was interrupted.

"Hey, Boss, we're taking her on to MCH. I'm riding with her. Get somebody to bring you."

"No, I wanna—"

"No! You need to be checked out yourself! Get somebody to—"

"I'll bring him!" a voice rang out. Tank shot a look at Conor. "You've been in the water. You're coming too."

The fish and game officer held up his hands. "But I'm—"

"Getting checked out. You're getting checked out!" Pops bellowed. "Won't take no for an answer! Get going!"

"Get in the truck," Tank said, pointing at his big pickup. "And you," he said, pointing at Jackson, "get in the back seat. I've got some clothes back there. Put on a shirt before you freeze."

He wasn't going to argue. She was on her way to the hospital. It didn't matter if he lived or died, as long as nothing happened to her and that baby. They were all that mattered.

CHAPTER 11

JACKSON DIDN'T CARE that Tank's shirt was too big for him. He also didn't care that he was in his wet socks. Who gave a fuck? He had to get to that hospital.

By the time they got there, she was nowhere to be found. "Where's my girlfriend? Pretty girl, about—"

"Meadows?" a nurse asked him, and he nodded. "She's in the back. They're working with her now. Let's get you and him," she said, pointing at Conor, "checked out first."

A nurse behind the desk stared at him. "Wait. By any chance, is your name Frame?"

"Yes."

"She was in here looking for you a little while ago."

"What?" That made no sense at all.

"Yeah. Was convinced you were here somewhere. Said somebody called her and told her you were here, that you'd been in an accident. We told her you weren't, and she was really upset."

That son of a bitch. It was hard to see for the blood rising behind his eyes. Craven Bradshaw had lured her out with the only thing that could've gotten her out of that house—the idea that something had happened to him. *When I find that little bastard …* "Jackson? You okay?" Tank's big hand clamped down on his shoulder.

"Uh, yeah. Yeah, I'm fine. I just need to see her."

"I know, but she's—"

"Where's Jackson? Where is he?" There was a commotion near the doors, and they all turned to see Gant come barreling through the second set of automatic doors. "YOU! You promised me you'd take care of her! You promised—"

"Hey, hey, hey! Take it easy!" Tank's voice was like melted butter as he stepped between the two men. "There's a lot here that we don't know, but just know this wasn't Jackson's fault. Somebody—"

"It was that fucking Craven Bradshaw, that's who it was," Jackson growled through clenched teeth.

Gant stared at him. "What's that little bastard got to do with this?"

"Everything, I'm afraid." Tank's voice was low and even. "Let's just get Jackson and Conor checked out and then we'll all sit down and talk, okay? Just chill out, G-man. It's gonna be okay."

"Is she all right?"

"They're working with her right now. I think we should …" Jackson could still hear them talking as a nurse led them toward the exam cubicles.

Twenty minutes later, they were deemed none the worse for wear, but Gant was nowhere to be found. "Where's—"

Tank pointed. "They took him back to see her."

"No. That should be me."

"Just hang on, okay? Just sit down and try to relax. I know that's—"

"Impossible! That's impossible! I want to see her and talk—"

"Hey! Calm down!" a voice called out from down the hallway and Buff came into view. "Her dad's back there with her, and I'll take you back in a minute, but you need to calm down. Sit down and take a deep breath." Jackson was still pissed, but he did as he was told.

Ten minutes later, they looked up to see Gant heading toward them. When he reached the men, he threw his arms around Jackson. As Jackson hugged him back, Gant leaned toward his ear and whispered, "We need to talk about what we're going to do about Craven Bradshaw."

Jackson's lips moved close to Gant's ear and he whispered. "Agreed."

THE ONLY SOUND COMING FROM THE ROOM WAS THE SOFT hiss of the oxygen they were giving her, and Jackson hesitated a mere second before he rounded the doorway. They'd moved her up to the obstetrics ward to keep an eye on her, and he was terrified for her and the baby. But when she saw his face, she smiled. "Oh, Papa-boo! I was so scared!" Then she promptly burst into tears.

Yeah, he was dirty and wet, but he didn't care. He sat on the side of her bed and drew her into his arms. "Angel, dear god, I thought I'd lost you. You feel okay?"

"Yeah. I was so scared! He was right behind me! I'm not even sure what happened, but I remember the water."

"Knocked your car into the creek."

"Who got me out?"

He side-eyed her. "I did."

"No you didn't. Was it Conor?"

"No. It was me."

"It couldn't have been you because …"

He stared at her. "Because why?"

"Because. Because … your brother told me what happened to you. In the service. In the prisoner of war time. I know why the water makes you nervous, why you made filling the watering troughs my job. You couldn't go into the water. You're too—"

Jackson pressed a finger to her lips to shush her. "You. You're my life. I didn't care if I died, as long as I knew I'd done everything I could to save you and the jumping bean." She giggled through her tears. "Baby, there's nothing—*nothing*—I wouldn't do for you. Do you understand now?"

She ran a velvety hand down his cheek, kissed his lips tenderly, then leaned back and smiled. "I do now."

WHEN JACKSON STEPPED OUT THE AMBULANCE BAY doors, Gant was standing there, waiting for him. He'd known Amethyst's dad would be right there. Gant only said one word: "So."

Jackson nodded. "So."

"I guess we need to work out a plan, huh?"

Jackson nodded again. "We absolutely do."

As they backed up to the building and leaned against the wall, Gant's voice was a low hum. "You got any ideas? I mean, I know what to do afterward, and I've got all the places anybody could need to do it, but we've got to get him …"

"Yeah. Never done this before. They were always shooting at me. But there's a first time for everything, I suppose."

"First time for what?" A voice caused them both to spin toward it, and they found Jack standing there.

"First time to … be a grandpa," Gant said.

Jack moved up to take the same stance beside Jackson as they all leaned against the building again. "I know full well what you were talking about, and I beat you to it."

Gant stared at him. "What do you mean, you beat us to it?"

Jack shook his head and chuckled. "He's in county lockup."

Jackson could feel his fury returning. "No! We can't let him—"

"You'll let him and you'll let me. I do *not* want either of you going to jail over that little piece of shit, do you hear me? I've talked to the DA and we've got a clear path to attempted murder, *two* counts. Sometimes, being in an anti-abortion state can have its benefits."

Jackson could feel his cheeks cooling. Maybe Jack was right. That Bradshaw asshole wasn't worth spending the rest of his life in prison over. "Okay. But I want to talk to him."

"Oh, that's perfectly fine. If I had my druthers, I'd let both of you in the cell with him to help him understand the severity of his behavior, but that would be wholly unprofessional of me, now wouldn't it?" Gant chuckled at Jack. "So for now, I've got it under control. He's going nowhere. He'll be arraigned tomorrow morning, and I have it on good authority that the judge is going to deny him bail. You know, flight risk and all that. So there you have it. Craven Bradshaw isn't a threat anymore, and his family is permanently embarrassed." Jack surveyed the parking lot from there under the *porte cochere* and sighed. "You're gonna have your hands full, Frame. You're not a young man, and you're gonna have a toddler to keep up with. You need your strength. I'll do the heavy lifting on this one now. Gentlemen," Jack said and gave them a tiny salute, then straightened and strode away from the building.

"I really wanted to kill that sumbitch," Gant grumbled.

"Me too. I'd blow up the jail, but I might kill some poor dick who had one too many to drink and fell off the curb and … Hey, Jack!" he called out.

The lawman turned. "Yeah?"

"Anybody else in the jail tonight or just Bradshaw?"

Jack tapped one temple with his fingers. "I know what you're thinking, Frame. Just put that thought right out of your head." In a funny little falsetto, Jack called out, "Girl, don't do it! It's not worth it!" Then he started laughing.

Jackson was laughing so hard he could barely breathe when he called back, "I'm not gon' do it, girl. I was just thinkin' about it. I'm not gon' do it!" Jack was still laughing as he disappeared into the parking lot.

Gant stared at Jackson. "What the hell was that about?"

Jackson chuckled. "Something on TikTok."

"TikTok? Do I want to know?"

"No," Jackson answered, shaking his head. "You do not."

HE'D THOUGHT HE WAS GOING TO DIE. THREE DAYS. They'd kept her at the hospital for three whole days. He went home that first night, took a shower and put on clean clothes, and went back. They didn't want to let him in, but a kind nurse interceded and he stayed the night.

Conor showed up the next morning and told Jackson to get something to eat while he sat with her. Instead, it was hot, black coffee and back to the room.

Everyone in town had sent her flowers, cards, and candy. He was waiting for the discharge papers when Dr. Everett wandered into the room. "Well, hello there! How ya doin'?"

Amethyst gave her a tired smile. "I'm okay, I guess. They're letting me go home."

"Ah. That's good. So, as your obstetrician, I ordered an ultrasound. Let's examine you and I'll see if there's anything I need to tell the tech before she gets in here." The doctor listened to her heart, checked her pulse, and pulled up her chart on the iPad all the doctors carried. "Oh, she's a he!" Dr. Everett said as a young guy pushed the ultrasound machine into the room. "We're just doing this as a precaution. She seems perfectly fine."

"Okay. Let's see what we've got here." He helped Amethyst pull up her gown, then squirted gel onto her belly and pressed the transponder to her skin.

Jackson and Amethyst watched the screen. It was black first, and then white things started appearing, and then it became something round like an apple. In the middle of it was something oval. As the tech pressed the transponder around, the oval thing took on more shape. "Oh, legs and arms!" Amethyst whispered.

"Yeah." The tech pointed to the screen. "Two arms

and two legs. See the heartbeat there? Nice and strong. Looks very good, don't you think, Dr. Everett?"

"Sure does."

Jackson pointed to a spot on the screen. "Okay. Two arms. Two legs. What's that?" The tech gave him a lopsided grin. "Oh. Oh!"

Amethyst caught on instantly. "Oh! It's a …"

"Congratulations. I do believe you're having a boy!" Dr. Everett sang out.

Jackson took Amethyst's hand and gripped it tightly. He'd never let her out of his sight again. Yeah, that was ridiculous, but he didn't care. Nothing could happen to her—to them. Ever.

THEY WERE HAVING MORE FUN THAN AMETHYST COULD have ever imagined. Being invited to spend the holiday weekend on the Gulf was a treat, and the house his brother's family lived in was right on the beach at the seawall in Galveston and up high to protect against storm surge. It was spacious and beautiful, and she fell in love with it the instant she walked in. Wyman and Chimlin treated her like she'd always been part of the family, and their kids were more than kind to her.

She wandered into the kitchen on Labor Day morning. "Do you need some help in here?" Amethyst asked Chimlin.

"No, no. I've got it, honey. Just sit and rest."

Boy, that's sure a lot of food, Amethyst thought as she looked around the kitchen. The house wasn't huge, and there was food on every available countertop surface, all over the table, and on a cart in the dining room. "Where's Jackson?"

"Helping Wyman with something."

"I'll just go—"

"No! Uh, I could use somebody to help make the tea. Can you do that?"

"Sure. I don't mind." That was weird. It was almost as though Chimlin didn't want her and Jackson together, and that didn't make sense.

She got the tea made and tried to go out the back door, but Chimlin redirected her toward the pantry. "Do you see juice in there? I need juice. In a big can."

"No. I don't see any juice."

"Keep looking. I know it's there," Chimlin called out.

"Okay." *There is no juice in here*, Amethyst told herself. *What is going on?*

Two minutes later, she heard Jackson's voice. "Where's Amethyst?"

"Pantry," Chimlin answered, and then she whispered something Amethyst couldn't hear.

"Okay. Hey, angel, come out here."

She stepped into the kitchen to find him standing there, grinning from ear to ear. "Hey! What's up?"

"Come with me." Jackson's hand reached out for her and she took it, then let him lead her toward the back door and down the stairwell. She could hear Chimlin following them. "I've got a surprise for you."

"A surprise? What kind of—"

"SURPRISE!" what sounded like fifty voices called out as they stepped out of the stairwell, and Amethyst's jaw dropped.

Of course, Wyman, Chimlin, and their kids were there.

But to her amazement, Gant and Lorna stood there, and beside them—Sapphire and her mom! "Oh my god! I don't believe it! Mom!" Amethyst rushed across the lawn and threw her arms around her mother. "I'm so glad to see you!"

"I'm glad to see you too, honey!"

"What am I, chopped liver?" her sister asked.

"Of course not! I'm so glad you're here!" Then she turned to Jackson. "Okay, what's going on?" She hoped she knew what his answer would be.

"I just wanted everybody to come for a visit while we were here so I could give you this." It was the little box she'd seen in his desk drawer, but she didn't have to fake a gasp. When he opened the box in the bright sunlight, it was like a thousand rainbows were escaping from inside the satin. "I hope you like it, and I hope you'll wear it."

"What if I don't?" she asked, teasing him.

Jackson grinned. "Then I'll call you a liar, wrestle you to the ground, and shove it onto your finger."

"Wow. Sounds like I should just say yes. But what am I saying yes to?"

"To wearing this ring. To being mine all mine. To letting me change your name. And to raising our baby together. Any of those things sound unappealing to you?"

She smiled. "Not a one!"

Jackson took the ring from the box and held out his hand. When she rested hers in his palm, he slipped the ring on her finger. "Miss Meadows, I'm asking you to be my wife."

"And I'm accepting."

"Good. And now, there's something I need to tell everybody here. I hope you'll be patient with me."

Amethyst stood there and watched, tears streaming down her face, as the bravest man she'd ever met told everyone there about the horrors he'd experienced in the military, about the daring rescue the mercenaries had provided, and about the night terrors he'd experienced ever since. When he finished, Gant quietly asked, "Jackson, how in the world did you make yourself go into that creek for her?"

"Oh, that was easy. Something greater than fear." He turned to Amethyst and smiled at her tear-stained face. "Do you know what that is?"

She nodded her head as she leaned against his chest and let the warmth of his arms staunch her tears. "Yes. It's love."

A week later, they stood in front of a judge at the county courthouse and made it official. Amethyst had never been one to dream of white gowns and big receptions and all of that. It didn't interest her. What she'd always looked for was love, real love, the kind of love that Gant and Lorna had. She'd finally found it. A cake wasn't necessary.

All she needed was his kiss.

He knew she'd loved being around the whole family, and it had been a great trip. They'd been back for three days, and he watched her closely. It was as though the visit had drained her, and she'd cried for part of the day. He could tell it was simple frustration born of weariness, and he'd asked a dozen times how he could help, but she just mumbled, "Hormones," and then went back to crying.

"Anything I can do?" She just shook her head. "I love you."

"Ohhhh, I love you too!" she sobbed, so he just let her cry.

When the tears finally stopped, Jackson sat down beside her, smoothed her hair, and kissed her temple. "Why don't we go out to dinner? We haven't done that in several weeks, and I think it's high time. How does that sound?"

"Good. I'll get cleaned up and ready."

"I've gotta shower, so you've got time. But I love you, angel. You know that."

"I love you too." His weight lifted from the side of the bed, and Amethyst watched as he crossed the room, but when he reached the doorway, he turned and smiled at her before he disappeared into the bathroom.

He insisted on taking her to her favorite restaurant in Medina, and she'd smiled and chatted with him the whole time. He felt like some kind of magician who could magically make sad women happy with food. He'd finished his pie when he asked her, "You about finished there?"

She looked down at her dessert plate. "Yeah. I can't eat much more."

"Okay. Let me get our check and we can go."

"I'm just going to the restroom. I'll be right back." It took some finagling to get out of the booth with her big belly, but she managed. As soon as she stood, she braced her back with her arm. "Lord, this kid is heavy," she mumbled.

"He's gonna be a football player," Jackson answered as she walked away. He said that at least once a day.

She'd almost made it to the end of the aisle when it happened. At first, she thought her bladder had turned loose, and then she realized it wasn't urine at all. "Oh, god." Looking down, she watched as the liquid puddled at her feet and filled one of her shoes. "Oh, god, Jackson, oh, god."

"What's … Oh, shit, baby. Um, okay, it's all right. You need to go to the restroom, right? Come on. I'll help you. Miss!" Jackson yelled at one of the servers.

"Sir, is something … Oh! Oh, I'll get someone to clean that up right away. Is she okay?"

"Yeah. We're going to the restroom. Could you watch her bag, please, and we'll be right back. Come on, baby. Let's go." When they reached the restroom door, Jackson pushed it open and called out, "Gentleman coming through!"

From somewhere inside, a woman called back, "Come on in. I'm only washing my hands. Oh, my, honey! Are you okay?"

"My water broke," Amethyst gasped out as she tried to walk and keep her shoes on. The right one was squishing as she walked. "Gah, this is grossing me out."

"Can I do anything to help?" the lady asked.

"Yeah, if you could keep everybody else out of here until she's finished, that would be good," Jackson answered. "Come on, angel. Let's get you sorted out and we'll go." Amethyst marveled at how calm he was, and she let him help her into the stall so she could relieve the pressure on her bladder. She'd finished and was about to wipe when the first one hit. "Ohhhhh. Oh, god."

"Yeah, your labor's starting. We need to get out of here. Come on, babe. Let's go." He practically lifted her to her feet and helped her out the bathroom door as the lady held it.

"You take care, honey. You'll be fine."

"Thank you, ma'am," Amethyst called back to the woman as she waddled out to the booth. The server handed Jackson his debit card and her bag, and they made their way slowly out of the restaurant.

By the time they got to the truck, she could feel another contraction coming on. "Ohhhh, god. Ohhh, that hurts. Yeah. Hurts."

"At least we're near the hospital. Let's just go on over there and see if they'll let us stay there."

"But I've got a long way to go!" she argued.

"But by the time we could drive back home, we'd probably have to turn around and just drive right back. That doesn't make sense." Jackson started the truck and cut the wheels toward the street.

"Why are you being so calm?" She was a little pissed at how unconcerned he seemed.

"Because you need me to be calm. And because I'm trained to deliver babies, so I know you're not going to have him in the next five minutes. Let's just go over there and let them look at you."

Thirty minutes later, she lay on a bed in the labor and delivery wing. "I just want to go home," she moaned as another contraction hit. "Ohhhh, ohhhh, ohhhh, make it stop."

A tall, heavy-set nurse glared down at her. "You've got a while yet. I'd suggest you get some rest if you can."

Amethyst gave her the stink eye. "Easy for you to say."

"Oh yeah? I've had seven kids. There are much worse things than labor, believe you me. Now, get some rest. I'll be back to check on you in a little while." As she ambled out of the room, Amethyst made little mocking mouth movements toward her.

"Hey, you should be nice to her. She may be the one

who decides if you get drugs or not," Jackson pointed out.

"I want some. I damn sure want some." There were voices in the hallway, and the door opened.

"Hey, baby!" Gant sang out and headed straight to the bed. His arms wrapped around her and she was glad to have her daddy there. "So he's on his way, huh?"

"Looks that way."

"You doing okay?" Lorna asked and smoothed Amethyst's hair with a soft hand.

She nodded. "Yeah, so far, so good."

They all chatted, punctuated by Amethyst growling and howling. Gant and Lorna went down to get some coffee, and Jackson gave her a knowing smile. "And now, my sweet wife, we've got to come up with a name."

"How 'bout … J.B.?" He scowled. "You know—Jumping Bean."

"Oh, no. Uh-uh," Jackson answered, chuckling. "Nope. We've got to do better than that."

"Okay. Um, so what was your grandfather's name?"

Jackson rolled his eyes and snorted. "Herschel."

"Oh, uh, nope. Okay. What about your dad?"

"Arlen."

She thought about it for a few seconds. "Well, that's a nice name."

"I don't really like it. What about your grandfathers?"

"I have no idea what their names were. They may still be alive, for all I know."

"Do you know who your dad is?"

"Gant Meadows."

"I mean your *biological* dad."

"Nope. If my mom knows, she's never said."

"Shit! You should probably call her and Sapphire!"

Amethyst laughed. "Whaddya wanna bet Dad already has?"

"Probably."

"Yeah, he can' … Ohhhhhh. Oh god. Uhhhhh, I want those drugs," she moaned.

"You've got a long way to go yet, angel. Names. Let's keep going. Um, did you have a boyfriend when you were a little girl?"

She nodded. "Yeah. Part of the Ren crowd. Jody."

"Sounds too much like Joey." She was about to say something when he said, "Oh hell. Hang on." He pulled his phone out and hit a contact, then waited, and Amethyst wondered who he was calling. "Yeah, Autrey, I need a favor. I need a name. The guy who pulled me out of that prison. If his first name is something we can live with, we'd like to name our baby boy after him."

Amethyst nodded. That would be grand, to honor the man who'd saved her husband's life in that way. She couldn't imagine anything more fitting for a new life. "Ohhhhhh. Ohhh, gawd, ohhhhh. How much longer?" she asked, panting.

"They're getting closer together, that's for sure. Do you want me to have them examine you, or do you want me to do it?"

"You can do it?"

"Of course I can do it. I told you, I'm trained to deliver babies. I could've done this at home."

"Then why aren't we?" she huffed.

"Because if anything went wrong … I didn't want to take that chance. If it had been your second or third child, maybe, but not a first. That's a risk I'm really not willing to take."

"Okay, okay. I get it. Yeah. If you can look and tell me what's going on, that would be good."

"Will do. Let me close the door." In a second, he was back and pulling on some latex gloves. "Okay, pull your knees up and I'll take a look." He didn't say anything for a few seconds, then patted her left shin. "Okay, put them down." When she'd pulled her gown down, he pulled the sheet up, rolled the gloves off, and patted her hand. "You're almost fully dilated. I'd say a couple of hours and we'll have a baby."

"Oh. Well, that's good. I'm just really tired." She glanced at the clock and realized it was almost eleven thirty. It had been a very long day and she wished she could get some sleep.

"So the key here is to wait until the next contraction and then try to nap. It won't be a long one, but anything will be better than nothing. I'll make sure you're not disturbed so you can drift off. You'll wake up with the following contraction, and then you can go back to sleep."

"I'll try, but I'm not sure that's going to work."

"Worth a shot."

A few minutes later, Gant and Lorna were headed home after instructing Jackson to call them when it was almost time. Sure enough, Gant had admitted that he'd already called Emerald and Sapphire, and they were both on their way. She was going to get to tell them her baby son's name and let them hold him.

Her baby son. Her and Jackson's baby son. The two dearest people in her world, Jackson and the baby, would be there with her in the house she'd come to think of as home. They'd be a family, the family she'd always wanted and never had until Gant had come into the picture. He and Lorna would be there to help her and Jackson if they needed it. For the first time in her life, she was putting down roots. She knew how much her mother had always hated the idea of that.

But for Amethyst, it was a dream come true.

CHAPTER 12

"HANG IN THERE, baby. We're almost there."

"We? What's this *we* business?" Amethyst ground out through gritted teeth.

"I'm right here. Trust me, if I could do it so you didn't have to, I would." He wiped her brow with a cool, wet washcloth. "He's almost here, angel."

"Okay, Amethyst, this time, I need a mighty push. Push and don't stop until I tell you to. Hear me?" Dr. Everett asked and slapped Amethyst's thigh with a gloved hand.

"Yeah, yeah. I hear you."

"It's about to happen. Okay, here we go. Get ready … Now!"

Jackson winced as she torqued down on his hand and scrunched up her face until he couldn't even see her eyes. She didn't yell or scream, just let out a thin, high-pitched "Eeeeeeeeeee."

"Keep going!" Dr. Everett yelled through the commotion in the room.

"I'm … trying," the young woman hummed as she strained.

"There, we …*got him!*" There was a mighty upheaval in the room as nurses ran to take the baby. "Daddy, want to cut the cord?"

He hadn't realized they'd ask that. "Uh, sure." The doctor clamped the umbilical cord off, and Jackson took the medical shears and cut right through it. It was impossible to tell anything about the baby. He was covered in all kinds of fluids and blood, and all of that mess made him look kind of blue. If Jackson hadn't known they were supposed to look like that, it might've scared him to death.

"Is he okay?" he heard Amethyst ask and in a split second, he was right beside her.

"Yeah, he's fine." *I need to hear him cry!* he heard a voice in his head say. "They're just taking care of him, suctioning out his airways, all of that—"

"WAAAAAAAAAAHHHHHHHH!" the infant screamed from across the room.

"There we go! Boy, he's got a set of lungs on him!" Jackson said, laughing, as the baby continued to wail. "How ya doin', angel?"

"I'm so tired," she whispered. "I really need a drink."

"Here you go." He held the cup with the straw up to her lips, and she took a long sip.

"We're almost done down here," Dr. Everett announced. "Just a couple more minutes."

A tiny brunette nurse stepped up to the side of the bed, the blanketed bundle in her arms. "Want to meet your little son?"

"Yes, please." Amethyst reached for him and snuggled him against her chest. "He's so tiny. Look how perfect he is."

"He really is." Jackson reached out and stroked his thumb down the baby's cheek, watching as the little thing's chin quivered. His text tone went off and without thinking, he pulled his phone out and tapped the notification.

Just as he did, someone called from across the room, "What's his name?"

Jackson held the phone up in front of Amethyst, and she nodded. "His name is Spencer," Jackson called back to whomever had asked.

"Spencer Lewis," Amethyst corrected.

"Spencer Lewis Frame! Got it!" whoever was filling out the paperwork answered.

"Welcome to the family, Spencer Lewis Frame," Jackson whispered to the baby and kissed its soft temple. Then he looked up into his wife's eyes. "I love you, my angel. I never knew I could love somebody the way I love you."

"I love you too. We're going to be okay, right?"

"Babe," he said as he kissed her forehead, "it doesn't matter where we are. As long as we're together, we'll be okay."

IT HAD ONLY BEEN FIVE DAYS, BUT IT DIDN'T SEEM LIKE there was a new baby in the house. It felt like he'd always been there, always been a part of their little family, and he was over the moon happy. As he watched Amethyst nurse the tiny child, he smiled. "I didn't know I could love somebody so much."

She looked up from under her brows and grinned. “Me or him?”

“Yes.” That got a laugh out of her. “But really, doesn’t it seem like he’s always been here?”

“It does. I can’t imagine life without him.”

He scooted closer to her. “I can’t imagine life without either of you.”

“Same here.” He’d fallen asleep, warm and full of milk, and she handed him to Jackson while she pulled her bra up and buttoned the front of her pajama top. “So what’s next for us?”

“Live our lives, I guess. You got other ideas?”

“No.” She chuckled. “Is that going to be enough for you?”

“Are you serious? I’m an old man. It’ll probably be too much for me.” He cuddled the baby close. “If this is all I do for the rest of my life, I’ll be happy.”

“Yeah, well, it won’t be all you’ll do. There are horses and a hog and goats, and grass to mow, and—”

“Sheesh, woman, you’re a taskmistress! Yes, it’ll all get done, all the laundry and the cleaning and the diapering and the bathing and—”

“Oh, who’s the taskmaster now, huh?” she quipped.

“We’ve both got our hands full.”

“Money?”

He shrugged. “We’ve got enough for now. I might eventually have to find something, especially if you go back to school, but for now, we’re fine. We’ll just take it a day at a time and I’ll make the changes if I see that they’re needed. But for right now, I’m here for you and this little man.” The baby’s bottom lip quivered as he slept and Jackson smiled down at him.

His son. His beautiful baby son and his beautiful

wife. They'd have the life he'd always wanted, the one he'd thought was destroyed. It had all come back to him with her love. He didn't know how anyone else felt, but he was happier than he'd ever been in his life, and another thought made him even happier.

If Cassidy could see him, she'd be happy too.

ABOUT THE AUTHOR

Deanndra Hall is a working author living in far western Kentucky with her partner of 30+ years, crazy little dogs, and maybe a snake or two. She's written for business, industry, religious institutions, non-profits, and owned her own graphic design business, as well as working as a fiber and textile artist. When she's not writing all things romance from sweet, simple plots to explicit, erotic suspense, she can be found working out at the local gym, hiking, kayaking, reading (of course), or working on a healthy recipe. And wherever she is, chocolate is sure to be nearby.

On the Web: deanndrahall.com

Email: Deanndra@DeanndraHall.com

Amazon: amazon.com/Deanndra-Hall

Bookbub: bookbub.com/authors/deanndra-hall

Facebook: facebook.com/deanndra.hall

Goodreads: goodreads.com/deanndrahall

Instagram: instagram.com/deanndra_hall/

Newsletter: Subscribe!

Pinterest: pinterest.com/deanndrahall

Twitter: twitter.com/DeanndraHall

Mailing address:

P.O. Box 3722

Paducah, KY 42002-3722

ALSO BY DEANNDRA HALL

Bluegrass Dynasty Series

Bluegrass Dynasty:

The Love Under Construction Novels

Laying a Foundation (Book 1)

Tearing Down Walls (Book 2)

Renovating a Heart (Book 3)

Planning an Addition (Book 4)

Bluegrass Dynasty:

The Citadel Novels

One Simple Mistake (Book 5)

One Broken Promise (Book 6)

One Poor Choice (Book 7)

One Wrong Glance (Book 8)

Bluegrass Dynasty:

The Legacy Novels

Atonement (Book 9)

Legacy of Pride (Book 10)

Legacy of Freedom (Book 11)

Legacy of Faithfulness (Book 12)

Legacy of Hope (Book 13)

Legacy of Memories (Book 14)

Legacy of Love (Book 15)

Bluegrass Dynasty:

The Moonlight & Moonshine Novels

Kindred Spirits (Book 16)

High Proof (Book 17)

Angel's Share (Book 18)

The Bliss Series

Adventurous Me (Book 1)

Unforgettable You (Book 2)

Incredible Us (Book 3)

Completely Mine (Book 4)

Undeniably His (Book 5)

Eternally Yours (Book 6)

Blissfully Hers (Book 7)

The Harper's Cove Series

Karen and Brett at 326 Harper's Cove (Book 1)

Becca and Greg at 314 Harper's Cove (Book 2)

Donna and Connor at 228 Harper's Cove (Book 3)

Savannah and Martin at 219 Harper's Cove (Book 4)

Cheryl and Samuel at 323 Harper's Cove (Book 5)

Tasha and Davis at 333 Harper's Cove (Book 6)

Lily and Brock at 343 Harper's Cove (Book 7)

Siobhán and Gabhain at 241 Harper's Cove (Book 8)

The Witch of Endor Series

Laid Bare (Book 1)

Ripped Open (Book 2)

Torn Apart (Book 3)

Bound Together (Book 4)

Books included in Susan Stoker's

Police and Fire: Operation Alpha World,

Badge of Honor

Bluegrass Bravery Series

Shelter for Sharla (Book 1)

Justice for Aleta (Book 2)

Shelter for Martina (Book 3)

Justice for Daesha (Book 4)

Shelter for Jerrica (Book 5)

Justice for Landee (Book 6)

Shelter for Tanna (Book 7)

Justice for Liella (Book 8)

Justice for Maisey (Book 9)

Shelter for Nita (Book 10)

Justice for JoElla (Book 11)

Refuge for Flora (Book 12)

Tarpley Volunteer Fire Department Series

Fighting for Carly (Book 2)

Tarpley Volunteer Fire Department Series 2

Fighting for Lorna (Book 4)

Fighting for Amethyst: A Tarpley VFD Novel

The Silent Cove Series

Awakening (Book 1)

Independent Novels

My Last Dom

The Celtic Fan

Rough Stock

ABOUT THE AUTHOR

Deanndra Hall is a working author living in far western Kentucky with her partner of 30+ years, crazy little dogs, and maybe a snake or two. She's written for business, industry, religious institutions, non-profits, and owned her own graphic design business, as well as working as a fiber and textile artist. When she's not writing all things romance from sweet, simple plots to explicit, erotic suspense, she can be found working out at the local gym, hiking, kayaking, reading (of course), or working on a healthy recipe. And wherever she is, chocolate is sure to be nearby.

On the Web: deanndrahall.com
Email: Deanndra@DeanndraHall.com
Amazon: amazon.com/Deanndra-Hall
Bookbub: bookbub.com/authors/deanndra-hall
Facebook: facebook.com/deanndra.hall
Goodreads: goodreads.com/deanndrahall
Instagram: instagram.com/deanndra_hall/
Newsletter: Subscribe!
Pinterest: pinterest.com/deanndrahall
Twitter: twitter.com/DeanndraHall
Mailing address:
P.O. Box 3722
Paducah, KY 42002-3722

There are many more books in this fan fiction world than listed here, for an up-to-date list go to www.AcesPress.com

You can also visit our Amazon page at: http://www.amazon.com/author/operationalpha

Special Forces: Operation Alpha World

Christie Adams: Charity's Heart
Denise Agnew: Dangerous to Hold
Shauna Allen: Awakening Aubrey
Brynne Asher: Blackburn
Linzi Baxter: Unlocking Dreams
Jennifer Becker: Hiding Catherine
Alice Bello: Shadowing Milly
Heather Blair: Rescue Me
Misha Blake: Flash
Anna Blakely: Rescuing Gracelynn
Julia Bright: Saving Lorelei
Cara Carnes: Protecting Mari
Kendra Mei Chailyn: Beast
Melissa Kay Clarke: Rescuing Annabeth
Samantha A. Cole: Handling Haven
Sue Coletta: Hacked
Melissa Combs: Gallant
Lorelei Confer: Protecting Sara
Anne Conley: Redemption for Misty
KaLyn Cooper: Rescuing Melina
Janie Crouch: Storm
Liz Crowe: Marking Mariah
Sarah Curtis: Securing the Odds
Jordan Dane: Redemption for Avery

Tarina Deaton: Found in the Lost
Aspen Drake, Intense
KL Donn: Unraveling Love
Riley Edwards: Protecting Olivia
PJ Fiala: Defending Sophie
Nicole Flockton: Protecting Maria
Alexa Gregory: Backdraft
Michele Gwynn: Rescuing Emma
Casey Hagen: Shielding Nebraska
Desiree Holt: Protecting Maddie
Kathy Ivan: Saving Sarah
Kris Jacen, Be With Me
Jesse Jacobson: Protecting Honor
Silver James: Rescue Moon
Becca Jameson: Saving Sofia
Kate Kinsley: Protecting Ava
Rayne Lewis: Justice for Mary
Heather Long: Securing Arizona
Gennita Low: No Protection
Kirsten Lynn: Joining Forces for Jesse
Margaret Madigan: Bang for the Buck
Trish McCallan: Hero Under Fire
Kimberly McGath: The Predecessor
Rachel McNeely: The SEAL's Surprise Baby
KD Michaels: Saving Laura
Lynn Michaels: Rescuing Kyle
Olivia Michaels: Protecting Harper
Wren Michaels: The Fox & The Hound
Annie Miller: Securing Willow
Kat Mizera: Protecting Bobbi
Keira Montclair, Wolf and the Wild Scots
Mary B Moore: Force Protection
LeTeisha Newton: Protecting Butterfly

Angela Nicole: Protecting the Donna
MJ Nightingale: Protecting Beauty
Sarah O'Rourke: Saving Liberty
Victoria Paige: Reclaiming Izabel
Anne L. Parks: Mason
Debra Parmley: Protecting Pippa
Lainey Reese: Protecting New York
KeKe Renée: Protecting Bria
TL Reeve and Michele Ryan: Extracting Mateo
Elena M. Reyes: Keeping Ava
Deanna L. Rowley: Saving Veronica
Angela Rush: Charlotte
Rose Smith: Saving Satin
Jenika Snow: Protecting Lily
Lynne St. James: SEAL's Spitfire
Dee Stewart: Conner
Harley Stone: Rescuing Mercy
Sarah Stone: Shielding Grace
Jen Talty: Burning Desire
Reina Torres, Rescuing Hi'ilani
Savvi V: Loving Lex
Megan Vernon: Protecting Us
LJ Vickery: Circus Comes to Town
Rachel Young: Because of Marissa
R. C. Wynne: Shadows Renewed

Delta Team Three Series

Lori Ryan: Nori's Delta
Becca Jameson: Destiny's Delta
Lynne St James, Gwen's Delta
Elle James: Ivy's Delta
Riley Edwards: Hope's Delta

Police and Fire: Operation Alpha World

Freya Barker: Burning for Autumn
B.P. Beth: Scott
Jane Blythe: Salvaging Marigold
Julia Bright, Justice for Amber
Anna Brooks, Guarding Georgia
KaLyn Cooper: Justice for Gwen
Aspen Drake: Sheltering Emma
Emily Gray: Shelter for Allegra
Alexa Gregory: Backdraft
Deanndra Hall: Shelter for Sharla
Barb Han: Kace
EM Hayes: Gambling for Ashleigh
India Kells: Shadow Killer
CM Steele: Guarding Hope
Reina Torres: Justice for Sloane
Aubree Valentine, Justice for Danielle
Maddie Wade: Finding English
Stacey Wilk: Stage Fright
Laine Vess: Justice for Lauren

Tarpley VFD Series

Silver James, Fighting for Elena
Deanndra Hall, Fighting for Carly
Haven Rose, Fighting for Calliope
MJ Nightingale, Fighting for Jemma
TL Reeve, Fighting for Brittney
Nicole Flockton, Fighting for Nadia

As you know, this book included at least one character from Susan Stoker's books. To check out more, see below.

SEAL Team Hawaii Series

Finding Elodie
Finding Lexie
Finding Kenna (Oct 2021)
Finding Monica (May 2022)
Finding Carly (TBA)
Finding Ashlyn (TBA)
Finding Jodelle (TBA)

Eagle Point Search & Rescue

Searching for Lilly (Mar 2022)
Searching for Elsie (Jun 2022)
Searching for Bristol (Nov 2022)
Searching for Caryn (TBA)
Searching for Finley (TBA)
Searching for Heather (TBA)
Searching for Khloe (TBA)

The Refuge Series

Deserving Alaska (Aug 2022)
Deserving Henley (Jan 2023)
Deserving Reese (TBA)
Deserving Cora (TBA)
Deserving Lara (TBA)
Deserving Maisy (TBA)
Deserving Ryleigh (TBA)

Delta Team Two Series

Shielding Gillian
Shielding Kinley
Shielding Aspen
Shielding Jayme (novella)
Shielding Riley
Shielding Devyn
Shielding Ember
Shielding Sierra (Jan 2022)

SEAL of Protection: Legacy Series

Securing Caite (FREE!)
Securing Brenae (novella)
Securing Sidney
Securing Piper
Securing Zoey
Securing Avery
Securing Kalee
Securing Jane

Delta Force Heroes Series

Rescuing Rayne (FREE!)
Rescuing Aimee (novella)
Rescuing Emily
Rescuing Harley
Marrying Emily (novella)
Rescuing Kassie
Rescuing Bryn
Rescuing Casey
Rescuing Sadie (novella)
Rescuing Wendy
Rescuing Mary
Rescuing Macie (novella)
Rescuing Annie (Feb 2022)

Badge of Honor: Texas Heroes Series

Justice for Mackenzie (FREE!)
Justice for Mickie
Justice for Corrie
Justice for Laine (novella)
Shelter for Elizabeth
Justice for Boone
Shelter for Adeline
Shelter for Sophie
Justice for Erin
Justice for Milena
Shelter for Blythe
Justice for Hope
Shelter for Quinn
Shelter for Koren
Shelter for Penelope

SEAL of Protection Series

Protecting Caroline (FREE!)
Protecting Alabama
Protecting Fiona
Marrying Caroline (novella)
Protecting Summer
Protecting Cheyenne
Protecting Jessyka
Protecting Julie (novella)
Protecting Melody
Protecting the Future
Protecting Kiera (novella)
Protecting Alabama's Kids (novella)
Protecting Dakota

New York Times, *USA Today* and *Wall Street Journal*

Bestselling Author Susan Stoker has a heart as big as the state of Tennessee where she lives, but this all American girl has also spent the last fourteen years living in Missouri, California, Colorado, Indiana, and Texas. She's married to a retired Army man who now gets to follow *her* around the country.

www.stokeraces.com
www.AcesPress.com
susan@stokeraces.com